By the same author

Frames of Mind
Heights of Folly
Courting Trouble
The Disenchanted Circle

Falling Apart

by

Philippa Bunting

PINE MARTEN PRESS

The Pine Marten Press

First published in 2017

ISBN 978-0-9933493-3-1

Typeset and cover design by GSB (Edinburgh)

To my dear parents.

Chapter 1

Mr Tipler stared at Constance with a stricken face. He pointed down the long unlit passage. Standing at the end was a hefty wooden trunk where someone had thrown a pile of sheets.

Dido was choking with laughter, hand to mouth. 'It was a trick!' she said. 'I played a trick on poor Mister.'

Mr Tipler was small and thin, and the most nervous person Dido had ever encountered. The stairs were dark. Catching sight of the sheets under the passage window, his abiding fear of ghosts had unmanned him.

'A very silly trick,' Constance said, descending a short flight of stairs before her. 'You'd better apologise, Dido.'

Dido hopped down another three stairs from her bedroom to join them on their landing – a slight fair child with grey-blue eyes and an intent expression. 'I'm never scared,' she said. 'I wish I could be frightened stiff.'

'To hear the missus talk, you'd expect to meet a ghost or two,' Mr Tipler said, speaking with a stutter. 'She's seen things all right. After old Mrs Burnett went to live away, and he died.'

'Who's he?' asked Dido sharply.

'Your granddaddy.'

Constance said, 'Into bed, Dido. You and Hal should have been asleep much earlier. You're getting into bad habits.'

In the hall below, the grandfather clock launched into its mechanical seizure before the strikes, gasping and whirring. Nine o'clock. Constance went downstairs and stood in the hall for a moment, lost in thought. She heard Dido call to her brother to have bad dreams. Then there was silence.

She passed into the house-keeper's sitting-room. Mrs Tipler was seated beside the Aga, rubbing her legs. She was a stout woman and not tall, with a placid face and normally cheery expression.

She groaned for her employer's benefit.

'I could cut my legs off,' she gasped. 'They ache that much.'

'Perhaps they're hot,' said Constance. 'Legs tend to ache in hot weather. Keep them raised when you can. But about tomorrow, Mrs Tipler: I'd be glad if you could make the beds in the spare room. You know the best linen is in the bathroom wardrobe.'

Releasing a gratified sigh, Mrs Tipler began rolling an elasticated stocking down her right leg. Constance moved to the door again. Glancing up with the stocking in her hand, Mrs Tipler regarded Constance: a good figure neatly dressed, hair lightly waved, blue eyes in a heart-shaped face. She's a nice looking lady, ran the thought in Mrs Tipler's mind. Nicely spoken. She began peeling down the other elastic stocking.

'Colonel Burnett is joining us. It may be only for a few days, until he has everything more organized. But the children are very excited.' A silent moment passed. Constance sensed the unasked query concerning conjugal wishes and rights. 'He'll be here on Saturday, back to his childhood home after so long . . . and the horror of these last years.'

'Mr Tipler will be pleased,' the house-keeper assured her with easy self-involvement. 'He's been that curious about some of the stuff in this house – the blunderbuss, and that whopping sailing boat, and the old gramophone records. He's amused by the family snaps too.'

Constance nodded and withdrew. She knew perfectly well that the Tiplers had made themselves at home and very comfortable at Westbourne House when her father-in-law died early in the war. There were numerous stories circulating in the neighbourhood about their ruthlessly enterprising stewardship.

Constance went into the drawing-room, and opening the little bureau, took out a creased note written on fragile paper, addressed to the children. It was from John, in Burma, to them, in Natal.

'Dear Hal and Dido,

'Thank you very much for your two letters. You are both becoming quite good writers, and four pages is a very long letter for any small boy.

'There are millions of Japs to kill yet, but the British and Americans, Chinese and Indians are getting on well and presently we won't have to kill any more. The postcard I sent I picked up on the battlefield. There are some more which I will send you. They used to belong to a Japanese soldier but he left them behind when he ran away.

'I expect Mummy has told you that my Daddy in England died not long ago and you might go and live in the house where we used to live. I think you would like it.

'Outside there is a big garden with two little spinneys, a croquet lawn and a tennis court and a vegetable garden and a summer house and another summer house. There is a garage and a stable and a tool room. There is a place for pigs and chickens and two fields where you could ride your ponies. There is a dog kennel and a tiny house in the garden down a secret path where I used to have a museum. There is also a cemetery where dead dogs and cats are buried.

'Perhaps you will see these things one day, and you will be able to explore for yourselves. There is also a hayloft over the garage which you get into by means of a ladder. This is rather exciting and very dirty.

'Love from Daddy.'

Nothing about the sister who had shared these memories.

Constance could hear John's voice clearly in the tone he had used in the letter. Mention of the house in Lincolnshire had greatly enhanced the mystery of their new home. Now John himself was expected in two days, after what he alluded to as his 'good' war. As a veteran of Kohima, he was lucky to be alive after it.

At breakfast next morning Dido said, 'Does every child's father write letters about killing people?'

'Only in wartime,' said Hal. He was nine to his sister's seven. He was a slim dark boy with deep green eyes in contrast with his Anglo-Saxon sister.

Dido considered. 'Is it the same as ordinary boasting ?'

'No.' Constance used her off-hand voice. 'Of course it isn't. Men in the Army usually don't like to speak about these things at all. Violence in battle is much too shocking. No-one should want there to be wars, or to have to gain by them.'

'I might make it my ambition to kill people,' Hal remarked, spreading margarine frugally over a slice of toast. 'People really dedicated to it get promoted and some end up knighted.'

'I spent ages yesterday kissing dead flowers,' Dido said.

'You'd have been exterminated in another century for being so soppy,' Hal told her through a mouthful of toast. 'Or locked into an asylum.'

'I've asked a couple in for coffee this morning,' Constance said. 'The Crawleys from the farmhouse near Goggles Causeway. I'm hoping to hear something about a pony Mrs Crawley spoke of on the phone. An old pony called Daisy, who taught their children to ride.'

'Oh – can it speak?' asked Hal with affable irony. He felt himself matured beyond the riding days of Mooi River. Exercise with bikes was more virile and less hazardous than with brute animals.

'You wouldn't understand her. But I will,' said Dido. 'Can Mrs Crawley ride her round this morning?'

'She certainly won't do that. But we can discuss how Daisy is delivered. I gather she used to love hunting and gave quite a mettlesome ride even up to her retirement.'

'She'll soon be back in retirement then,' said Hal. 'But Dido can always chat to her about the cruelty of hunting.'

Dido, who fell into every trap, lunged at him.

Katie arrived in a modest little Vauxhall, sweeping round the gravel drive and crunching to a stop by the bow window where Constance stood watching. She left a pair of gun dogs in the rear of the car. Grasping her handbag, she hurried through the porch and into the hall where she and Constance embraced. Katie was a bustling homely person who met everyone beyond halfway with goodwill and advice. She had shrewd brown eyes, a square face with freckled skin, and wore shiny blobs clipped to her ears. When Constance went through the house to see Mrs Tipler, Katie accompanied her, greeting the housekeeper and asking how they all did for soft fruit that season.

'I'll bring a pot of coffee right away,' Mrs Tipler promised, putting a newly baked Victoria sponge on to a plate.

'So John will be here on Saturday?' Katie said, sinking into a comfortable drawing-room chair.

'He will. The precious time we've waited for. To be together again.'

Mrs Tipler brought in the tray and set it down beside

Constance. 'Lovely aroma, fresh coffee has. . . and Mr Tipler can't abide coffee! He has a fastidious stomach.' She left the room, slowly closing the door.

'She's very cheerful for one who's no longer lady of the house,' Katie remarked.

Constance handed over a cup and offered the cake. 'She seems to have adapted; but I'm wondering how long I want her to stay. They're an odd couple.'

'Well, John couldn't have a lovelier wife,' Katie declared. 'And I'm sure he'll lose no time in assuring you of it, my dear. Bear in mind, you got him through his ghastly war.'

'An unimaginably awful time. But John is modest to a fault always, and he insists his war was good. The truth is, he was a scrupulous officer, always dedicated to the welfare of his men, and a man with ideas too . . . which meant he was hand-picked for action at Tobruk and Kohima. Later on they wanted him in Malaya and Singapore . . . and as escorting officer at the ceremony for the surrender of the Japanese.'

'You must be very proud of him. Sad to think his father didn't live to be proud too – though one knows that things weren't easy between them.'

'I gather John never got on with his father. Nor Unity with her mother.'

'I never knew John or his sister well when they were young.' Katie pinched some loose cake crumbs into a ball. 'But I do remember that Unity was a wonderful horsewoman. Passionately fond of animals. Which reminds me – little Daisy. We can get her boxed over tomorrow. She's lived outside all her life and is very hardy. One of the men can bring her.'

Leaving the drawing room, Katie heard young voices across the hall. 'May I tell them she's coming?'

They found Hal and Dido sitting one on each side of Mr Tipler on the dining-room settee, Mr Tipler nursing a musical-box on his knee. He glanced up with furtive pleasure, then back at the revolving cylinder. Resounding gently in the wooden box was 'The Prince of Wales,' which happened to be Mr Tipler's favourite among the eight tunes, and he told them so.

'There used to be a list on the inside of the lid,' Hal explained. 'The first one is called 'The last Rose of Summer,' not very logically you'd think.' He tilted his head sideways, regarding his mother and her friend as the tinkling notes rippled in their ears. Like Mr Tipler, the children were clearly spellbound. 'It's very valuable,' Hal informed the ladies.

'I'm sure it is,' Katie agreed. 'I'm sorry I can't stay to hear the other seven tunes. I've told your mother that you have a pony coming to live with you tomorrow, Dido.'

'Yippee,' said Dido. 'I know I'll love her.'

'I hope you'll both enjoy riding and looking after her,' Katie said.

'I've decided I'd rather have a bike,' Hal replied. 'A Raleigh, if possible.'

While Constance was waving Katie away, Hal was scrutinising Mr Tipler across the musical-box at close quarters. 'Your eyes aren't joined up,' he said, blinking his own eyes.

'That's because one of them wanders.'

'Oh, you are lucky!' exclaimed Dido.

'Why is he?' Hal demanded.

Dido reflected. 'Because everything he sees must be so interesting.'

The glassy ripples of sound had stopped. Mr Tipler tenderly lowered the lid of the box, then using a positive tone, he said, 'Mrs Tipler married me for my special eye.'

'I like your stutter even more,' Dido told him. 'It makes me really listen when you speak.'

Chapter 2

Constance approached the gate of her next-door neighbour which bore the name Trullers. Mrs Dunbar was the widow of a Scottish minister and had lived in Royal Deeside for many years. Constance knew that Mrs Dunbar suffered from ill health and was seldom known to leave the house.

She rang the bell. A deep silence. She rang again and began to hear muffled movements with creaks, and then the rattle of a chain. The door opened to reveal a lady a little taller than herself, swaddled in an elaborate pale blue housecoat with frills at cuffs and hem, and whose hair lay over one shoulder in a thick untidy coil. Her presence was a disconcerting blend of the tawdry and the regal, and her large face had been smothered with rouge, powder and lipstick.

'Please come in Mrs Burnett. I'm sorry I have no Mrs Ablewhite this morning. I am not blessed with her help every day.'

Her pronunciation was rather grand, with the faint huskiness suitable to poor health.

'It was so kind of you to have asked me over,' said Constance. 'You must think me most unfriendly – but there's been a lot to do since we arrived.' She held out a basket of fruit from the garden, and Mrs Dunbar accepted it graciously and laid it aside. 'I believe you're unable to get out very much. I hope you'll let me know if I can help.'

Mrs Dunbar indicated a chair, and sat herself in what was clearly her established centre, where a soft shawl was draped across its bulky back and a tartan rug over the seat. Her feet, now thrust forward, were clad in feathered mules.

'I'm no better than an invalid, Mrs Burnett. My mind is peopled with once beloved friends who have lost touch – who are no doubt stimulated by change and excitement. I spend most of my days in my bedroom. Hence my *dishabill.*'

'I can imagine how frustrating it is to be so restricted,' said Constance.

Her hostess spread conspicuously ringed hands with a sigh, then managed a smile. 'I have concerned myself for years with your family. Their joys and sorrows have been mine . . . at one remove. Your father-in-law was a complex personality and in my view, never really understood. A lonely person – like myself.'

'Well – I never met him.' Constance spoke with caution.

'They were too much alike, father and son. Both stubborn. That mouth' – Mrs Dunbar's mouth replicated it. 'Now – Florence was a good time girl if ever there was one. Her father always spoilt her, and being a wealthy man, she was used to every extravagance.'

Her mother-in-law a good time girl! Constance said, 'I became very fond of Florence. She went out to South Africa on holiday, you know, and was caught by the war.'

'A delightful lady – but an unorthodox parent! She made no secret of favouritising John over Unity. I expect you're aware that as a young boy, John wasn't strong. He had a weak chest, and missed all of one term at school. Yet his mother made it a rule that even in winter he must be tough. So, wrapped in coat and scarf,, outside he would go. He used to spend time at the railway station, talking to the staff and picking up knowledge. Or he'd hang about the brickpits – and the slaughter-house. Not the usual way into a medical career, one might suppose.'

'Knowing how to drive a steam engine saved his life in Greece,' Constance said. 'His childhood stood him in good stead later on.'

'Not a happy family. Not happy.' Mrs Dunbar shook her head with its tangled loop of hair. 'But your husband grew up to be a fine tall man. His mother's face and his father's figure.' She languidly coaxed the shawl around her shoulders.

Constance said, 'Perhaps you'll have a meal with us some time. John may take a while to settle down after his experiences. But tell me about your years in Scotland.'

'The visual beauties were very explicit. Glen Lyon and the Castles of Mar. Spiritual beauties were more elusive. We all carry our little burdens of sorrow in this life.' There was a heavy pause. 'You've been offered nothing to eat or drink, Mrs Burnett. But I am helpless without Mrs Ablewhite!'

'Oh, I seldom have morning coffee. And please do call me Constance. I should be going now anyway – we're expecting a pony to be delivered this morning from the Crawleys.'

'Dear Katie Crawley. A rather fraught domestic situation, I suspect. I don't know how her young people turned out. I can't remember the last time I spoke to her. She and Florence were very much in each other's confidence. Katie missed her when Florence went to live in Oatlands Park Hotel.'

'Curiously enough, it was at Oatlands Park I first met John,' Constance said. 'He went to see his mother when my family were spending a holiday there.'

'Fascinating how things turn out.' Mrs Dunbar gazed pensively at Constance as though with second sight. 'The dictates of angels. I'm afraid I used to feel sorry for Henry Burnett. Deserted by his wife, and then his daughter's tragedy. That surely hastened his death.'

These allusions to her family misfortunes prompted Constance to glance at her watch and repeat her need to leave. 'I can collect my basket another time.'

'Oh – your nice fruit dear. Perhaps the children could fetch the basket? Children are a fount of wisdom, I always feel. I should like to meet them.'

It struck Constance what a pity it was for Ernestine Dunbar to be both an inveterate gossip and a recluse in the same period of her life. She had certainly indulged herself in the former art that morning.

No pony had arrived. The afternoon passed, and still no-one called. Dido was anxious. 'I've been waiting and waiting with chopped apple and it's all turned brown.'

Hal was disgruntled. 'I could've gone down with Mr Hillis. He's got another litter of piglets at the piggery. You realize Daisy may not have any teeth.'

Constance said, 'I'm sorry Mr Hillis won't be here when the van arrives. He's so pleased we're keeping a pony.' Will Hillis was the gardener who had worked in the Westbourne gardens for the major part of his life. She turned her head. 'Wait a minute – I can hear something now.'

It was indeed a small horse-lorry, nosing down the tarmacked drive beside the house. Expecting the Crawley's man, Constance saw Roddy himself climbing out of the driver's seat, a stocky figure with thick greying hair and florid complexion. He moved towards her with arms extended, and folded one round her shoulders. 'My dear, I hope you haven't been on the lookout all day. We were short-staffed, and it was remiss of me not to warn you. Well now, will you chaps help me bring Daisy down the ramp?' His voice was rich with the comforts of life.

Hal and Dido hastened to the rear of the lorry. Roddy lowered the ramp with a thump and the grey pony turned her head and whinnied.

'No answering call, alas.' Roddy went to untie the halter rope and gently urged her to start down the ridged slope. With a clatter of hooves on hollow boards, the pony descended. Dido, beaming, took possession of the rope while Hal kept aside with a neutral expression. Together they all walked Daisy through the gate into the home paddock. 'You'll need a pony for this young chap. And why not for yourself, too?' Roddy suggested, his eyes travelling over Constance's form. 'I can see you handsomely mounted and taking them into the woods. Katie and I will keep our antennae out and let you know if anything suitable comes up.'

He slipped the halter over Daisy's head and she immediately stepped a few paces away, sniffing at the grass while in motion. Leaving the children to stare at her, Roddy hung her halter over the gate post and again extending an arm, moved Constance nearer the house. He said, 'Katie's sure you'll be an invaluable addition to local society . . . snapped up by our member of parliament and courted by all our worthy institutions.'

'Heaven forbid,' Constance demurred, turning to detatch a straggling briar from her shoulder. 'We're still discovering what's in the house, and what needs to be altered. John's coming tomorrow.'

'Splendid! Think what pleasure he'll have, seeing his family here. Mixed memories for him I suppose – his father and sister no longer alive . . . and his mother . . . ?'

'Poor Florence became ill on her return from South Africa. She's now in the London Clinic. Yes – very mixed memories.'

'Well, my dear, you'll be a great comfort to him. He's a lucky man. But I mustn't hold you up, and I've plenty I should be doing.

Our farms are flourishing, D.V., and making their contributions. Should be a good harvest this year.' Roddy went round the lorry to the passenger seat, and brought out a clean but elderly saddle and bridle. 'Daisy's luggage – with our complements. She'll pull that trap of yours, by the bye. I've left the harness with it.'

'Thank you very much Roddy. And do thank Katie. We'll let you know how the children get on. They rode continually in Mooi River, most often without saddles. A dear friend of ours had a string of horses and ponies – and a polo ground.'

'Sounds the ideal life.' Roddy laughed. 'Glad you've come back though. Take care of yourself, Connie.' He kissed her, climbed into the lorry and after reversing into the back yard, drove away.

'Our father's coming home not a minute too soon.' Hal spoke with light irony, balancing on a rotten apple branch lying in the grass, while his sister stood ogling Daisy.

'In other words, he's late,' said Dido. 'Try speaking clearly.'

'Some things are best left obscure. You go on talking to Daisy. She may answer if she stops eating.'

'That's a stale joke, Hal.'

'Are you pleased with her?' asked Constance, coming through the gate.

'Oh so pleased!' said Dido. 'Ponies don't show their age at all. She's perfect.'

'Look in her mouth,' said Hal, 'and wait till her legs buckle under her.'

Daisy's head came up rapidly as Constance drew near, her eye and nostril flared. Then she resumed snatching at the rough orchard grass.

'Ride her with respect,' said their mother. 'Remember Mrs Crawley's remark about her being spirited.'

'Mr Crawley was showing a bit of spirit,' said Hal, glancing down.

Constance moved close to Dido and stroked the pony's back. 'Ride Daisy in the field first, before you take her on the road. All your experience has been in great spaces on the polo ground – with no traffic. When Daddy's here we'll brave the English roads together.'

'We'll have a father tomorrow,' said Hal incidentally. 'Very normal and very weird. I hope we like each other. Love doesn't necessarily mix with blood, does it?'

'Think of oil and water,' said Dido. 'I'm actually quite nervous. I'd broken my arm when he came to Mooi River and I think that annoyed him. He soon went off to Granny Burnett in Durban.'

'He's probably nervous too,' said Hal, his vision expanding. 'After being in the thick of a war, men do suffer nervous attacks. You know he was in the RAMC, don't you? The Royal Army Medical Corps. Which means he was dealing with smashed legs and arms.' He paused, envisaging the carnage. 'We'll be the last straw I expect.'

'Well, I hope not,' said Constance. 'You may be sure he's longing to get to know you – and re-live his boyhood here. An ideal therapy, I should think. The one thing that matters is that we show him our love, and are determined to make him happy.'

'We can always escape into the field and train Daisy.' Dido watched the pony swish her tail and stalk abruptly towards a far corner.

Chapter 3

Awaiting her husband's arrival, Constance was filled with an optimism that was appropriate, but unreliable. An inkling of John's mood at that moment would have helped. For all those months in Egypt and South Africa, waiting anxiously for news, sending reassuring letters and parcels, helping to pack parcels for the troops, welcoming soldiers on leave for meals and civilized facilities in their Durban flat, she had done her bit. Then the memory returned of John meeting her on the station at Pietermaritzburg and greeting her with 'Your dress is too long!'

'Will Father remember his way round everywhere?' asked Hal, standing in the bow window.

'I'm sure he will. It's not so long since he came . . . perhaps the time I was with him on a visit to meet his family. Before he went abroad.' Constance tried not to keep glancing outside. 'You're sure both the gates are open, Hal? And I think you should call him Daddy, rather than Father.'

'He isn't like that yet. I don't know him enough. Father is safer.'

'I might call him Dad,' said Dido, 'and watch how he takes it. What about the Tiplers? Does he know them – and what will they call him?'

'Colonel Burnett of course.'

Dido shuddered and clutched herself. 'I'm greatly dreading our father. What will we talk about? I hardly know anything about war! We'll have nothing in common.'

'He'll be interested in Daisy,' Constance suggested. 'He can watch you riding. He enjoyed the ponies in Mooi River.'

Hal said, 'He only lasted a few days. Then off he whizzed to Granny in Durban.'

'Will you and he have anything in common?' Dido asked her mother, as the doubt occurred.

'They'll have us in common,' said Hal. 'And that will be the trouble!'

Constance said, 'We're all a bit anxious, I expect. I wish it were a more straightforward home-coming. Your father and I have been through a bad time, each in our own way, and suffered from being apart from each other. We must try to get back to how we were before the war. But I expect Daddy won't want to talk about those experiences.'

Hal said, 'I'd have thought the war would make it easier. I'd be really impressed by the things he'd done; and you two could be sorry for him.'

'It would educate us to hear about it,' said Dido, balancing on one foot and stretching the other out behind her. 'I'm so against wars happening.' She stood erect with another sudden thought. 'The war's been over for ages!'

'Yes, it's well behind us. Daddy's had time to get over it and become his old self again.'

'Where was he doing that? Why weren't we all here sooner?'

'They wanted him to re-establish medical services in Singapore.'

Hal was still preoccupied at the window. 'It's like waiting to meet my head teacher.' He drummed his fingers against the sill. Then he raised a shout. 'He's here! There's a car turning into the drive!'

Constance drew a deep breath, rose and walked to the hall, the children passing through before her and into the porch. They heard distressed gravel and a great turbulence of combustion engine roaring into silence.

What greeted them was a grand convertible Bentley, its driver stepping out with an almost bashful smile.

He said, 'Hello!' – standing tall and well dressed in a country suit. What a metamorphosis! Constance thought. No military trace. He moved towards her and gave her a light embrace. He waved his hand towards Hal's head and then Dido's, and watched them climbing into the car through his open door.

Constance laughed. 'It's lovely to see you John – and what a magnificent way to arrive. Is it yours?'

'I'm afraid it is. I'll fetch my bag.' Sheepishly he went to the back and lifted a suitcase from it. 'Don't meddle with the controls, you two – and shut the door when you get out.'

Constance led him into the house, saying, 'I expect you'd like to put your things in the bedroom and have a wash.' She began to ascend the stairs and he followed, looking about him with a quizzical face.

'How are you John?' Constance asked, her tone full of the endearment she couldn't express. If she could only be her natural self, free to touch him at will . . . She hesitated on the landing by the steps to Dido's bedroom, then turned into the passage and entered his room. Hal and Dido came up at speed behind them, and saw their father place his bag on a low table.

He said, 'Does it matter which bed?' standing between them and looking askance. He had the finely combed black hair, open face and wide spaced eyes of a matinee idol . . . who was acting the part of a diffident suitor.

'Whichever you prefer,' said Constance. 'There's no difference.'

Dido said, 'He's our first visitor.'

'Oh, not a visitor!' remonstrated her mother. 'This is Daddy's home, where he grew up. We'll leave you for a few moments John, and have tea ready downstairs.'

'Where did you sleep when you were a boy?' Hal asked.

'In the same room you have,' his father replied.

'So Aunt Unity had my room.' Dido made the easy statement without qualms. 'I wonder if she kept it more tidy than me.'

'Than I,' Hal corrected. 'Aunt Unity certainly couldn't have been untidier.'

'More untidy,' countered Dido.

'Come on children, and leave your father in peace,' Constance urged, taking the lead downstairs.

There was much talk concerning the Bentley sports car. John was sparing in his answers, still using the wry delivery of a child with a bad conscience. He left out the narrative of it's purchase, but supplied ready mechanical facts to his son's questions. Mr and Mrs Tipler had both been introduced, and Mrs Tipler now made a stately appearance with the tea trolley into the drawing-room.

'We hear your mother is poorly,' she said with tactful modesty. 'Such a nice lady, I thought her. Trusted us implicitly with all her lovely stuff. And it was a trust not misgiven.'

Constance thought of the many items absent, probably

broken, according to the agent's inventory. She said, 'We manage as best we can with food rationing, don't we Mrs Tipler? These egg sandwiches look delicious. Mr Hillis's hens from the piggery? How generous of him!'

'There's a trick in every trade,' was Mrs Tipler's sage comment before she withdrew.

'Whatever that means!' said Hal. 'What does it mean?'

'Nothing specific – but it sounds good,' John told him. 'If you join the army one day, you can expect to be mystified by lots of utterances.'

'The front bedroom is a much better size for two people,' Dido observed, intent on the practical. 'Much sunnier.' She waited for a response.

'The room I'm in was considered special in your grandparents' day, because visitors were given it,' John said. 'And I was never allowed to sleep in it as a child.'

Hal said, 'Mr Tipler tells us this house has ghosts. He and Mrs have heard a noise going up the stairs like someone dragging a stick against the bannisters. Mister lives on his nerves. He has to sleep with a light all night.' Then, because he wanted to know, and to help the conversation along, he asked, 'Did your parents see ghosts? Or hear them?'

'I never asked,' his father replied. 'One never asks crucial questions at the right time.'

'We ask endless questions. But we hardly ever have proper answers.'

'We're told that people living here had a pet monkey and it threw their baby out of our mother's bedroom. On to the drive,' Dido volunteered. 'And it died.'

Constance smiled. 'I haven't heard that story.'

John said, 'Have you discovered my old museum?'

'Yes, we found it at once. It's a lovely place. It has that dank kind of stink – like crypts in churches,' Dido recited, with her father's lisp. 'We added an old truncheon to the collection, and an Egyptian horsehair fly swat, and the Japanese sword you found. And some ancient coins. And two of my teeth.'

'And your Japanese postcards,' Hal went on. 'And a bird's skull, and a Boer war button, and Egyptian pottery two thousand years old. And your practice skeleton.'

They all ate egg sandwiches for a moment. Then Constance put her plate aside. 'You remember Ernestine Dunbar, John? She'd be so pleased if you'd look in on her some time. She's rather a lonely soul, and she has a real affection for your family. She's obviously missed having them next door.'

'Old Floppyguts!' John exclaimed, brushing crumbs off his mouth and shirt front. 'Is she still alive? Good heavens – She was an elderly fixture in that house when I was young. Never seemed to go out. Mourning for the good minister – but full of resentment against him.'

Constance glanced up with eyebrows raised, at his frivolity.

'Why Floppyguts? Can we call her that?'

John said, 'Probably better not. It started long ago, I can't remember how. She's a most respectable person, with great amounts of hair on top and a vast bosom.'

The children digested this in silence.

'Tell them about your dog,' suggested Constance.

'Dear old Peter. He was a mongrel – medium size, thin, with a short rough coat – and he could clear a five barred gate.'

'Can we have a dog?'

'You may certainly have a dog.'

Constance said, 'Don't forget what a tie they can be.'

'What d'you think?' Hal asked his sister. They were in the garden, cycling round flagged paths that criss-crossed the extensive lawn and were punctuated at regular intersections by rose and clematis arches.

She didn't hesitate. 'He's trying to behave like a father and I think he's nice. Don't you?'

'Too early,' Hal spoke curtly. 'We'll see if he gets a dog.'

John stood up when the children left. 'After driving from London, a walk is what I need.'

'I'll come with you.'

They passed the car and strolled over the front lawn. 'There was a fine tulip tree here, bang in the centre. My father had it cut down, the old vandal. Have the children found the croquet things yet?'

They hadn't. John discovered the dusty old box in the harness room. 'Needs a lick of paint,' he said. 'That's a job the tiddlies can do. I see the pony trap's still here, and someone's been keeping the harness in order. You must get yourself a horse, and a mount for Hal. It's good for children to work with animals, and develop an understanding for them.'

Constance reflected that he was more apt to display affection and tolerance towards animals than human beings. 'Katie and Roddy Crawley were helpful in letting us have Daisy, and bringing her over.'

'They used to do some horse trading at the Ram Jam – and at the Haycock.' John stopped at the bottom of the side drive, and leaned over the gate. 'How are the Crawleys then? Seen much of them? Roddy was always a bit of a charlatan. She's all right.'

'Oh – I'm fond of Katie. She's been terribly kind. . . and they wouldn't take a penny for Daisy.'

John chuckled, his eyes on the pony coming slowly towards them with a mean expression. 'I gather Roddy avoided being called up. Weak back, weak eyesight –things of that sort.'

'Defective people did help to keep us in food,' Constance demurred in a humorous tone. 'But wouldn't he have been too old?'

John turned his head and looked into her face. 'How are you, Stupe?'

'Very well . . . now you're safely back. I've dreamed of you returning, and getting to know the children better. I wish you'd tell me how you really are. Despite all you've been through, you look as handsome and young as in the days at Oatlands Park! I think you're marvellous.'

Ever dismissive of praise, John replied, 'Mother is dying, you realise.'

'Well, I'm afraid I do. I've visited her twice, but she wasn't well enough to speak much. I just sat and remembered the happy times in Durban when the children and I went for lunch with her at the Cumberland. It made such a difference, having her there.' Sitting with Florence in her private room, it had struck Constance that the mother's bias towards her son in his marital quandary had reproduced the sort of chill connection between herself and Florence that Unity would have known only too well.

'I'll have to go back to London next week, and see to a good many things.'

'Of course.' Inadmissible questions were no sooner in her mind than swept out. With no emotional support, and before the need for legal aid had arisen, her brief was to remain silent on his immediate past – and on their future. Empathy was her best protection. She said, 'Some day before winter we might take Hal and Dido for a trip to Cornwall. The West Country's so beautiful, and I'm tired of hearing them sigh for their beloved Natal: the cheerful faces, the colour, the warmth, the smell of burnt grass in the donga, the mealie plantations . . .'

'That's not a bad idea. I've been thinking of buying a car for you, by the way. You're going to need one.'

Constance felt a surge of spirits. 'What a wonderful offer! I was planning to find one locally.'

'Leave it to me. I've something second-hand in mind. How are your parents?'

'Considering what they'd gone through, we were made very welcome. But they're both a bit shaky and look older. You can imagine my relief in seeing them. Mother's found an attractive house near the sea front, with tenants in the basement, and they fitted us in with them on the other two floors. Prayer is a wonderful thing John; I never ceased to pray for them – and for you – and for a good many people.'

John regarded her with incredulous eyes, startled by the faith of a woman who was in other respects a normal being. He was suddenly transported back to school chapel, hearing the chaplain intoning over the serried ranks of young fellows doomed to die within a decade. He prepared to reply to his wife, assuming that the words would come, then finding his mistake. He knew she had a deep acceptance of religion, which he himself might once have defended. But in his case, the power of prayer seemed to have dissipated on the battlefield.

He said, 'You do know, Stupe, that nothing much will ever be the same again?'

Chapter 4

John had seen his mother in the London Clinic, and she hadn't displayed any interest in how Constance and the children were adjusting to life in her old home. There was no rancour, since she remained fond of Constance at heart; but she was loath to make any imaginative leap back into that Westbourne world.

Hal and Dido had almost forgotten they had a father returning to the house. They'd been on extended cycle rides, explored the dangers of the brickpits with its willow-edged small lake, and proved to Daisy that her will was stronger than theirs: for halfway down one particular lane she refused to approach what only she knew was the slaughter-house at the end.

When they heard the Bentley being garaged with customary roars and cumbersome negotiations, they walked rather than ran to greet John. They felt an awkward duty thrust upon them, for all the goodwill in the world. As Dido was apt to keep repeating, they were just not good at having a father yet.

He drew his suitcase from the back of the car, and smilingly asked them what they'd been up to. Hal said, 'Oh, nothing much.'

'You surprise me. I imagined you discovering the brickpits. Plenty to do up there. But you have to be careful. You can cut your feet on the rubbish in the ashes – and the pond is pretty deep.'

'Oh yes - we did go there, and the ashes were really hot. We found old gramophone records: 'Dancing with tears in your eyes,' and 'What d'ja do Sunday, Mary."

'They're a bit scratched, and the edges are broken, but you have to love them.'

They went into the house together. 'Where's your mother?' John asked, determined to be gentle and good-humoured with her.

Constance met him in the hall. The children slipped away to play their exhumed records. Searching his face, she thought how tired he looked. 'Were you comfortable at the Club?' she asked.

His mouth became poutingly small, and in a self-deprecating manner, he answered, 'Oh – it was shabbier than I remembered, and under-staffed. Food pretty awful.'

'Lunch will be in half an hour. You might like a drink beforehand.'

'No – no thanks. I'll just sort out these things.'

He took his case upstairs. Constance went to the kitchen to supervise Mrs Tipler with vegetables from the garden to go with shepherd's pie. Visiting Florence will have saddened him, she thought. It was possible he was worried about money too; the London Clinic was an extravagance. But finance and dying were not the easiest subjects to debate. Had he been meeting someone in London? In which case his feelings would be full of conflict.

John stood at his bedroom window and watched his children cycling the flagged paths in slow-motion, randomly chattering. In his mind he saw himself and his sister playing, affection between them also.

He had still not come down. Constance walked slowly up the stairs, holding the bannister rail and remembering the rattling stick up the rods at night. She had heard it with vague curiosity and said nothing to anyone in the morning.

'John!' she called, 'can you come for lunch?'

He came with a demure obedience. They found the children in the dining-room, arranging period records inherited with the house.

Dido said, of the one currently playing on the gramaphone, 'It's Paul Robeson singing Ol' Man River. And he was a communist!'

'But he has a beautiful voice,' replied her mother.

'Why 'but?'' challenged Hal. 'It's good to be a communist. It's only luck he can sing well.'

'He made a lot of money with his voice,' John said. 'Are you telling me he gave it all away?'

Hal shrugged. 'Probably some of it. To the poor – and to the cause.'

'I love 'You are my Heart's Delight' and 'A Room with a View' and 'So Blue,' Dido said. 'And 'Just Two Hearts and a Waltz Refrain.' And 'Dancing with Tears in my Eyes.''

'They sound rather a sentimental lot,' said her father.

'My favourites are 'Pick me up and lay me down in dear old Dixeyland." Hal was shuffling through the discs with casual pride. 'Dear old Mooi River' is what we say. And 'Canterbury Chimes' and 'Bells of London' and 'Mr and Mrs Brown at Wembley' are quite funny.'

'We can sing along with the woman who does 'Rusty and Dusty,'' Dido boasted. 'About a boy and his poor little puppy-dog. We do her mincy voice. Put it on, Hal.'

'Here's 'Shepherd of the Hills,'' he said, and was about to oust the communist when Constance informed them that shepherds' pie was standing in the hatch. No matter how apt, the song could wait. They took their seats round the table.

'Help your mother bring the dishes over,' John said. 'You must pull your weight. Do you clean your own rooms?'

'Oh yes, they do,' their mother asserted.

'Do you?'

Hal and Dido glanced at each other. 'We make our beds. And we mop the edges of the rooms.'

'It seems wasted work,' Dido added. 'Over and over again. We could do it once a month.'

With a gesture, John declined the duty of serving for them. So Constance filled the plates and he said, 'Forming healthy habits with self-discipline is something everyone should learn. You're old enough to understand that. It's surely what you're taught at school, Hal?'

'Alas yes,' Hal replied, in jaunty tone.

'And table manners? Look at your knife and fork! Sticking up from your fists like weapons. Put your knife down – you don't need a knife with mince.'

Hal laid his aside with a clatter, and Dido followed suit. They resumed eating after an ungainly transfer of forks to right hands, and with eyes cast down in mirth.

Feeling personally chastened, Constance asked in open tone how the afternoon would be spent. 'Will you two give Daisy some exercise? Daddy hasn't seen her going over the jumps.'

'I had an idea to put her in harness, and take you for a drive in the countryside,' John said, the voice of authority replaced by one of diffidence.

'All of us?' asked Dido, cautiously excited.

'No. Your mother.'

Constance indicated to Dido to help stack and carry plates from the table. Hal remained seated, meddling with his pudding spoon and fork. When Dido slid the four plates off the table with unpractised zeal, half the cutlery fell to the floor.

John struck the table with his hand. 'Why on earth can't you be careful! It's not helping your mother to behave like a clumsy clot.'

'I should very much like a drive round the country,' Constance said brightly, after a pause, and Dido had been reduced to a resentful nonentity. 'You and Hal might cycle to meet us, Dido. We could suggest an approximate time.'

'What a fidget you are,' his father told Hal. 'Leave that spoon alone.'

'Does one use a spoon with rhubarb crumble, or just a fork?' Hal asked with feigned anxiety. Dido had recovered enough to smother a laugh. There was a pause while three bowls were passed round.

'Of course you use your spoon,' John told him. 'Don't be fatuous. I suggest you catch the pony and groom her, and take her to the harness room at two o'clock. Then we'll hitch her up to the trap and fix a time when we expect to be home.'

'If we can't be riding, Hal and I often do manure stirring,' Dido said. 'We sit on the gate with sticks and stir manure in the trough, and it smells mmmmm! My second best job in life.'

'That's a rather silly contribution to our meal,' John said. 'It's distasteful to talk about manure at table. Surely you know that?'

Hal and Dido stared down again with solemn force. There was silence; and then lunch was over.

By two o'clock, Daisy was tied outside the harness house, roughly brushed and with her hooves picked out. When John and Constance joined them in due course, they seemed at ease, with smiling faces. Constance wore a tweed skirt and light jacket, and the beret tilted at an angle on her head had an RAMC badge pinned to it.

'Well now, Ragbag,' was John's greeting to the pony. 'You're to do some interesting work today.'

A shadow of betrayal crossed Dido's face; then she gave a laugh and hopped over the bucket of grooming tools. 'She doesn't know that name,' she said casually.

Hal said, 'But she has a tongue in her head. If she doesn't like it she can say so.'

'Hal thinks Daisy can talk,' jeered Dido in self-defence.

John brought out the trap, and gradually they got the pony into harness and between the shafts. 'She seems placid. Not the virago I was hearing about.'

'She's been used to pulling carts around the farm,' Constance said. 'It's the hunting horn that sets her on fire.'

'I wish I was coming with you.' Hal stood at Daisy's head, fondling her nose. He said it only to curry favour, imagining an hour's painful conversation . . . and in accordance with a habit of hiding his true feelings.

'We should be nearing the house in an hour and ten minutes, if you want to meet us on your bikes,' his father told them, consulting his watch. 'Hold her head now.' He helped his wife up the step and into the snug embrasure of the trap. Following her, he gathered the reins, and Daisy gave a shake of the head and walked through the wrought iron gates and across the road.

'This is a good idea,' Constance said as their pace quickened to a trot. 'Used you to drive your pony as a boy?' She had seen photographs of John and Unity mounted on smart ponies with a nattily dressed groom, standing by. She could imagine the young John wanting to know how to fit harness.

'Someone would drive into the village quite often, perhaps on market day. We'd drive through the woods occasionally, to exercise one of the animals. Mother was a deft driver, though she never rode.'

'Did you set out together as a family?' Spoken with a touch of wistfulness: Constance carried an image in her mind of continual bickering between his parents, which must have eroded John's childhood. 'I imagine you taking a picnic in summer.'

'Good heavens, no.' He flicked the reins as if impatient at such folly, and Daisy responded with a toss of the tail and lowered head as she increased her pace. 'It was a working outfit. Not one for pleasure.'

'I do wish I'd met your father. It's unsatisfactory having no idea of him. No photos – even in a group!'

'He meant little enough to me, so why should he mean

anything to you?'

'Well – it might have helped . . .'

'Nonsense, Stupe! It's no good expecting me to entertain you with family memories. I assure you, they'd be as boring as others of the kind.'

'That's not fair, John. You were pleased to know my family; and it was important to me that they met you. A perfectly normal situation.'

'Nothing is perfect, and no families are normal. Are you warm enough?' He put a rough arm round her for a moment, shifting on the seat.

'I certainly am, thanks. It was quite warm while you were away. I expect London was hot?'

He shrugged. 'I wasn't much outside.' They trotted steadily on for nearly a mile and then he said, 'We're collecting a puppy, by the way. A Labrador.'

'Really? What a surprise for the children!'

'It's a place about two miles from here. Hillis put me on to them. The children must understand the responsibility an animal entails.'

'And the extra work, indeed.'

She felt an urge to draw him out over all he had undergone in the war. Ask him about the precious plank he'd slept on in his ever damp and filthy uniform – until someone stole it. His rescue of his batman under fire – the man's head blown off beneath his arm. Incidents mentioned matter-of-factly in letters, written whenever possible in small, immaculate writing. No hint of self-pity. His good war. Sympathy over it would be anathema to him. Constance felt they were in a party game, each acting a different narrative, with a prohibition on the use of certain words. She reflected that there were many types of happy marriage, and hers was one of the semi-detatched, baffling, humiliating examples.

Would the best thing be to throw caution to the winds and say, John, if you want to ask anyone to Westbourne for the day, then do. As he withdrew his arm to control the reins, she imagined him uttering a dismissive laugh. She could hear him add, But it's typical of you to suggest it, Connie.

She sat with her fantasy tribute in silence; and then the trap veered away down a narrow lane, and Daisy was brought to a halt.

It was a modest cottage, owned by a couple who grew commercial mushrooms. The wife took her visitors down a passage and into the kitchen where an immediate eruption of dogs greeted them from a corner. Led by their mother, five well grown puppies milled about them and competed for attention. Their owner said 'They're more or less house trained,' and waited for attachments to be formed.

John stooped down. 'What do you think, Connie? This one's a fine chap.'

Constance touched the puppy about his face and neck as he struggled in John's arms. He was certainly a sturdy build and a strong colour. His four companions clamoured for attention.

'He's lovely,' she agreed. 'Just as well the children aren't here. They'd have wanted the whole litter.'

John paid for the dog, received its pedigree, and was assured that injections and worm treatment had been administered. They took their leave, the pup tucked inside his jacket.

Constance held the reins going home. John glanced at his watch. 'Those two will have to mark time a bit for our arrival.'

They were there, circling around at the side of the road, half a mile short of the house. They lined up behind the trap and kept the same pace, curious about their parents' outing. Then they caught sight of the puppy's head thrusting from under John's jacket.

'Oh, you've done it,' cried Hal. 'You've got us a dog!' His tone was one of vain hope justified. 'What's his name?'

'Or is he a she?' demanded Dido, striking a femininist note.

'He is a he,' their father replied. 'We have no name for him yet. What name do you suggest?'

'Goggle – like the Causeway,' Dido produced at random, seeing the dog's wondering eyes.

'Rory,' said Hal – a name he preferred to his own.

'He shall be called Prince,' said their father.

The children peddled in silence, exchanging looks. Constance said, 'You can buy a collar and lead for him tomorrow from Bannister's. It's never too early to begin training.'

'Is he house-trained?' Hal asked. 'Or Mrs Tipler won't be so impressed.'

'You two will be responsible for any messes.' John checked his lap, to be sure none had occurred already.

'Mister will be excited,' Dido said, as the vision came to her. 'He can't be nervous of a puppy.'

Chapter 5

John had spent most of that day outside, coming and going from the garage area, and measuring lengths along the wall between their ground and Mrs Dunbar's garden. He was reserved throughout lunch, and hurried out afterwards. When four o'clock gave her an excuse to follow him to the party wall, she found a quantity of stones had been delivered over the grass.

'Are you building something?'

He wore his self-deprecating expression and shrugged, much as Hal often did. 'Just thought I'd put a bit on to the wall along here. Bring it up to a decent height.'

In Constance's view, the existing barrier was adequate, being of handsome stonework, and against a part of the neighbouring garden which never seemed to be used. She said, 'Well, you've given yourself an undertaking. Can you get Will Hillis to help you?'

'I thought Hal could help. It'll teach him something useful. Hillis has enough to do, keeping up a garden this size.'

Would there be a positive reaction from their son? Uneasily expecting not, Constance asked John if tea brought into the garden would give him a welcome break.

He shook his head, mouth formed into its humourous pout. 'No thank you.' He gazed towards the two well grown pear trees where a hammock hung, and said, 'They've done well. Right from the first, they gave splendid crops of pears.' He looked aside at a smaller, very elderly tree, and commented on the lavish crop of greengages remembered from his childhood. 'Unity and I used to lie on the little bank there, luring wasps into a special glass container with jam and vinegar. They came in droves, and fell into the vinegar until the base was a mass of struggling dopey bodies. It fascinated us – as something surreal.'

'Did either of you get stung?' asked Constance, open to hearing they too had suffered.

'Oh yes,' he confirmed. 'No harm in that.'

'We've been giving pounds of fruit away to various people. And I've done lots of bottling.' Constance paused to draw strength to herself. 'John, I feel there's a social call I'd like us to make together. To Haverfield.'

'What –to the Measures?'

'Yes. Bunty knows you're here. She and Max want to see you. Either we go there, or I ask them here. After all – the children are your nephew and niece . . . Unity's family.'

'I can't remember their names. They won't want to meet me.'

'Of course they will! Bunty's been very friendly, and kept in touch. They'll wonder what's wrong if we make no effort.'

'Max is awful. You go and see them.'

'How can I go on my own now? What excuse can I give?'

'Warfare dulls a man's social graces. I haven't the heart to be sociable.'

Constance's sympathy was touched. 'No-one is easier and more fun than you in company.' In the old days, she amended to herself. 'And we won't mention Unity.' Struck with a sense of foreboding, she added, 'We need only stay a short time.'

'Tell them I'm healing my nerves by placing one stone on top of another. I'm building a wall.'

'Well – I'll ask you again later.' She waited long enough for him to see she had a smile on her face, and then returned to the house.

'Mrs Tipler's the kindest person I know – not counting family,' Dido exclaimed as her mother entered the staff sitting-room. 'I absolutely love her!'

Mr Tipler, appearing from the scullery, sniggered. 'But you're not married to her, duckie.'

Finding this not only obvious but improper, Dido resumed, 'Your wife is the kindest. She's been on all fours and let me put Daisy's saddle on her – and then I mounted! But the girth was too tight.'

Mrs Tipler, busy with her hands, showed no embarrassment, while her face glowed unhealthily. The puppy had left its basket to welcome Constance and she asked after its progress.

'A promising start with his evacuations,' Mrs Tipler said. 'He's catching on. But it's the catching on with his teeth I don't care for.'

'He does nip,' Dido said. 'Mister almost lost a finger.'

'Mr Tipler,' corrected Constance. Then, 'That's something else Prince will have to learn. And you must never treat poor Mrs Tipler like that again, Dido. Now take your saddle and put it back in the harness-room.'

'I'm none the worse, and maybe a bit better,' chuckled the house-keeper. 'I'll need to watch my waistline, won't I?'

'Remember Hal using someone's old toothbrush to clean his bike?' Dido said lightly, gathering the saddle and its girths into her arms. 'He thought it couldn't be one that was wanted.'

'Course it wasn't,' Mrs Tipler assured her, with a look towards her husband, 'Get that dog out quick! He's about to perform again.'

'If we're going on this visit, may we please go!'

John, standing in the hall, had raised his voice, though he knew all his family were near at hand. The grandfather clock cleared its throat and commenced striking the hour.

Hal and Dido emerged from the dining-room, with last snatches of their conversation dying away. Their father's eyes regarded them critically, and rested on his son's feet.

'You've forgotten to clean your shoes.'

Hal could find nothing to say, as he never cleaned them. Looking down, he considered the fronts were quite white enough.

'Do you normally go out to tea in gym-shoes?'

Hal shrugged. 'We don't normally go to tea.'

'I think a pair of black school shoes would be more suitable ... with the backs as well as the fronts polished. But we're running late already. So those will have to be seen – and will let you down accordingly.' John turned to his daughter. 'Show me your hands.'

She held them out, and he took them in his own and examined the fingers. 'I've noticed you bite your nails. It's a disgusting habit.'

Hal said, 'People mostly do that when they're made to worry about life.'

Ignoring this remark, John elaborated further. 'No-one will ask you to marry them.'

'Well, I wouldn't want to marry a fusspot of that sort,' Dido said defensively. She thought, I'd rather bite my nails.

Constance hurried into the hall from the drawing-room where she'd been delayed on the phone. She apologized, looking a little flustered. They all went outside and walked to the garage. Their drive to Haverfield in John's Bentley lasted barely twenty minutes, and the silence was broken only by short exchanges between Constance and John. The children communicated silently, and stared at the passing countryside. Being in an open sports car, they were all blown about, and Constance was glad to have a scarf.

Drawing up before the house, they were confronted by a dark bay pony standing near the front steps and held by a fair-haired girl of about thirteen. She was joined by her father, strolling up from an adjacent barn.

'Hello there,' he greeted. He was of average height, dark haired, and with an acquiline nose on a narrow face that seemed ill matched with his muscular body. His eyes were large and very bright, and with his olive skin he had an attractive appearance. He was not dressed for a tea party.

Constance called 'Max! How are you?' and went forward to receive a formal handshake that was abruptly translated into a clumsy embrace. Then Bunty came down the steps, gave Constance a warm hug, and waved a hand at her step-daughter. 'This is Serena, our budding horse-woman.'

'And this is Chocolate,' said Serena in her flutey voice.

John shook Max by the hand, nodded Hello to Serena, and stepped back to survey the house and grounds. 'Farms still doing all right?'

'We're still in business . . . whatever else the world is up to. Are you interested to go round?'

John liked action, and to see how things worked. They set off together. Bunty called, 'Don't go too far – tea at four o'clock!'

Hal and Dido were brought up to Serena and they gave each other uneasy glances.

'Dad!' Serena shouted, 'Can you turn Chocolate into the starvation patch for me?'

Max returned as though failing to fathom why he should, and led the pony off between himself and his brother-in-law. Bunty ushered her visitors up the steps with an awkward movement, a tall, willowy, rather hesitant person in a simple old-fashioned summer dress. 'James is somewhere . . . Poor children, they're counting the days left of their holidays like misers. Of course they love school, but it's been such a lovely hot summer for them. James!'

A pause bringing no sign of James, Bunty took Constance into the drawing-room and sat near her in a way that suggested a comfortable dialogue without children or men involved. 'Go and do something upstairs,' she said to Serena, who hung at the door with her guests. 'After tea, you'll probably want to go outside.'

Serena swung on her heel and started dutifully up the stairs. James appeared above them, and leaned over the bannisters. 'So you've come,' he stated.

'Well – we have,' Hal confirmed. 'But it wasn't our idea.'

'Come and listen to our musical-box.' Serena herded them into a large playroom, and lifted down a box of greater proportions than their own. Hal and Dido watched her press the handle up and down to set the roller turning with a mixture of awe and pique.

'We've got a musical-box too,' said Hal. 'It plays eight tunes.'

'Ours plays nine,' replied James, promptly. He was a small boy with brown hair and the same large brown eyes as his sister. They were both dressed in shorts and aertex shirts.

'I just love all our tunes,' said Dido. 'Not one is boring. They're all special.'

'This one is lovely if you listen to it properly,' said Serena. 'Our nine tunes get more and more special.'

They bent their heads close to the vibrating box to listen; and when Serena lowered the lid, the visitors decided it was less nicely decorated than their own.

'Bunty's your step-mother, isn't she?' asked Hal.

'Yes. Our mother's dead,' answered Serena.

The Burnetts digested this, mindful of stories they had read in younger days. 'I expect your step-mother really wishes she could turn you out,' Hal said. 'At the beginning she will have, anyway.'

'No she didn't,' James said roughly. 'She was always glad to be our mother.'

'Not in the way our mother's glad to have us.'

'How do you know?' James glared at Hal, doubts assailing him.

Hal said, 'Your father probably prefers Bunty now, to both of you.' He tilted his head on one side, considering. 'Unity was our aunt as well as your mother,' he added, as though defending the line he took, and trying to show solidarity with them.

'We know that, silly,' Serena replied, shaking her long hair to one side in dismissal. 'We're cousins.'

'Distant ones,' Hal said quickly, his tone cool. 'Meaning we live near each other, but we don't meet.'

'We're finding our father quite difficult,' Dido said, in conciliatory tones. 'We fall into every trap.'

Max had taken John as far across the fields as seemed practical, and explained their crop system. They were in the great cow shed when John broached the subject of his sister.

'It was ghastly losing her,' Max said, shaking his head and gripping a wooden hurdle. 'Never suspected any such thoughts in her mind. She seemed a well-balanced person – interests of her own, and all that.'

'I imagine she was upset when our father died,' John put to him as a question. 'They were always close.'

'Heavens yes. She took his death badly. But in the main, she was sound as a bell. She just had a highly-strung side to her. Stroppy as a mare on occasions. Of course we used to have rows . . .'

A long pause followed.

'I expected you to look after her,' John said, meeting Max's eyes.

Max moved away from the partition as if stung by his brother-in-law's tone. What on earth right had he to take that pompous attitude? He said simply, 'I adored Unity. And I encouraged her love of reading. Did you know she had a regular order of books delivered from Hatchards? She had accounts at Harrods and at Fortnum and Masons too.' He thought, and not funded by her mother – who spent her money on luxury liners and hotels . . . and right now, at the ritzy London Clinic. 'You can take it from me,' Max said 'I looked after her very comfortably. I'm sorry to hear Florence is dying.'

'I think the world of my mother,' John said mildly, 'and I hope she's not going to die.'

Voices reached them from the house. 'Tea time! Do come!'

Bunty had the paraphinalia arranged about her. She stood over the trolley, teapot in hand. The children came pushing through the door, and were dispatched to call the men again.

Max and John lingered at the foot of the steps. 'Connie's looking as attractive as ever,' Max was saying. 'Now you'll be happy to make up for the years apart.'

John made no reply but thought, I'll be happy if you'd mind your own business.

They entered the house and went each to a separate cloakroom. Bunty had poured the tea, and laid the task of passing sandwiches on James and Hal. Serena was draped negligently across a comfortable chair and was required to vacate it for her uncle as he came into the room. Dido perched on a stool and found it beyond her to balance a plate, and hold a cup, and eat and drink.

'Pull that little table over,' Bunty advised. 'Perhaps you children would prefer fruit juice?'

John sat in the comfortable chair, and seethed with discomfort. Max had caught him on the raw over Constance; and all that sanctimonious claptrap about Unity. I too love my wife, he thought. He rested his eyes on a portrait of Unity hanging in the room: The artist had posed her, gazing over her shoulder as she sat in evening clothes, three-quarter face; a small mouth, large grey eyes and with an expression that was both quizzical and entreating. A very personal focus. Marrying Max had been a mistake; but how could she have shot herself?

The Measures family went outside to see the visitors leave. While the adults talked, James ran to the Bentley in excitement, ready to stroke the gleaming metal and imposing lamps, but resisting the temptation. Hal, whose attitude towards the growling monster had been ambivalent, now strolled over and rested an elbow against its windscreen with casual swank. 'You can touch it if you like,' he told his cousin. Then the others arrived.

'You must admit Stupe, it was a pretty awful business. Max is still the same ass he ever was,' John said in a low tone, driving back.

He had spoken affectionately. Constance, for whom the afternoon had been a pleasure, felt her heart lift.

She laughed. 'Bunty made it all very easy. And the children seemed to get on together. Was Max so dreadful? I thought he welcomed us warmly enough.'

'He has a nice line in hypocricy, you mean. If you could hear his comments now, you'd sit up.'

'Our cousins didn't think much of us,' said Hal. 'But that was because we refused to be brow-beaten.'

'What d'you mean?' John asked.

'They behaved like superior people. But they aren't really. Anyway, we've got a lot of the same blood.'

'Couldn't you just enjoy seeing their rooms and being together?' Constance asked.

'The point is,' Dido explained, 'we saw their pony, but they haven't seen Daisy. They knew no better.'

'Well, James liked this car,' said Hal.

When John went to Dido's room to say goodnight, she was sitting up with a book on her lap. 'You did well with your cousins,' he said. 'You should see them often – make friends with them. Now sleep well.' He moved to the door.

'Will you go to Hal now?'

Her father smiled, and she returned to her book.

Looking in at the room along the passage, he found his son sitting on the bed with parts of a balsa wood model aeroplane around him. John walked to the window, glanced out and returned to see what the model was. He said, ' We'll make a good job on that wall in the next day or so.'

Hal uttered a sound between a laugh and a jeer.

'I like to see you and Dido leading the sort of life I led with my sister.' There was a pause. ' Will you want to take up riding again? I've offered to find your mother a horse, and you could all go out together.'

'It wouldn't be the same as Mooi River.'

'This part of England is famous for its hunting and hacking. Think it over.' Another pause. 'One experience you won't have, which I did: your tonsils taken out on a kitchen table – in the Tiplers' sitting-room.'

'Wasn't there a hospital in those days?'

'Yes – over in Stamford. But much less fuss and bother getting it done here.'

'Are you going to work in Stamford?'

'No. London.' John was trying the wings against the body of Hal's plane. 'I suppose it's school again in a week or so. How are you getting on? We must have a talk about it before you go back.'

Hal's shoulders twitched. He said, 'Dido's got to go as well. But her school's only in the village. She's never been to any school before.'

'And I have to go back to London. We all have work to do. Well, you've earned a good sleep. Thank you for your help at that charade today.' He gave his son a conspiratorial smile and handed him the model plane.

Hal nodded, and retreated into bed.

Chapter 6

John had begun his project of building the wall. Hal's cooperation wasn't so much sought as coerced. In vain did his mother urge him to make the best of it, pick up some useful skills, stow away for term-time some boasts of the achievement. He hung about close to his father, fetched and carried, pushed the wheelbarrow, mixed mortar with lime and even placed one stone with increasing brutality on top of another.

The hours passed. Constance carried glasses of pear juice across the lawn to them. Dido came and went with tactless freedom; then announced she'd go for a ride. Three hours crawled by, then another meal imposed a break. Hal kept an embittered silence throughout; Dido vividly described her ride up the road, and how lovely the countryside appeared, and how Daisy was a tease . . . refusing to go along that lane again.

Hal ground his teeth. Their father said, 'I'll tell you why. She knows the slaughter-house is at the end of it. She's a clever little mare.'

Dido looked stricken. If anything was sinful, a slaughter-house was.

Hal said, 'I can think of worse places to pass the time.'

Constance lifted a serving spoon. 'What are you doing this afternoon?' she asked with an encouraging expression.

'We'll be hell-bent on getting that wall finished,' John answered, draining his glass of water. 'No more to eat thanks. We don't want to waste time.'

'What about you, Hal?'

Hal glared at his mother. For a moment he seemed about to speak; then he shoved his chair back and slouched after his father, turning at the door to scowl at Dido.

'It's not the way to treat him. I know Hal,' she told her mother.

'Hal's like Daisy – he won't be forced.'

'I think you're right.' Constance began to stack the plates. 'Fathers should make it fun to do useful things. Your father's a wonderful leader of men – but not yet of boys, I'm afraid.'

Opposite Westbourne House were Almshouses built in red-black brick round three sides of a garden square and forming a picturesque small-scale scheme. Constance had occasionally called on the elderly inhabitants of these cottages, asking them about themselves, hearing accounts of their lives. She would tell the children some of what she heard, and the protagonists emerged as colourful characters. It soon became clear to her that among the old women, two or three were apt to malign each other; but taken individually, they all had idiosyncratic strengths. The old men didn't gossip, but retired more into their modest homes where they smoked. Old man Belcher could be seen several days a week pushing his small handcart up or down West Road. No-one knew on what business he was bent. One watery-eyed man confided to Constance that a gypsy had told him he should never go to bed; and for twenty years he had slept in a chair. Thin Miss Poole was the spryest member of the cottages, with her long floating hair and wavery speech. Mrs Baxter with the swollen legs kept a fat white Jack Russell terrier for company. Miss Elliot, it was rumoured, had cut off her neighbour's flower heads to clinch a disagreement.

Lunch being tidied away, and Hal having trailed his father morosely back to their building site, Constance told Dido that she wanted to look in on Mr Fewings, who slept in a chair.

'Collect some pears, and we'll take them together. Mrs Tipler will find you a bag.'

'Can't we visit Miss Poole? I'd like to make her hair into plaits.'

They went to see Mr Fewings.

He was sitting outside in a sunny patch, pipe in hand. He smiled a toothless smile at them, and insisted on returning indoors so they could sit down. 'You said your chest was bothering you last week,' Constance reminded him. 'How is it now?'

Mr Fewings promptly coughed, knocking his fist against his brown woollen cardigan. 'Not so bad,' he said between gasps. 'Can't complain.'

'But would you do better to take some cough medicine?'

Constance asked, showing him a bottle she'd bought for the purpose.

'Na.' He shook his head. 'I don't hold with that stuff. Nat'ral med'cines is what works, and I get that in baccy.' And he waved his pipe at her.

Dido was touching the back of his armchair, fiddling the antimacassar into line. From behind his head, she said, 'I've got a lovely pillow I could bring you to sleep on.'

He was chuckling. 'What'ud I want with a pillow, lass?'

'Well –for your head . . .'

Before she could persuade him further, there came a tap on the door. A man looked in.

'Hello Uncle Ned!' he said, and came fully into the room. 'Just passing, and thought I'd see how you were doing.' He smiled at Constance. 'I'm Oliver Seaton – Ned's nephew. He's mentioned that you visit from across the way.' He gestured. 'You are Mrs Burnett?' He had pleasant features and the deep voice of a large male person.

Constance shook his outstretched hand. 'I pop in now and then. We have some good chats don't we, Mr Fewings?'

'He won't have my pillow,' said Dido ruefully. 'He ought at least to try it, even if he won't sleep on a bed.'

'Old dogs can't do new tricks,' said Mr Fewings placidly.

Constance stood up. 'I'll come back next week.'

Oliver Seaton laughed. 'A surfeit of well-wishers. I'm very glad to meet you both,' and he smiled at Dido. 'I hope we coincide again at Uncle Ned's. But don't leave. I can sit over here . . .' and he pulled up a stool and squarely sat on it. 'I'd like to hear how long you've been living locally.'

'Don't mind me,' said Mr Fewings. 'The lass can talk to me about pillows.'

'I never give up,' Dido assured him.

'Do you live nearby?' Constance asked Oliver, laughing despite herself.

'Just over in Edmorton. Matter of six miles.'

He seemed familiar to Constance already; a man of goodwill. There was much laughter between them all before Constance put the pears in a bowl on the sideboard and took her leave.

'That was jolly nice,' said Dido, closing their iron gate after them to prevent Prince wandering on the road.

'They were both nice,' her mother agreed.

'But think – no beds!'

'Oh, I expect Mr Seaton has a bed.'

'I wonder how Hal is.' Dido frowned. 'He'd have talked Ned into having a pillow. He's good at persuading. Unlike our father.'

The wall builders hadn't been jolly. Hal stormed through the back door late in the evening, his face dark with anger, and went straight upstairs. John remained in the garden clearing up the remnants of their day's work, and brushing Constance aside when she came to see the results.

'Do encourage Hal to feel pride in what you've done,' she urged. 'It is rather a splendid job! He looked so tired and cross a moment ago.'

'It's no good pandering to them,' John answered.

'But encouragement!' she reiterated. 'He was a help, I presume? He's spent most of the day fetching and carrying for you?'

'He did quite well.'

'Then please do show him you're grateful! That you couldn't have done it without him.'

'But I could,' John said. He grasped the wheelbarrow and running it close to her legs, set off across the lawn.

John took trouble in seeing his children at bedtime that night. He went to Dido first, and sat on her bed, and asked what book she had on her lap.

'It's Doctor Dolittle,' she said. She passed the book to him and lay down.

'Would you like a chapter read aloud?'

Giving her assent, she became spellbound by the voice he used, and the manner of his reading. Her eyes never left his face as she listened. With his slight lisp, she thought he sounded the very being of Doctor Dolittle, and with his love of animals and gentle, funny manner; a total obverse to the father Hal had spent the day with. Before he closed the book, he turned it to share the pictures with her.

'Now sleep well.'

She slid under the covers and he moved to the door.

She sat bolt upright again. 'If you go to Hal, will you be nice to him too? He's not used to building walls.'

'He's done it very well,' her father said. 'I'm most grateful to him . . . and I will certainly try to be nice.'

Chapter 7

John ran the Bentley to the curb in Gloucester Road and drew a deep breath of satisfaction mingled with nervous anticipation. He glanced up at the red brick Victorian block of flats, swinging the car keys lightly against the dash-board. Then he stepped onto the pavement, locked his door and crossed the road.

Vera received him with a cry of pleasure and drew him into the flat she shared with another nurse. He caught her round the waist and embraced her in his own manner, his soul shedding all its anxieties and burdens.

Vera sat him down on the chintz covered sofa and tucked herself beside him, taking hold of his hands. She was a scale larger than Constance, with dark hair in a mildly wavy style and blue eyes set well apart. An attractive face, a Jersey cow in human form, with a certain tilt about the nose. Her voice held a faint West Country lilt, and she was apt to display a quirky self-confidence.

'How are you enjoying St Thomas's?' he asked. 'How's morale?'

'Theirs or mine? We never have enough staff or money of course; but I love the work – and I'm touched to think of the days when a youthful John was there as a student. When do you start at Millbank?'

'After Christmas.' He took a deep breath. Vera's eyes were very bright, and he stared into them. 'I've been missing you.'

'Can you really say that? I've been imagining you with Constance – and getting to know your children. Has it been happy, living with them in your childhood domain?'

'Domain!' He laughed at her word, and leaned back against an over-stuffed cushion. His fondness for Constance, their war-time interdependence, Hal's need of him, was all at the back of his mind. He leaned over and kissed her and glanced about him. 'You did well to find this flat.'

A good Wilton carpet covered the floor. She had hung her commemorative Spode plates, each with a different flower design, across one wall; two ornamental poodles stood on the mantelpiece, tributes to a dog she had kept and who had gone to a higher sphere; and of prime importance to her, the family pieces of silver, arranged to be noticed.

Vera had an arch manner of regarding him, and a ready chuckle in her voice. She said now, 'I did well for you in Singapore.'

'You made an excellent impression on me.'

She continued to regard him with a teasing smile. 'You were such a bad colour. Yellow ivory.' She now leaned across to kiss him. 'But you were no malingerer – like one or two of them.'

He made a wry expression. 'Despite you, I didn't much enjoy being ill.'

She played with the fingers of his hand. 'It's nice to think of you a student again. Remember telling me how you drove from Edinburgh to London for a show and back that same night, ready for lectures next morning.'

'Hey ho,' he said, ironic and rueful. 'I'm a dull old stick now. Don't expect merry japes of that sort.'

She quizzed him seriously. 'Tell me: how are you? Is it a case of living on your nerves with the family? Are you still having nightmares?'

'Health perfectly reasonable.'

'I don't want you to be anxious. Or guilty.'

'I won't be anxious or guilty.' He turned away from her on the sofa and held his head in his hands. 'I just don't know what I want. I wish I could appreciate that I'm alive, with my wife and children – in the old home.' He thought, Westbourne has no sentimental pull for me. Unity and I weren't happy children. Our parents barely communicated, except to argue. And having pleurisy each winter wasn't a lot of fun.

'Anyone would consider you were lucky.'

'I daresay. But I don't feel it. That's what is so stressful. Made worse by resenting my brother-in-law.'

'You said you weren't going over there!'

'I know.' A rueful note again. 'Constance contrived it so that we all went, much against my better judgment. Max has a talent for bringing out the barbarian in me.' He raised his head, stood up and drew her to her feet. Neither of them spoke for a moment and he thought, I doubt if any marriage is quite right. My past seems something of a dead loss – but I've no confidence to go another way.

'You ought to make a few ward rounds at Thomas's,' Vera said, 'and witness the misery and mutilation in some of the beds.'

'That's the stuff to give me. I need a good kicking.'

'Exactly what I had in mind.' She smiled into his face, and put her hands behind his neck.

To think that in one mood he could indulge his selfishness with marital betrayal, and in another, indulge the dark satisfaction of throwing his life away. Despising himself, he began to laugh.

She jerked her chin upwards when he didn't speak, and pursed her mouth in imitation of the one he often made. Then he enclosed her in his arms.

Mrs Tipler was weeping. Constance could no longer ignore the fact. Knocking on the sitting room door, she went inside. She put a hand on the house-keeper's well-upholstered shoulder. 'What's the matter?' she asked.

The tears stopped as at the touch of a switch. Constance wondered if alcohol could be part of the trouble. 'Have you been drinking?' she asked, receiving no answer.

Mrs Tipler looked up with a tear-sodden face, and nodded vigorously. 'You're right! Beer turns me into another woman, Mrs Burnett. I become a brute, though it's not in my nature to be rough.' She sniffed and rubbed a handkerchief over her face. 'I'm the life and soul one moment, and the next I'm full of anger. Over nothing!'

Constance had decided she must arrange a change of position for her. The Tiplers' trips down to the Nag's Head, and her subsequent mental state, was a deciding factor. Prince had begun demonstrating a wish to enter the pub when out with Constance and the children, and Mr Hillis had explained it was because the Tiplers took him in on a regular basis, and treated him to his own quotas of beer.

Constance pulled up a chair beside the distressed woman, and explained what was in her mind.

Dido, meanwhile, had heard the sounds of sobbing in horror.

She felt herself caught between an urge to rush in and comfort the person for whom she had such an affection . . . and a need to keep her distance. She had little confidence in her own powers. She delayed getting undressed and stood listening to the weeping with an uneasy curiosity. Then she crept down the stairs, aware of her mother going into the Tiplers' room and hovered inside the china pantry. Moments later she slipped bare footed through the back door to collect her shoes in the yard, and with a rude shock was confronted by Mister, clinging to the fence in front of the raspberry, gooseberry and currant bushes. He looked like a man flung into outer darkness, and made more spectral by the twilight surrounding them.

Dido asked, 'Are you all right?' He was never all right – never jolly or purposeful or cross – but this utter despair struck Dido as awful. He was either panting or crying, and she could see tears running from his eyes when she peered at him. 'Have you been sick?'

'He replied, 'Sick at heart, more like.' He was clutching the fence as if about to fall.

Dido stared. 'You seem a bit weak. D'you need some food?'

He shook his head. 'I'm not hungry. I'm sore.'

'Why?'

'I've been hurt.'

'Who hurt you?'

'Swear not to speak to your mum or your brother?'

'I swear!' said Dido.

'It's the missus! She starts on the beer, then she lets me have it. Loses her temper – she's got a filthy temper.'

Dido, picturing her dear Mrs Tipler letting Mister have it, was dismayed. 'With words or fists?'

'Both,' said Mr Tipler, glancing nervously at the back door of the house. 'It's a habit, after the beer. In between, we rub along.'

Dido thought of her bitten nails, and of this poor man's sufferings, and decided again that she'd never get married. She said, 'Your wife's been kind to Hal and me. And she works so hard.'

'She shouldn't drink,' he said roughly. 'When I warn her not to, she clouts me.'

It was a profound disillusionment . . . and Mrs Tipler being so much bigger! Like Hal thumping her, but worse.

She picked up a shoe in either hand. 'Cheer up,' she said, hopping round him on one foot. 'At least you don't have to go to school.'

Chapter 8

Constance was writing letters at the drop-front bureau in the drawing-room. She heard a Land Rover pull up, doors slam shut, then came an imperious tattoo on the inner front door. She hurried to open it and was rewarded with an embrace in the hall.

'Gracious Roddy, you're a man in a hurry,' she said, detaching herself with an ironic smile. 'Are you sure now, this isn't going to be a nuisance?'

'By no means, Connie dear.' He retained his hold on her upper arm. 'Always plenty of time to serve a beautiful woman. Thirlsby's a mere stone's throw away! And as Katie will have told you, we're calling on friends. Katie knows someone in every damned town and village in the county, and we sometimes like to check they're alive.'

Katie tapped on the open door and joined them. 'We're running late as usual. How are you all? The children still at home?'

'Not for much longer. Dido's starting at the village school, so I shall be missing them both. I'm most grateful for your help with the Tiplers. John's promised to produce a more practical car for our use. Meanwhile, it's awkward getting around.'

'Isn't John back yet? I'm keen to have that natter with him,' said Roddy, rubbing his hands, and darting glances up the stairs. 'Best get together one evening. We'll have them to dinner – eh Katie?'

'John's in London. His mother died yesterday, and he'll be staying for her funeral.' Constance hesitated, hoping they wouldn't know she wasn't attending. 'I don't suppose you'd like coffee before you leave with the Tiplers?'

To her relief, Katie said, 'No, I think we'll get on our way, dear. But we're so sorry about John's mother. Probably a relief for her – and that makes it easier for John and for you.'

'Yes, I'm sure that's true.' Constance felt an involuntary emotion rise in her as she spoke. She added rapidly in a low voice, 'As I explained on the phone, the job I've found for Mrs Tipler is a last chance. She's determined to give up alcohol and to govern her temper in future. Dido will miss her. It's a great shame.'

Constance went into the dining-room. She looked through the open hatch, and was told that the Tiplers were ready. She then called upstairs, where the children had been hanging about to make their farewells. They appeared on the landing and descended slowly. Mr and Mrs Tipler arrived, each carrying cases.

'I understand we're taking you to members of your family?' Katie said. 'Will you have somewhere of your own to go to soon?'

Mrs Tipler shook her head. 'We can't take advantage of my niece. But she insists we don't rush into anything. I've got this post at the old folk's home in Market Deeping, doing lunches. A new start all round, you might say.'

'And a blessing on it!' Roddy spoke in a glass-raising voice with spontaneous lack of wisdom. Mrs Tipler's fondness for beer had gone before her to Market Deeping; promises had indeed been made and a regime undertaken.

'We'll see what comes up.' Mrs Tipler shook her head again. 'You can't rush into finding digs.'

'People are a trial and a trouble,' said Mr Tipler, complexly.

Hal said, 'Are we going with them?'

'No room – and we're not coming straight back,' Roddy said crisply. 'Here – give me that case,' and he took Mrs Tipler's bag from her and went to the door.

'Say goodbye, children,' said Constance.

'Goodbye,' said Hal. 'I'm sure the old people will like your cooking.'

Dido was pale and reluctant. Hal went forward and shook the Tiplers' hands. Mrs Tipler put her arms round Dido and said, 'We'll look in sometimes and see you all. Don't let that Daisy get too fat for her saddle!'

Dido allowed herself to laugh. 'Goodbye Mister,' she said. 'Look after yourself.' For a mad moment she was tempted to lend him their musical-box.

'Drop in and see us, Connie,' Roddy called from behind the wheel. 'Don't wait for John.'

The Burnetts stood on the gravel watching the vehicle depart. Hal glanced at his sister's face. 'Are those real tears?' he asked, incredulously. 'I'm sad, but only a *bit* sad.'

They wandered into the porch and sat on the oak seat, then returned outside and watched their mother talking to Mr Hillis beyond the great yew tree. After some idle minutes, Hal gave Dido a friendly kick. 'Shall we go and see Floppyguts?'

She said morosely, 'That's not her name. It's Ernestine.'

They climbed the aggrandized wall, something Hal had intended to do for his own satisfaction, and were greeted by a barrage of yapping. Towards them over rough grass came a pug. He was oatmeal in colour with a black head, and his bulging eyes shone. The children sank to their knees, laughing. When they walked towards the garden door of Trullers, the pug trotted at their feet. Hal pointed to a bird bath standing in an over-grown flower-bed. 'Let's read what it says.'

The lettering under the bowl read: The kiss of the sun for pardon, the song of the birds for mirth. One is nearer to God in a garden than anywhere else on earth.

'That'll be her husband,' Hal said. 'I bet he wrote it.'

'Come on,' said Dido.

Under Roddy Crawley's influence, Hal knocked loudly with his knuckles. Somebody approached, opened the door, and came out. It was Mrs Ablewhite, a middle-aged lady wearing an overall and carrying a packet of soap flakes.

Dido said 'Hello!' and Hal at the same time asked if they could pay Mrs Dunbar a visit.

Mrs Ablewhite said, 'She's not expecting you then?'

'No,' said Hal, 'It's a surprise.'

'Well – I'll go and tell her.' Mrs Ablewhite disappeared into the house, and they heard voices in muffled exchange. The room they were in was furnished with rattan chairs and tables, some with pots of flowers on them, and there was a general sense of dead petals and dust. The air was not fresh. The pug was panting with expectation.

Voices grew louder and they heard, 'Bring them in here Mrs A, and we'll have some cocoa if you please.'

Mrs Dunbar was regally seated in her favourite armchair. She was draped in a magnificent wrap of Indian silk, under which were layers of still more lustrous garments. Her knees were smothered in what appeared to be a small, heavily embroidered bedspread. Her hair was impressively coiled to a height, but allowing much casual escape from the main structure. Pins and slides were in evidence, and a tired bow was fixed to one side. Mrs Dunbar leaned graciously forward with a sweep of her braceleted arm and said, 'Find somewhere to sit my dears, and tell me about yourselves.'

Dido, inhaling perfume, felt she was being wafted far beyond the mere confines of the house next-door.

'Can we call you Ernestine?' Hal asked, as if the optimum footing for their elevenses couldn't be too quickly established.

Mrs Dunbar regarded him steadily. She said, 'You *may* call me Ernestine since you ask nicely . . . grammar apart. Not so many people are entitled to use my Christian name nowadays. I rather like it.'

'So do we,' said Dido, for Hal's benefit.

'And how is your dear mother? And has your father settled into family life now?'

'Father's mother has just died,' said Hal. 'We're very sad, because she was our grandmother in Durban.'

'I'm sorry to hear it.'

Mrs Ablewhite returned with a gilded tea trolley, and dispensed cocoa into a modest-sized cup for Ernestine, and two breakfast cups for the children.

'The biscuits over here please, Mrs A.' Biscuits were passed round and the pug, who was rapidly reaching a second climax of excitement, circled the company with staccato jumps.

'Our mother never told us about him,' said Dido, reaching a hand to the dog. It was ignored since it held no food.

'He was probably taking Mrs A for a walk when your mother came.' Ernestine languidly broke a chip off her biscuit and tapped it on her plate, while the pug watched. 'His name is Willoughby,' she told them. 'I was inspired to call him Hereward. I needn't remind you that Hereward the Wake was born in this town.'

'You do need,' said Dido, under her breath.

'Now then little fleshpot, that is greedy. Just be good and play at being a proper dog.' Ernestine smiled complaisantly at her guests. 'When he's happy, he's positively radiant!' She cupped her hands round his face, then pushed him down. 'I saw your father's splendid car come, and then drive away again. I also saw you and your father bringing our wall up to a great height.' She waved at the biscuits and the children helped themselves, and the pug watched them expectantly. 'He's a fine man, your father – very tall and handsome. Reminds me in turn *of his* father.'

'No-one seems to have known Grandpa Burnett very much,' said Dido, with intent to be enlightened.

'He was not understood. It's my belief his wife failed to understand him. A rather tragic man – and he would have been a *lonely* one . . .'

'But what?'

'Oh, I used to keep an eye on him. We kept each other company now and then, when your grandmother took herself off to Surrey; and went abroad. I was more mobile in those days. He was a very dear gentleman, was Henry Willoughby Burnett. It was a poor marriage. But it's all conjecture.'

'We know Granny Burnett was rich.'

'I mean – a mistaken marriage. She was rich in wealth yes.'

'Aunt Unity loved Grandpa Burnett,' said Dido, also using conjecture. 'After all, he was her father.'

'Unity was a daddy's girl – and she made a bad marriage too,' said Ernestine. 'History does repeat itself.'

'That's what our mother says. Granny Burnett used to give us lunches at the Cumberland Hotel in Durban.'

Fondling the pug on his lap, Hal said, 'Dido and I long for South Africa. We miss it every day, the people and the polo ground and the grandstand where Johnny Gibson's ponies were tied up in the shade. And riding bare-back – and searching for potholes.'

'And the donga where we found snakes – and the rivers I fell into,' said Dido.

'Johnny Gibson liked our mother very much. He had the express train to Cape Town stop at Pietermaritzburg to say goodbye to us when we took a ship to England,' Hal recited.

'You have led a fascinating life,' Ernestine said. 'But then, so have I.'

'Can you do a Zulu war-dance?' Dido asked, after a silence.

'I can not,' Ernestine asserted. 'But if you can, I should be most interested.'

Hal rolled Willoughby on to his sister's lap, and took up a position. 'I'd rather you didn't look,' he said.

'It mustn't upset the pug,' Ernestine warned. 'But we'll let him do his little war-dance won't we, Willoughby?'

Feeling hampered by Willoughby's nerves and an audience clearly intent on watching, Hal changed his mind and sat back in his chair. 'I'm doomed to be in school in two days,' he said.

Ernestine held out her hands. 'I've forgotten everything I learnt at school, dear boy.'

'Then it's a short-cut not to go – and think how much money they'd save!'

'Very true. But don't quote me,' Ernestine said. 'You've got a better memory than I have, I expect. Now away with you, or your mother will be anxious.'

'Thank you for the drink Ernestine,' said Hal, standing up. 'I agree it's a nice name. Better than the one our father calls you!'

'And what is that, may I ask? ' She waited a moment, while Dido cringed; then with a pure countenance, Mrs Dunbar suggested 'Mistress?'

Hal looked puzzled.

'I used to do some teaching, a long time ago. I was a teacher before I was married. ' She blew them each a kiss. 'You may leave by whatever route you wish. Come and see me again.'

'Not a common type,' said Hal, as they passed through the gate with Trullers on it.

Chapter 9

At one fifty-five, Constance brought the children to a stop under the clock on Victoria station with Hal's school trunk and small case. John arrived punctually on the dot of two. It had the makings of a nightmare episode: Hal feeling sick from the journey to London and with the dread of swapping rhythmic home life for the agitations of term; Constance anxious on his behalf; Dido conflicted between pitying her brother and envying him.

John gave his wife a perfunctory clasp, and patted his son on the back. 'Looking forward to seeing all those other criminals again?'

Hal, not troubling to simulate cheerfulness, twitched his shoulders and pulled a nonchalant face.

'I wish I could be a criminal,' said Dido, hopping round the luggage trolley. 'I so want to wear a uniform!'

'You'll be a local one, lucky thing,' said Hal. He was pale, and wore his inscrutable air with deliberation.

'They say that school days are the happiest in your life, and I'm just getting hints that it may be true,' his father told him; which seemed to Hal of little comfort for their present or for their future. John turned back to Constance. 'Everything go all right on the way up?'

'Perfectly. We took a taxi across from Kings Cross. Will you have time to spend with us this afternoon?'

'Only for a cup of tea. As a matter of fact, I've got to meet a chap in Whitehall, and then attend a course at Millbank. But next week I'll be at Westbourne – bringing that little runabout I promised you.'

'How wonderful. We'll look forward to it.'

'I'm looking forward to the holidays,' Hal said within himself.

'The Tiplers have left us,' Dido told her father. She repressed a natural impulse to take his hand.

John glanced down. 'Yes, I heard. The nasty part was the beer you know. Be warned, you two.' Aside, he said to Constance, 'Get yourself some help in the house. What you need is a young girl who can clean and do some cooking. It's a very big house for you to run on your own.'

'You might tell me how the funeral went,' Constance said. 'Were there many people? Anyone I know?' She still felt a grievance that he hadn't wanted her at the occasion to support him; which in normal circumstances would have brought them close. He should have understood her own wish to make a final gesture to Florence. She, who had been Florence's replacement daughter. It was brought home to her again how terribly hurtful and insensitive John could be.

'Not a big crowd. Ivo Collard, who was staying at the Cumberland while Mother was living there. He talked a lot about you and the tiddlies. But come on, oughtn't we to be moving?'

'Yes, I think we should go to the platform and look out for the staff.'

They rolled the luggage across the station and down the platform. Hal was quick to spot several boys with their parents, and oh . . . his heart lurched, there was Mr Mattingly. Probably feeling as wretched as the boys he was rounding up.

Dido was hit by a minor panic of her own. Hal was going, and she'd be alone by herself at Westbourne. How awful for him being forced to go away, and yet appear so offhand! And how much she'd miss him for three whole months . . .

She and Constance hugged him, and John clapped him on the back again. The trunk was put on board, and catching sight of a harmless classmate, Hal suddenly darted off and climbed into the train.

John said, 'I'm sorry, we don't have a lot of time. Better go at once and find a place to sit for half an hour. Hal won't want us waving to him.'

Reluctantly, Constance hurried back down the platform, hearing doors slam and a whistle being blown. She glanced over her shoulder, and saw the train gliding gently away.

She might just have time to hear more of Florence's departure.

It was Dido's turn for school. She felt perfectly calm and a little excited. Soon she would know what school was all about. Ernestine would be interested!

Constance walked her down that first morning. The village school was run by an elderly lady called Mrs Dawtry, who was pleased to enroll a pupil 'who spoke well.' 'My South African accent has gone now, hasn't it?' Dido said as they approached the school gates. 'Such a pity.'

It was a small, traditional stone building, typical of the period, with a concrete playground. Children were running about in all directions. Dido slid into a queue near an open door, and Constance hurried away.

Dido found herself neither above nor below the standard of her class. There were thirty-nine other pupils. Dido was asked to stand on a desk and recite Stevenson's 'Shadow' and was much taken by the words 'arrant sleepyhead.' She made friends with a capable big girl, and a small boy who had his hands hit by a ruler but refused to cry, rubbing at his eyes for several minutes. They read a book about Martin Pippin in the Apple Orchard.

'I think school is really nice,' Dido commented at home; and then, 'I'll write to Hal about it.'

Constance sat at her desk, absorbed in writing to her parents in Hove, and to friends in Natal. She spent much of her time answering letters, giving and commenting on news, and reviewing the pages covered by her unvarying writing. She was interrupted by a shrill ring of the phone.

'Connie? Hello my dear. It's Roddy here. Katie and I fancy a day off, and a picnic in this invigorating autumn weather seemed just the ticket. We thought to have it at Grimsthorpe and we'd like you to join us. What do you say?'

'I say that sounds a lovely idea.' She swiftly weighed inclinations to accept and to refuse. 'I couldn't get away before one o'clock, which is when Dido's back from school.'

Roddy hesitated. 'All the jollier! What's a picnic without a child or two? I was under the impression they boarded?'

'Our son's a boarder. But Dido and I will come with pleasure. She should be home at one. Shall I speak to Katie? I'd like to ask her if I can bring anything with me to eat. Or drink.'

'Bring nothing. Only your charming self. I'll be with you around quarter past one.'

He came in his muddy Land Rover, and he came alone.

'Where's Katie?' Constance asked through the car window, with a sense of unease.

'Migraine,' Roddy informed her briskly. 'Poor girl, she gets them rather frequently. Sent her love – and is sorry to be such a spoilsport.'

'Well, I'm very disappointed for her,' said Constance with emphasis. 'Jump in the back, Dido. You're sure it's all right for a dog to come too?' She seated herself beside him, glad to have her daughter's company. 'It certainly is gorgeous weather – and the trees are such rich colours already.'

'How far is Grimsthorpe?' Dido asked, leaning over their shoulders.

'Four, five miles. Hungry, are you?'

'I had a dream about Mister last night,' said Dido. 'It wasn't very nice. I can't remember what he did.'

'Shot off to hide, I expect!' Roddy laughed. 'We ought to have warned you, Connie, that her drinking was notorious. I bet she was a formidable woman in her cups. Don't you think they were like a couple on the old saucy seaside postcards?'

Constance laughed too. 'Well, they were rather. But she could be very kind and patient, couldn't she, Dido?'

'I loved her,' said Dido. 'Until she turned nasty.'

'Most of us turn nasty at times in our lives,' Roddy assured her. 'Humans are like that. Just a few hardly know how to be nasty . . .' He gave Constance a quick smile. 'Less of the wicked dust on them.'

They were passing a handsome coaching inn, and shortly afterwards swung off the road and up a private drive past the castle. 'Next summer you'll be able to bring Daisy here and give pony rides. And rides in the trap. They hold quite a decent fête in the grounds.'

'What a marvelous approach,' Constance exclaimed, seeing the expanse of lake spread out below them as they headed down the hill. 'Trees all around – and a wood beyond. The perfect place for a picnic. Does nobody mind our being here?'

'The old Earl's perfectly happy for responsible people to enjoy coming. After his time, I daresay it'll be different. I've been here and found him fixing a fence with a piece of string. They say the old boy loves knitting socks.'

He parked beside the track, and switched off the engine. 'Well Connie – good to have you in the neighbourhood. John's missing out badly! Get him home soon – there are more important people than me who want to see him. However – let's unpack the goodies!'

Constance found a rubber-lined rug, and laid it down. Roddy dumped a battered hamper of food on the grass, and asked Dido to find a box with plates and mugs. 'We've got a thermos of coffee for later – but how about a glass of vino to lift the tone?'

'Thank you,' said Dido, to go one above Hal.

Roddy gave a dark chuckle. 'Oh no my dear, I mustn't lead you astray. Think of Mrs Tipler! I was offering it to your mother.'

'D'you know, I think I'd rather wait for the coffee,' Constance said. 'I certainly never expected anything as elaborate as this spread. Look at these delicious sandwiches, Dido. What a pity Katie isn't with us!'

Roddy was giving her his full attention. 'I'd like to hear more about your antecedents. Families are so interesting. My forebears were either dignitaries or charlatans. I won't ask where you see me fitting!'

'Much better not,' Constance agreed.

'Katie can number one or two cranks and screwballs in her family tree. Plus a creative blighter here and there. Now you, Connie dear, chose a murky family to throw your lot in with. Take Max Measures: Your father-in-law couldn't stand him. Then Henry himself was a black sheep, according to John's grandfather.'

'History does repeat itself,' observed Dido.

'Out of the mouths of babes.' Roddy smiled dryly. 'Rumours went round after Unity's death. Dreadful how people talk in ignorance.'

'I feel sorry for Grandpa Henry.' Dido pushed her fair hair aside and held Roddy with slate blue eyes. 'Unity loved him though.' She was stroking Prince's head as he sat salivating at the food.

'So I've met another genealogist!' Roddy lifted his wine glass and tipped the contents down his throat. 'Write it all in a book. 'The family I never knew.''

He turned his back on her to face Constance. 'My intention was to learn about your forebears.'

Constance said, 'A de Mouton on my mother's side is said

to have come over in 1066. They established themselves with a Sussex Estate in the sixteenth century. I've nothing to fill the gaps with.'

She then began to laugh, and after a moment Roddy joined in.

Dido was thinking, Hal didn't much like Mr Crawley. But Mr Crawley was very nice to their mother – and that pleased her. She remembered how Hal had struggled to keep his teeth from chattering on Victoria station. If only he was here now! Dido ran to the water's edge with the Labrador running beside her, and kicking off her shoes, waded to and fro under the over-hanging trees. This was like the brickpits, only hugely grand and not so spooky. Hal had written one letter so far, saying that school was all right. He was getting quite good at soccer, and his class had been taken up on Beachy Head where people went to commit suicide. And had Daisy any messages for him?

That stupid old joke, thought Dido.

Chapter 10

John had returned in a 1938 Jaguar four-seater convertible, with the intention of leaving it for family use.

Constance had driven in every imaginable condition in Egypt and in South Africa, including places where there were markets in full swing, chickens and children and goats haphazard on unmade roads. She had complete confidence in herself, and she enjoyed being in charge of a car. But this one was beyond her experience.

John said, 'I thought we'd go for a drive in the country for as long as it takes; and you can get used to her.'

'Very well,' agreed Constance stoutly. 'She looks quite a handful. I hope I can manage her!'

'Come and meet Coral. She lives here now the Tiplers have gone.' Dido, just back from school, took his hand and urged him down the passage. Coral was in her sitting-room, knitting. She stood up when they entered, and shook hands with the Colonel. She was an attractive young woman with red hair cut in a short geometric style, light green eyes and a lively demeanour. Her figure was full but comely.

'How are you getting on?' he asked in an open way, not expecting a considered reply.

Coral answered enthusiastically.

'And are you courting? Or should I say, being courted?'

Coral smiled at the quaint expression. 'Well, I am as a matter of fact.'

'Alf is tall and handsome,' Dido informed her father. 'Though I haven't seen him yet.'

John said, 'I wonder how long you'll want to stay with us?'

'A few months anyway, I expect,' Coral said.

Dido said, 'Coral's teaching me to do French knitting. I want to make a trick bridle for Daisy. I'll give a performance when it's finished.'

'I live in suspense,' her father said. 'Don't tell me that's a trick bridle,' and he pointed to the dark blue shape hanging from Coral's needles.

'No, this is for a child in my family. I've nieces and nephews and a younger brother and sister.'

'And I'm teaching Coral to make a gunda-gunda,' said Dido. 'Those things with cotton reels and soap and an elastic band and a stick. Hal and I had them in Mooi River.'

'A sound exchange of skills,' John said with shy pomposity. 'We might need gunda-gundas if your mother's car breaks down.'

The lesson began that afternoon. Dido and her dog climbed into the rear seats, and Constance went to the driver's side. 'I'll take her to begin with,' John said, and sat himself behind the wheel.

They drove along the Stamford road, and the old Jaguar engine roared mightily, and the wind savaged their hair, and Constance kept clutching her protective headscarf. Coming to a long straight stretch, John pulled the car over and opened the door. 'Your turn.'

Replacing him on the right, Constance wriggled a little, then glanced obliquely at her feet. 'The pedals seem very remote.' Before her lay the great expanse of gleaming black bonnet. The engine was still running. Dido and Prince sat in high expectation, enjoying the growl and vibration.

'I'd better shove the seat forward,' John said. Constance stepped out on the road. He made the necessary adjustment. They both sat back inside. 'Now engage first, and work up the gears in your own time. You'll soon get used to the feel of it. The steering's a touch heavy, but once you've grasped it, you'll be away!'

Constance's feet moved over the pedals in an attempt to locate them freely. She took a breath, and tried to put the gear gingerly into first. It resisted, and then as they drew away, the car began to jerk and thrust. The engine cut. 'Start her again,' John said.

Constance steeled her soul to do better justice to herself. She succeeded in making a reasonably smooth departure and reached top gear, intent on the steering wheel now, with its unaccustomed responses. They covered a mile, and another. 'Now pull in at the next lay-by,' John ordered.

Constance did as bidden. 'Switch off,' he said. They sat in

silence. Prince began to fidgit for exercise. 'Now carry on and we'll go over to Stamford. You must practice in more traffic.'

On the way to Stamford, Constance developed an ache in the small of her back, and her legs were growing tired. The driving position was not proving a happy one.

'Those shoes you've got on aren't suitable,' he told her. 'Couldn't you have worn a flatter pair? Heels don't help.'

Dreading congestion in Stamford, Constance made no reply. She felt her face become hot. They passed a sign giving three miles to go. 'Are you sure you want me to take you through the town?' she said. 'I'd prefer to feel comfortable in her before being hemmed in.'

'Nonsense – you've done a good seven miles. You know how to drive in traffic. You know the rule of the road. One car is very like another after driving as long as you have.'

'Perhaps this car doesn't like women,' suggested Dido.

'In that case I'll tame her,' declared her mother.

They entered Stamford, and it was market day. Constance found herself trapped between a lorry carrying cattle, and a tractor with trailer.'You can pass – give a signal!' John hissed. Constance bungled it, and dropped back in line.

'Oh, good Lord – how feeble! ' John heaved a sigh and pointed to the roundabout lying ahead. 'Take the third turning.'

They continued uneasily through confined streets and action-packed squares, the car uttering hostile gasps whenever she accelerated suddenly, and lunging at corners as if out of control. 'Please John,' she said in a flustered tone, 'I really need to go somewhere quiet.'

'Carry on along this road and we'll leave the town centre. I can't think why you're making such a meal of it.'

He directed her out of Stamford and they drove mile after mile through countryside and villages. Dido longed to be home. Prince tried to climb across her to breathe the air on her side. He was panting, and she gave a series of deeply unhappy sighs. To Constance's relief, she noticed they were close to the hamlet where Prince had been born.

'Stop that melodramatic fuss,' her father snapped, leaning into Constance to read the petrol gauge. Dido fell back in her seat with a martyred expression and the dog trampled her lap.

'We'll have a shot at manoeuvering,' John announced. 'Stop again when you see an opening.'

Constance drove stoically on, missed an opportunity and received his exclamation in silence. When they halted, her foot slipped off the clutch and the car burst into silence. 'Oh bother!' she said in frustration, and made a valiant effort to extend the length of her legs.

John put her through the routine of three point turns during a merciful lull in passing traffic. Dido allowed herself a subtle groan. Another twenty minutes passed in purgatory. Her father's voice became increasingly sour. Her mother's stressed legs had begun to tremble.

Dido sprang forward. 'Don't try any more! It isn't worth it. He's bullying you!'

John swung round and smacked her leg. 'Mind your own business! Don't say another word.'

Dido mouthed the word 'Bad!' then sank into herself, her eyes filling with tears. Constance said, 'John, we've had enough. I'm afraid I haven't made a very creditable start, but it will come – with a few more sessions.' She opened the door. 'I'd be glad if you'd drive again now.'

John ungraciously climbed out and replaced her behind the wheel. 'I thought you'd enjoy a car that's a bit more interesting,' he muttered. 'Perhaps you're not up to it.' He had liked the dashing image of her in charge of this machine. He realised his loss of patience had been fatal; but exasperation still seethed within him. They made the final miles in silence.

Dido vanished into her bedroom the moment they were home. She sat at the small table in her room, and pulling a scribbling pad towards her, wrote in her own spelling, employing a pencil with heavy pressure, 'Dear Hal, if you think it's bad at school it's better than here. I wished I could be on Beachy Head this afternoon. We have a different open-air car now and our father made our mother learn to drive it and he was livid when she made slips. Prince and I were in the back and hated every second and I got a slap. Mum hated it even worse. Fathers are trouble. He thinks he's still a soldier. Mr Crawley (Roddy) took Mum and me and Prince to Grimsthorpe Castle for a picnic. I paddled and Prince did too.

Roddy was keen to make Mum like him but I know you don't. We can take our boat there sometime. Coral is here and is nice and we're knitting for Daisy who is a poor dumb animal in case you didn't know. Lots of love, Dido xxxx

John came into her room to say goodnight, but didn't offer to read. Dido lay under the covers, with the book put out of sight. She didn't want her feelings for it contaminated.

'Has it been a nice day?' he asked.

'The morning was,' she said.

'What did you think of your mother's new car?'

'I liked it.'

'It's called a Standard Swallow.'

'I know.' After a pause, she said, 'I thought you'd be happy with us.'

'Oh, but I am,' he said. And after another pause, 'It takes a bit of practice, that's all. Like learning the ways of a strange car. I rely on you to help me along.'

Chapter 11

They were like two friends staying in a hotel, meeting for breakfast and asking respectfully what each was planning for the day.

Constance brought the tea-pot and toast-rack to the dining table. 'Did you sleep well?'

'I can't say that I did.' He woke sometimes, drenched in the cold sweat of fear; then would tell himself he was perfectly fit.

'If you were dreaming, you must have been asleep. I can envy you your night.'

'You wouldn't want my dreams.' John spread toast with butter and marmalade.

Constance sat still for a moment. 'No, I was better awake,' she conceded, and took a slice of toast herself.

'Where's Dido?' he asked, looking vaguely about him.

'Oh, she left for school ten minutes ago. She enjoys walking down with another child from West Road.'

'I thought I'd get a ladder out and repair the pony shelter in the paddock. The roof's pretty bad.'

Constance laughed. 'The children and I spent one hot morning cleaning out that shed in the summer. I had to open a fete in the afternoon, and left myself barely time to wash and change – let alone compose my little speech.'

'I'm sure you did it gracefully,' John said.

'It was all right. But what worried me more was Hal using the Japanese sword to hack at the nettles and thistles round the shed. He was brandishing and swiping so fiercely I had to put a stop to it. Mr Hillis finished the job with the heavy mower.'

'Pity Hal isn't here to help me on the roof,' said John.

Constance couldn't share his regret. Hal was now in Hove with her parents for half-term. She said, 'Do get Hillis to help you.'

There was a tap at the door and Coral appeared. 'Excuse me

interrupting – but can I introduce my fiancé Alfred? He's just outside.'

Constance and John turned to see a young man come forward and stand shyly beside his red-headed girl. He was tall, with a narrow, spare physique, and seemed to be someone of slow action and gentle disposition. He gave a nod to the couple at breakfast, and a glance down on Coral.

'Congratulations to you both,' said John.

'We plan to be married before Christmas,' Coral explained. 'I just wanted you to meet Alf first.'

'What's your line of work?' John asked.

'I'm a jack-of-all-trades down at the Nag's Head. But one day I'd like to have my own pub. We'd run it together.' He gave Coral's plump waist a squeeze. 'She's ever so good with people – keeping order, and that.'

'Well, the best of luck to you both!'

'Where are you thinking of living after the wedding?' Constance asked. 'I hope we're not going to lose you too soon?'

Now it was Coral who glanced at Alfred. 'We haven't anywhere arranged . . . Alf wondered if you'd possibly let him be here with me – just to begin with – till we find something else?' She eyed Constance and then John, and darted another glance at Alf. Her expressions and movements were as quick and alert as his were phlegmatic.

Her employers' eyes met. John thought, Connie might have seen this coming . . . He refrained from commenting.

Constance said, 'I suppose we could manage for a limited time – until you find a place of your own.' She thought, history repeating itself. She added, 'But really, only on a temporary basis.'

'Alf's very handy outside,' Coral promised, looking brightly from one to the other. 'He'd make himself useful around the place.'

'Let's think about it,' said John, pushing back his chair.

Coral took the hint, and urged Alfred into retreat. 'Thanks ever so much anyway,' she said, and closed the door behind them.

'Well!' Constance spoke with fatalistic humour. 'We *were* taken unawares.'

'No sooner do we rid ourselves of the Tiplers, than we double our trouble with a publican,' said John.

'Until the New Year – then we think again. But it's not exactly what I had in mind.'

'I too have a plan.' John stood and threw down his napkin. 'I thought we'd go back to Stamford. You can have another run in the SS. I'd like to give you lunch at the old George Hotel by the bridge. Years since I was there. What's the fat fellow called? Daniel Lambert! His portrait used to hang in the porch, and his vast chair stood in a corner.'

Constance said, 'By all means. Let's go and see him.'

Before leaving she asked Coral to supervise Dido's lunch, and make it clear to her that if she rode it must be within the grounds.

They drove off at half-past twelve, and this time Constance felt confident at the wheel and relaxed in her husband's company. It was not a day of rich autumnal colours, but the low cloud and mild air corresponded with her mood of calm and her lack of undue expectations. She would not be bullied or bamboozled. Emotions under control.

Daniel Lambert, in his immensely tight green and cream costume, still hung in his customary place; but his chair had disappeared. 'He weighed fifty-two stones. I've never forgotten that,' said John happily, as if it augured well for their meal. They chose a table overlooking the garden. 'We'll go out afterwards and see if that monstrous wisteria's still flourishing. Now Connie, is there anything you fancy here . . .?' and he handed her a menu. She was struck by his use of Connie: he had always called her Constance before the war, as her family did – and she preferred it. Only friends of her youth called her Connie.

'I shan't manage more than one course,' she assured him.

'Oh, come on. I want this to be a special meal. Make an exception.'

'Well – the crab sounds tempting. Followed by roast beef.'

The dining room was filling up. It was well heated and the tables in their stiff white cloths garnished with fresh flowers had a festive air. She went on, 'How sad if this place suffers the fate of a lot of old hotels over the country . . . becoming run down – or shut down. The George is so well known, with its obese Mr Lambert.'

John fulfilled his intentions by ordering a bottle of wine. When it came and was poured for them, he raised his glass. 'Here's to us . . . and to everything being for the best!'

She drank. A rush of emotion seized her after all, and she

acknowledged his toast without the faintest idea what it promised.

'Do you think Hal's going to do all right at his school?' John asked.

'It was your school, and it doesn't seem to have changed much over the years. He seems to have made a good start . . . despite what he says when he goes back each term.'

'He needs to have some proper discipline. That much is obvious. A male environment. I get the impression that he's quite sensitive under the bravado. His sister shows more pluck.'

'Yes – Dido's the one to climb trees and push herself further. It was she who climbed on to a derelict barge at Tongue End. They'd cycled along one of those monotonous fen lanes between poppy fields and she fell into the stagnant water.' Constance suddenly recalled Dido aged three, going up to a large Egyptian who was ill-treating a goat and saying, 'You leave that goat alone.'

John said placidly, 'That's all right. Any normal kid takes risks. I like the fact that they're independent and resourceful.'

'But Dido's been having bad dreams. She seems to have lost some of that assurance.' Constance laid her knife and fork down and gave him a steady stare. 'Neither of them know where they are with us. They expect us to stay together, and to have you as a father. But the atmosphere makes it far from certain! And you must realize John, how confused I'm feeling.'

He continued to eat. He said laconically, 'Join the club.' Then he smiled at her. 'This is a happy meal, remember. Things will work out.' He took her hand across the table. 'You must know you'll always come first with me, Stupe, whatever happens. I'll never love anyone as much as I love you.'

'But I don't know it! I would have to be psychic to understand what you really feel.'

By the time they'd finished both courses, a group of men arrived, and after some hesitation and guidance from a waiter, they moved towards another table overlooking the garden, across the room from the Burnetts. Glancing at them, Constance recognized one of the men. After a moment's concentration, she saw it was Mr Fewing's nephew. She was in no mood to express interest and make introductions, and felt it would anyway be inappropriate; so she kept her eyes turned from their direction. It appeared to be a working lunch – or a celebration. How, she wondered, should their own lunch be described?

'I feel it's only fair to ask you to tell me your intentions as soon as possible,' she said on impulse, sounding misleadingly dignified. 'Fair to us both,'

John insisted on sweets and coffee. In silence they drank, glancing about them with self-effacing disinterest.

'Is there another woman, John? I want to know.'

John said, 'Let's look at that wisteria.'

He paid the bill and they strolled out to inspect the gigantic stem which curled round the back of the building like a horticultural reptile. 'Pity it's not in bloom,' he said. 'I've always loved wisteria. It's very English.'

Lucky wisteria, Constance remarked to herself. I too am English – and I'm still here. You don't know the meaning of the word love.

'It's splendid,' she agreed, and added with a touch of sarcasm, 'like you.'

'Oh, I've spent all my splendor,' he replied.

Constance, glancing at the hotel, saw Oliver Seaton facing out from his table, and their eyes met. He lifted a hand. She was obliged to salute back.

'Who's your friend?' John asked.

'Not a friend,' she answered. 'He's the nephew of someone in the Almshouses.'

John drove the car back in fading light and a rapidly gathering mist. Constance hurried into the house, which stood unlit and silent. She called upstairs to Dido. There was no answer. Going through to Coral's room, she found her sitting on the settee with her young man, quietly chatting, each with a hand on the other's thigh. Coral struggled upright. Prince leapt to his feet to greet them.

'Do you know where Dido is?' Constance asked.

Coral's gaze swung down to Alf and then back to Constance, and she said in a surprised tone, 'No I don't! Isn't she in her room?'

'No, she isn't. Did she take Daisy out this afternoon?'

Alf had levered himself to his feet. 'She had the pony bridled and went out some time ago. She was riding bare-back.'

'I hope you told her to stay in the fields?'

Coral and Alf regarded each other. Constance left them to their consternation and went into the other rooms, switching lights on everywhere. Having garaged the car, John now appeared in the hall. 'We can't find Dido,' she told him.' It seems there's a limit to how independent children should be.'

She hastened back into the front garden where all was foggy darkness, calling Dido's name in every direction. Then she heard screams coming from across the road. With a chill in her veins, Constance ran over to the Almshouses, and was confronted by a pale phantom hurtling towards her which took the form of Daisy, her small hooves striking the gravel, and reins flying free. Then through the fog floated the unearthly apparition of Miss Poole in a white nightdress, still uttering piercing cries, while her long grey hair fluttered out behind.

Constance, having failed to catch Daisy's bridle, was poised to comfort Miss Poole when she heard John shouting her name. She found him outside the garages, Daisy held by the bridle. But still no Dido. 'I'll walk up the road in case she was riding that way and had a fall,' he said without undue distress. His calm tone was a relief to Constance. She took the pony from him, led her to the paddock and set her loose.

Twenty minutes later, father and daughter arrived at the house. Dido was without coat or shoes, and very wet. She ran to her mother. 'I went to the brickpits,' she muttered. 'It was dark, I tied Daisy up and I climbed the tree that Hal and I go to and hid on a branch over the water. And then I fell in.'

'How deep was it?' asked John.

'Very deep. But I clutched the tree and dragged myself out . . . and there was no-one else there.'

Constance and John exchanged glances.

'That bad Daisy just bolted! She was thinking of the slaughter-house.'

Dido began shivering. She was dressed only in jodhpurs and a jersey, and fear of her parents' reaction to the escapade was mounting.

'Let's go upstairs and run a bath,' Constance said.

'I'll write and tell Hal,' Dido said.

John had thought, I'll go up and read her another chapter. But full of conflict over his wife, his children, his past and his future, and angered by his daughter's anarchy, he said, 'On no account write a boastful letter to your brother. Have a bath, get dressed, and come downstairs for a hot drink.'

Chapter 12

John was finding the ramshackle shed roof a gratifying challenge. The work was physically rewarding, he was self-motivated, it was a temperate climate, and it was work to good purpose. He felt he was at last regaining his health. Night times were the trouble. He couldn't sleep for worrying about Constance. He found Dido and the presence of Coral in the house inhibiting to his efforts to reconcile his new life with Constance's. He recognized his need to control them all, find fault with them; while aware of a pernicious inferiority in himself. It was the darkest sort of humiliation to feel the worthlessness of his future now that the war was over. Here he was, spared – and causing distress. Alone by choice for most daytime hours, he often imagined himself in company with men he had associated with during the campaigns in Burma; acquaintances from all levels, people he had regarded as friends: so many now dead. But he silently talked to them. He had been at his best at full stretch in the war; he felt at his worst needing to commit himself to this life.

When Constance suggested he get Hillis's help with the roof project, he tried to put his thoughts into words. 'It makes me happy to mend a roof.'

'It would make Mr Hillis happy too.'

'He's got acres of our garden to inspire him with happiness.'

I could as soon say to you, why should I send the children away to school when I can see to their needs myself? This idea, equally irrational, Constance left unspoken. It merely revealed to herself how sorry she was that Hal had to be absent. Poor sleep didn't help.

Constance felt guilty too for losing her husband's affections. For failing to secure a statement of intent from him during that over-vaunted lunch; and for being so preoccupied with her troubles as to risk her daughter's safety. This was how she saw it now: Dido's fall into dangerous water seemed like an uncanny reinforcement of confusion in the child's mind. Why didn't her parents love each other? Was she, Dido, part of the problem? Was she better out of the way?

Life in Egypt had been good. They'd been sociable. Constance had never experienced the least innuendo of unfaithfulness concerning John. Their second child had arrived. Dido was born in Alexandria – though John had chosen to be out sailing rather than to be at her side for that difficult birth. But strains must have begun then; and in Mooi River, he had deserted them to go to his mother.

Dido started for school that morning with light steps and a merry air, despite the brickpits misadventure. On her return, and when he came in for lunch, John spoke to her.

'I want you to tell me something. Did your mother say anything to you about where you were to ride yesterday?'

Dido held him in a steady gaze. 'She may have said in the field.'

'But you chose to go right up our busy road and then down a quiet lane.'

'Really nice and really quiet.'

'But if Ragbag had thrown you and trampled you and kicked you in the head, what then? Hardly anyone goes there.'

'The slaughter men were nearby.'

John considered that concept. 'You were told to stay in the home fields.'

'I did ride there. At first.'

'So that seemed all right?'

'Yes!'

'That's what I call chop logic . . . in other words, deliberate deceit. So you're completely in the wrong. It isn't all right defying your mother and being disobedient.'

Dido squirmed. She was suddenly cast down, though the whole long morning at school had been happy and successful. After a stultifying pause, she rallied to say, 'I've been up there before. With Hal.'

'Precisely. So that in the event of trouble, real or imagined, you had a sensible brother who could help you out.'

The sexism stung her. 'I call that chop logic!'

'Indeed! Why?'

His paternalism was crushing. Dido hesitated. 'Boys being better than girls.'

'No – that's not what I was saying. You're both too young to go exploring on your own. I'm thinking of your mother. You broke her rule, and caused her worry. Now go to your room and spend the next hour there. And no riding today.'

Dido climbed the stairs in high dudgeon and low spirits, and shut her bedroom door with a bang. She threw herself on the bed and lay for the count of fifty. Then she rolled on to the floor and noticed how much dust had collected under the bedsprings. Shutting her eyes against the sight, she felt a drowsiness settle on her, and struggled up. Sleeping now would further demean her. She chose a book at random from the line along her mantelpiece then changed her mind and dropped it. Perhaps by looking through the books between her bedroom and Hal's, she'd be breaking curfew with only limited risk. Those shelves held a variety of classics, reference books and adventure stories dating from her grandparents' era. Dido knelt down in the passage and trailed her finger along the spines.

Hearing a door open below, and footsteps, Dido's finger halted on a faded green book she thought likely to have pictures. Tugging it out, she slipped into the safety of her room and flopped back on the bed. Pages of thick rough friendly paper with big print, and every so often shiny photographs of towns, villages and features. It was a testimony of love for Fenland countyside. Dido flipped through euologies and illustrations alike, and was about to slam the book shut when a letter fell out on the eiderdown. She pounced on it and sat up to read. The single page was good quality cream paper, discoloured in places. The writing slanted forward and gave the impression of speed. Printed at the top was Haverfield House. Dido looked for a signature and it was Unity. Her unlucky aunt.

'Dearest Father,' she read. 'Writing this letter is a selfish act when you've been unwell and have troubles of your own. I need to write because if I came to see you I wouldn't find the words and your sad face would inhibit me.

Different from trying to explain to Max. Then I become catatonic. I'm a bad mother and a bad wife. You tried to like Max on my behalf, but I've told you so often how disparaging he is. You've heard him yourself . . . 'You're better with horses and dogs than with children.' But Max wasn't very interested in a family, it was always the farm that made him happy. I make him violent. We've both been unlucky in our choices and our personalities. Forgive me for everything. I can't think straight. My head's full of dark noise. Fondest love, Unity.'

Dido sat with the letter in her hands, deciphering it bit by bit, then considering the substance. Unity loved her father, but not her husband. Dido's mind jumped to the hour spent with her cousins, and she mellowed towards them; why had they been hard to love? Any number of reasons. What about herself and her own father? He couldn't manage love.

She folded the letter carefully and placed it under one of the two pottery bookend owls on her mantelpiece. Then she passed the time drawing until her mother called her down.

'You wanted to know when I was visiting Mrs Baxter, do you remember? I'm going now, to take her the last of the apples.'

They walked across to the Almshouses, Dido carrying the small apples with their pale pink-green skin and soft pink-tinged flesh. As they approached Mrs Baxter's cottage, Mr Fewings emerged from his, and greeted Constance.

'My nephew came in an hour back. Brought some provisions, he did.'

'That was nice of him,' said Constance.

'Decent chap, Oliver. Always has been.'

'I saw him yesterday in Stamford. At the George Hotel, as a matter of fact.'

'Oh, ah. He's an agricultural engineer, is Oliver. Grandstands his tractors and harvesters at the Peterborough Show each year. Has his office in Edmorton – his Works, he calls it.'

'Then I expect he was with a group of colleagues,' said Constance. 'I'll come and see you again soon, Mr Fewings.' She moved away, and Dido called over her shoulder, 'I forgot to bring you my pillow!'

'Get away, you Jezebel,' he called back.

They were invited to take seats in Mrs Baxter's little sitting room. 'I see you going to call on old man Fewings t'other day,' was her opening remark.

Dido's attention was taken by the stout Jack Russell terrier curled up in its basket. She went to it with bent knees and extended hand. The dog lifted its lip and growled.

'Willoughby's much more friendly!' Dido said, drawing back.

'I see Mrs Ablewhite take that pug down the road most days,' Mrs Baxter informed them in perjorative tones. 'Very fat it is. Those women spoil him rotten.' She eased her swollen legs.

'Has the District Nurse visited this week?' Constance asked.

'Yes. She's a nice young thing. Makes me a cup of tea. Tells me to keep m'legs up. Then she's off! She's that busy.'

'Shall I bring this stool over?'

'No no.' Mrs Baxter tugged her tight skirt lower to her knees. 'I'm very well as I am. How are you doing then, Mrs Burnett? Settling in to the district?'

'Thank you, yes. My daughter's going to school here, and we're feeling at home in the house - though it gets a bit cold in the evenings.'

'Been abroad, haven't you? Aye, you'll be feeling it. What's happened to the couple that looked after the place for Mr Burnett? I hear they've run off.'

'Nothing dramatic. They've gone to live with relatives.'

'Funny pair they were! Liked a few down at the Nag's Head, she did. Gave her husband a hard time – so says Ma Elliot, who picks things up.'

'What's he called?' Dido asked, sitting close to the terrier with her hands clasped.

'Snap,' said Mrs Baxter.

Dido pulled a lugubrious face.

'Never see Mrs Dunbar put her nose outside now,' Mrs Baxter continued. 'She likes to be thought an invalid. But it's just she's lazy – lets Mrs Ablewhite run round her and do her every bidding. In the days when Mr Burnett was alive, she couldn't keep away. Thought the world of him, she did. Not that I'm one to heed rumours.'

'He was lonely,' said Dido, venturing a finger towards the alert little dog. Snap growled. 'And Mrs Dunbar's lonely too. But Willoughby keeps her company.'

'I'm afraid she's riddled with arthritis,' said Constance. 'She also has a weak heart. I'm sorry for her.'

'Naughty old thing,' said Mrs Baxter in cabalistic tone, and the topic dropped.

'I haven't seen Mr Hare lately,' Constance remarked. 'Perhaps he doesn't get around much these chilly days. I'll look in on him before I go home.'

'Shouldn't bother dear. He's ever so shy. Never likes to have people poking their noses. Any chance of a cup of tea – if you'd like one?'

Constance was pleased to make tea. They drank from assorted vessels, Dido still on the floor. She made no further verbal effort, but sat watching Snap and mulling over her aunt's painful letter. Poor Grandpa, with no wife and such a sad daughter. Thank goodness for Floppyguts.

Sitting with her parents at supper, she said abruptly, 'Did Aunt Unity bite her nails?'

'Not that I remember,' said John. 'Why do you ask?'

'I wondered.' Dido didn't enlighten them. A little later, she said, 'I won't marry. But if you want grandchildren, Hal might have some. He quite likes girls.' It seemed unlikely to Dido that either her mother or father would have the least wish for more children of any kind.

'What is catatonic?' she asked as they were leaving the table.

They were at a loss. 'A surprising word for you to use,' said Constance.

'It means deranged,' said John. 'Not a bad word. A not irrelevant word by any means.'

'That's what I thought,' said Dido.

Dido returned to her room and sat at the small table by the window she used for drawing. She remembered Granny Burnett in happy circumstances in the Cumberland Hotel, Durban. Then it came to her that her grandmother really had died, and could be visited no more. Tears filled her eyes and spilled down her cheeks. She held her head in both hands, and felt it full of dark noise.

John went to Constance's bedroom late that night. She was disconcerted and confused. Very little was said. They were like fumbling, embarrassed beginners and nothing was achieved.

He left well before morning.

She lay remembering their early marriage in Chiswick, he still a medical student, using her body to practice on: mapping out biological areas in coloured pens . . . and she liable to laugh and wriggle while being drawn on. She remembered their love-making in those days – and finding it rather more comic than romantic. A faint sense of disappointment – of much-ado-about-nothing. Was she a frigid person? She didn't think so. She was instinctively ready to express her love for him and for the children physically: she'd just never been one to hug and kiss in a sentimental way. She'd always felt critical of mothers who embraced and kissed their children constantly. She felt that children of all ages deserved respect.

But there was certainly an absence of romance in her marriage . . .

Chapter 13

Coral and Alfred were married. As Mr and Mrs Sherwood, they arrived at Westbourne House a week later, with a modest amount of luggage.

That same day, a strange man with a bicycle presented himself at the house, and informed John that his mission was to regulate the two grandfather clocks. He was tall and thin and dressed in dark clothes. Dido watched with interest as he attended to his meticulous duty in the hall.

The clock man spent more time on the drawing room specimen in its walnut case. The fascination here was its glass window in the case door, through which the swinging pendulum could be seen; and a marble bubble in the pane of glass.

'That chap's been cycling up West Road to fettle our clocks twice yearly for thirty-two years,' John said. 'A well ordered life, by most standards.'

'A survivor from a past age,' Constance said, having seen their visitor away. 'Now I've something of an anachronism to show you.'

She held out a printed slip of paper which required her to fill in how many head of cattle, how many sheep, how many acres of land she possessed. Enclosed with the form was a certificate stating that Mrs Burnett's farms had achieved standard A in their grading, and that if she would be good enough to advise local farmers on any issues, they were sure her services would be much appreciated.

'Splendid!' John said. 'I hope you'll lose no time in advising that juggins Roddy Crawley on running his three thousand acre farm.'

'Indeed I will,' Constance joked. 'I can just imagine his reaction! While I think of it – shall we ask them for drinks or a meal after Christmas? We could have the Measures as well. And what about your old family doctor, Ralph Gallatly?'

John pulled a face similar to the one his daughter showed to the Jack Russell. 'Let's think about it,' he said.

'Hal will be home soon,' said Dido. 'I cannot wait to see him. I want him to ride Daisy in my trick bridle.'

'Yours and Coral's bridle,' Constance murmured. 'Of course – Hal hasn't met Coral yet – let alone Alfred.'

Before Hal's return, Coral and Alf presented themselves to Constance with another request: Coral, plump, fresh and guileless, Alfred improved both in complexion and confidence.

'Would you mind if Alf brings his dog here? He's an obedient animal , and no trouble,' Coral began, winsomely, head to one side. 'You wouldn't need to see much of him.'

'What breed is he?' Constance asked.

'He's a lurcher – quite a handsome fellow,' Alf said. 'I've had him since a pup and he'd pine to go anywhere else.'

'Does he have a kennel?'

'I could fix him up with a beer barrel. The Nag's Head'd let me have one, and I'd make a base for it. With straw in, he'd be fine.'

Constance waited for John to veto the proposal. He said nothing. Of course – where animals were concerned, he could afford to be soft. They presented no threat.

She raised an expressive shoulder. 'Well – I've no objection to having him if he lives outside. If it's really cold you could let him into your sitting-room. We'll see how it goes. Of course, Prince may feel his nose is out of joint.'

Coral and Alfred both thanked her warmly. 'He's called Race,' said Alf, proudly. 'And he runs like the wind.'

'Prince won't mind him,' Coral added. 'Race is ever so gentle.'

So Race the lurcher joined the family. His kennel appeared at the end of the side drive by the rear of the house. 'An adrenalin machine,' was John's laconic comment.

Shortly after the dog's future was established, the phone rang and Dido, who was in the drawing-room intent on making a collar for Mrs Dunbar's pug, answered. She swung round, the phone held away from her, and announced to her parents, 'It's someone called Vera.'

John moved to take the call.

'Who's Vera?' Dido asked.

Constance, without hurrying, went to the open door and through it. Dido continued to coax the French knitting into a greater length from the cotton reel by means of little tugs. She could hear her father saying, 'Not in the car. I'll take a morning train up tomorrow.' His voice held a note of asperity.

'I'll ring you from the club,' John promised.

'I'll look forward to seeing you arrive with Hal,' Constance replied. 'Don't go spending money on Christmas presents, will you? We've decided to keep it all low key this year, don't forget.'

'Very wise, dear Connie. By the way, do take the SS out for a nice long run somewhere, won't you? Treat yourself to lunch at the Ram Jam. Good for you and the car.'

The idea played in her mind. She said, 'Well, here's your train,' and raised her face to kiss him. Driving home from the station, she toyed with the thought of taking Katie somewhere for lunch. Standing on the platform of their modest local station, she imagined John as a boy left to his own devices, cheerfully consorting with porters, guards, engine drivers and probably the station master, eagerly learning the tricks of the trade, as Mrs Tipler might have said. No self-pity in the young John. No sentimentality, even then.

John took the tube to Gloucester Road station and walked from there to Vera's block of flats. He rang her bell and climbed the stairs, feeling his other self transforming him. She opened her door cautiously. Never inclined to flamboyance, even in his alter ego, John took her shoulders and kissed her briskly on the cheek. Vera might have been Constance; but pleasure lit his face.

She urged him away from the door, girlishly bossy. 'Shhh! My flat-mate's still around. But she's off to her folks this afternoon until after New Year. Let's take a walk to the King's Road – or to Earl's Court.' She fastened her swing-back jacket, pulled the door shut and dropped the key into her bag. Down the stairs they went together, arm in arm. 'We'll have dinner at the RAC Club this evening,' he told her. 'I must phone Constance from there. Don't let me forget.'

'I must do some Christmas shopping,' Vera informed him. 'We'll go to Liberty's in Regent Street because it's so glamorous now; and Oxford Street, which is fun and probably cheaper. Have you much to buy? Hamley's is a wonderland for children's presents.'

'I could get one of two things, I suppose,' he said, reluctant to contemplate a spending spree, while instantly inspired to find a luxury item for her in Liberty's.

'You are an importunate woman, ordering me up to London today. You're old enough to know better,' he said, with more sincerity than mockery, his conscience pricking him. 'Insisting on rights you don't have.'

'I have no rights. But I do have you.' She nudged him in the side with her elbow.

'And I certainly have no rights to anyone or anything. I love my wife – and I'm in love with you. A dismal situation.'

'You put a very brave face on it.' She looked up at him with her particular blend of efficient nurse and jolly country lass.

John telephoned Constance from the RAC Club when they had sat over a pre-dinner drink. Vera stayed in the lounge, surrounded by her festive gift bags, sipping a dry Martini, smiling in a detached way at any passing male. She wondered what John was finding to say to his wife.

She asked no questions when he came back, and they were preparing to go to the dining-room when someone approached John and laid a hand on his arm.

'Good Lord – it's you!'

He turned to find Ivo Collard behind him. They grasped each-others' arms, exchanged platitudes, then John gestured to Vera and introduced them.

'Ivo and Mother were both living at the Cumberland in Durban, between '42 and '45.'

'Dear old London's still parochial enough for friends to run into one another,' Ivo said. 'Thanks to your mentioning this place at Florence's sad do, I've been coming here to see friends, and avoid abusing my brother's hospitality. I'm a bit adrift, you see. Got to decide where to replant my English roots. Suffering from a bad dose of nostalgia for Durban days . . . and the old friends there.'

'What are you doing for Christmas?' John asked.

Ivo shrugged. 'Not a big date in my calendar. No other family members, no kiddies. Thought I'd rediscover the Cotswolds – or the Lake District – when they're clear of trippers.'

'I gave you our Westbourne address didn't I? Connie's there, and I'm collecting our son off the school train and taking him back the day after tomorrow. Come and look us up some time, why not?'

He could sense Vera nudging against him.

'Most genial of you. Meanwhile, what are your plans? If you're having dinner here, would you be my guests?'

John and Vera's eyes met. 'How kind of you,' said Vera. 'We were actually on the point of leaving.' She bent to gather her packages.

'Ah well. That's a pity. It'll have to be cheerio for now then.' Ivo shook their hands in turn, his tall figure slightly stooped, his large long face very pleasant when he smiled, his light coloured hair receding a little. His age could have been anything between forty and sixty. 'Happy Christmas and New Year in the meanwhile.'

John followed Vera downstairs to the entrance, and out into the dark evening. 'That's scuppered our dinner here,' he remarked.

'Why did he have to turn up?' she responded, as if John had contrived Ivo's appearance from the blue.

'You heard what he said: London serendipity. I certainly never expected him.'

'Well – you've made your duty call as promised. We're free agents! Let's catch a cab and eat Italian food in Soho.' She took his arm in a conspiratorial clench and began to move away, a sharp eye open for taxis. John fingered the elaborate box in his pocket with the necklace Vera had chanced to exclaim over in Regent Street.

They returned to her flat with their senses fully engaged. The future and the past had lost any kind of focus. He didn't stay the night.

Constance and Dido finished supper and passed their plates through the hatch to Coral. 'You may decorate the Christmas tree this evening,' Constance said. 'Then promise me you'll go to bed, and go to sleep. No reading. Daddy and Hal will be here tomorrow.'

'I hope Hal won't mind the train journey, just with our father.'

'I'm sure they'll enjoy being together. An opportunity for Daddy to tell Hal what he's been doing in London; and Hal can talk about school.'

'And remember their happy days with the wall!' Dido spoke dryly. 'Anyway – people never talk about school. Like I don't talk about my bad dreams.'

'Have you had more bad dreams?'

'I do keep having them. Mrs Tipler's there, like a nice old person . . . then she suddenly gets ugly and attacks me, and Mister is there, shivering.'

Before Constance could respond, the front door bell rang and she hurried to answer, hoping it might conceivably be John.

'Forgive me for disturbing you, Mrs Burnett.' It was Oliver Seaton, Edward Fewings' nephew. 'My uncle's had a fall, and I think he should be taken to hospital. Could you possibly ring for an ambulance?'

'Of course I can. How bad is he?'

'He's had a nasty shock poor chap, and he may have broken something.'

'I'll call an ambulance straight away . . . and then come over.'

Oliver hurried back to the Almshouses. Reminding Dido to get to bed early, Constance crossed West Road to join him, and Oliver took her into his uncle's sitting-room where Ned Fewings lay on the floor with a rug over him, and another folded under his head. 'I don't like to move him.' Oliver said.

'Young Jezebel would laugh to see me like this,' Mr Fewings muttered in his weak voice. 'Tell me to go to bed, she would.'

'I'm so sorry, Mr Fewings. How did you fall?' Constance asked.

'Tripped over me own feet,' he said. Then he shut his eyes and appeared to doze.

'It's lucky I happened to look in. I'd been working late,' said Oliver. 'My own car's outside, but I thought it best to let the first aid chaps see to him.'

They arrived a short time later, and carried the old man, groaning vaguely, on a stretcher to the ambulance. They slid him in and hopped aboard themselves. Oliver turned to Constance. 'I'll follow down in the car and see what they think the damage is. I just don't know how long he'd been lying there when I arrived. I suppose you couldn't come with me? I've a pathological dread of hospitals. Must be the gypsy-warning in my genes!' He gave a self-conscious laugh.

Taken aback, but happy to oblige, Constance left with him and climbed into his Morris. They drove slowly after the ambulance for the short distance to the cottage hospital.

Ned Fewings was laid on a trolley and wheeled away, no longer aware of what was happening to him. Oliver Seaton watched him vanish along a corridor and his face became distressed.

'I've been very fond of my Uncle Ned,' he said simply. 'He's eighty-nine, you know.' He left it at that, and Constance, wanting a conversational distraction, alluded to the George Hotel, without mentioning John. 'I took a friend of mine there yesterday for lunch,' she added. 'She hadn't been for a while, and was astonished at how crowded it was! I was glad to see Daniel Lambert and the wisteria still there.'

Half an hour passed in the waiting room, before a doctor came to give his report. 'We'll have to Xray your uncle. I suspect he's broken his hip, and he's in a bad state of shock. We've sedated him now. If you ring tomorrow around nine o'clock, we'll be able to update you on his condition.'

'Thank you very much,' said Oliver, and with a glance at Constance, they both walked out to his car. He hesitated before opening the door for her and said, 'I suppose you wouldn't have a drink with me in the pub? I think I'm in shock too, in a funny sort of way. He's been like a dad to me. Your company for half hour would be wonderful.'

Constance hesitated. 'Why not come home with me and I'll make some coffee?'

He accepted gratefully, and they drove back up West Road to the house. Constance had a word with Coral, and joined him in the drawing-room.

He said, 'Don't tell your daughter I'm a funk over hospitals. If she was critical of Ned's phobia, she'd be withering about me.'

Constance laughed. 'Have you any other family living near?'

'Well no, you see. My parents died some years ago, and my wife more recently. We weren't blessed with children. So dear old Ned has meant a lot. He used to be a great companion, and always took an interest in my modest life. Seeing him in that condition rather knocked the stuffing out of me.'

Coral came in with a tray and disappeared again.

'Tell me about your business.' Constance invited as she poured from the coffee.

He told her that agricultural machinery was beginning to grow in post-war demand, and that things were doing pretty well generally. Medieval style farming with horses was becoming automated: heavier tractors compacted the earth, it was true, but saved weeks of the year and half the man power. Developments in fertilisers and pesticides too. She might like to go to the Peterborough Show next spring? Plenty to see and do at those shows – magnificent displays of prize cattle and sheep of course, and heavy horses . . . and even dog shows at some venues. A lot of fun for children, and a chance to buy good quality country clothes . . . and mouth–watering produce from the food stands . . .'

'I think we'd enjoy that sort of occasion very much. A nice family outing – and educational. ' She told him about the accolade she'd received through the post for her farming standards.

Laughing, he said, 'For my part, I'll have complimentary tickets sent to you for the spring Show. I've a feeling you weren't brought up in the country?'

'As a matter of fact, I wasn't. I was born and brought up in Hove. But I love the country, and my husband spent his childhood here. He could happily have turned his hand to farming – or to your line of business.'

'May I ask what he does?'

'He's an army doctor, and about to begin a training in eye surgery.' She didn't add 'in London.' Oliver nodded, and swallowed half an inch of his drink.

'I don't suppose you suffer qualms over hospitals then. Are you a nurse yourself?'

Now Constance laughed. 'No, no. I opened a small business after leaving school . . . with my father's help, and a sister as my partner. An employment agency.'

Oliver exuded complimentary surprise. 'What enterprising young women! Terribly brave. Did the agency flourish?'

'Well, it did! We had one or two encouraging notices in the local papers, and we never looked back.'

They sat now, looking back – dwelling in silence on that agency in a prime street in Hove. Oliver wondered if the sister had been as attractive as his companion.

Fifteen minutes later, he drove through the gates of Westbourne House.

The following day, he rang to tell her that his Uncle Ned had died during the night.

Chapter 14

'How did the term go?'

John greeted his son off the steamy train with an arm round the boy's shoulders. He took the small case from Hal and put it on their trolley. 'Let's find your trunk.'

Saved the trouble of reciting a three-month synopsis, Hal followed him to the guard's van, identified his trunk and watched it being hoisted up beside the bag. Together they made their way to the taxi rank, Hal dodging through crowds of boys, parents and general public who kept separating them.

At King's Cross the process had to be repeated. John consulted his watch. 'Still over half an hour until our Peterborough train. Are you hungry?'

'A bit.'

'I'll see if there's room in the station café. Wait here with the luggage.'

Hal stood with the porter, shifting his feet, feeling cold and socially awkward. His father came back and they returned to the café and had tea and a plate of sandwiches.

'Well, did you have a good term?'

'All right.'

'But glad it's over?'

'Oh yes.'

'Mum and Dido will meet us at the other end. We have to change trains at Peterborough first.'

Hal looked glum. He sipped his tea, found it too hot and picked up a sandwich. Hunched over the table, he nibbled it.

'What are the staff like?' John asked. 'Tell me about them.'

Hal lowered his sandwich. Still hunched, he pondered. Then he said, 'Quite good. Some of them.'

'Describe them.'

Hal suspended his sandwich again while he thought. 'There's Miss Martineau. She's the matron.'

'Is she all right?'

'Well – we call her The Martinet.'

'Why?'

'Oh – only because she's nice and it's a nice name.'

'Good Lord. Is that your idea of logic? What about the teachers?'

Hal took a bite of sandwich and used the time swallowing to order his thoughts. He could hardly remember any names, sitting there in the station on a metal chair with his father. 'There's Mr Hodgkins. He's the Head. So he doesn't count.'

'Logic again,' John quipped.

'Mr Dent does games. He's not bad.' Hal sipped his tea and after drinking, said with nonchalance, 'He thinks I'm quite good at running. And I'm getting used to football now.'

'What about history?'

'That's Mr Meads. He hates me!' Hal uttered the words with a brash laugh.

'Why does he hate you?'

Hal shrugged. 'Don't know! Don't think he knows.'

'Just has a short fuse I expect.'

Hal reflected. 'Yes. He's bored teaching us, so he keeps blowing up. Then he sits and stares into space.'

'Sounds likely that he was blown up – literally – in the war. Nerves shot to pieces, poor blighter. Hardly a rest cure, teaching you lot. History's a key subject though. You must get a grip on it.'

Hal nodded, washing sandwich down with tea. John looked at his watch again. 'I'm going over to buy a newspaper. Keep an eye on things.'

Hal waited in peace, surveying the station.

His father returned. 'Not much time now. We'd better find our platform.'

In the Peterborough train, they took a window seat opposite each other. John stretched his legs, feet either side of Hal's. He unfolded his newspaper. Hal again experienced a sense of release. He focused on the passing landscape as the train moved smoothly away from London and beyond.

Some while later, John glanced up. 'What are you counting?'

he asked.

'Churches,' Hal responded readily, revealing the tactic he'd devised to keep his parent in abeyance.

'Feel like a peppermint?'

Hal accepted a Polo mint from the roll John found in his pocket.

'Tell me who your best friends are at school.'

Hal wrinkled his nose, sucking his mint, then said, 'We don't have best friends really.'

'I had a great friend when I was there. But he was unlucky. Caught a bullet in the head in France.'

Hal noted his thirteenth church. 'D'you think thirteen's an unlucky number?' he asked.

His father took off his jacket. 'Why should any number be unlucky? Superstitious people just like a bit of horror in their lives. Another church look – did you get that one?'

'Oh – thank you!' He'd spotted it; but no harm in humouring his father.

'I'm just popping down the corridor. Won't be long.'

Hal's eyes remained fixed on the passing countryside. Then he stretched out his legs to see if his feet reached the opposite seat. Then he leaned forward and felt in his father's jacket pocket for the Polo mints. He slid a Polo into his mouth, then bent to recover a piece of paper that had come out with the sweets and fallen on the floor. A Regent Street jeweler's receipt for a necklace. Crumbs . . . a hundred and seventy pounds! Hal pushed it back into the pocket and gazed again at the view.

'Will we have to invite the cousins over for Christmas?' he asked later, with no vested interest but needing a topic on his father's level.

'Your mother was thinking of it I believe. But not on the actual day. Why do you ask?'

Hal gave his shrug. 'Just wondered. I don't specially want them to come.'

'You and Dido might be glad to know the Measures children. Can't grow up unsociable, you know.'

'We have enough of people at school.'

'Come on, tell me who you like in your class.'

Well . . . I have a sort of best friend, I suppose. Person called

Clover-Brown.'

'First same Clover?'

Hal burst into natural laughter. 'Of course not! I think it's Anthony – but we don't use first names.'

John's curiosity appeared surfeited at this point. He took up his newspaper again and screened himself behind it. Hal returned his eyes to the window and watched the countryside fly by. After some minutes, his lids grew heavy and he dozed. They changed trains at Peterborough, and little conversation was made before they arrived.

Hal sprang into life. He'd caught sight of his mother and sister waiting on the platform to greet them. Leaping from the carriage, he was ordered back with a peremptory reminder to collect his bag. John followed with his belongings, and arranged to have the trunk wheeled to where the Jaguar was parked. Constance was given a quick kiss in passing, and Dido a smile and a raised hand.

The children fell into easy exchanges of news. The Sherwoods, the French knitting, the lurcher dog and a knowledge of transforming beet into sugar came from Dido; the gross unfairness of masters, the filthy food, the beetle-ridden public swimming-baths came from Hal.

John let Constance drive them home from the station.

'I love Christmas at Westbourne!' Dido cried ecstatically. 'We've got a tree in the hall, and I've decorated it.'

'Do you know what a lurcher is?' Hal asked.

'A dog. I told you.'

'It means a mixture of breeds – a bastard.'

'Don't use that word,' John said, as they swung through the gates and drove to the front door.

'It's a real word,' Hal assured him, having recently adopted it into his vocabulary.

'Not in that context,' said John. 'Race is a mongrel. Now run and ask Alfred to come and help with the trunk.'

The children disappeared into the house. 'I've invented a bastard game,' Dido was saying happily. 'It's a mix of polo and croquet and you play on bikes, using mallets and balls. The bike gets a bit battered.'

Prince ran out of the sitting room to see Hal.

'Hello Woggo!' he said. He still disliked the name Prince. Race came out too. 'Hello mongrel.'

Coral levered herself to her feet as the children entered her sitting room. She looked flushed and tired, and she had kicked her shoes off. 'He's called Race . . . and you must be Hal. I'm Coral. Alf's my husband, and he's not back from the Nag's Head 'till later.'

Hal shook her hand. 'Does he drink a lot?'

Coral laughed. 'Alf isn't drinking. He works there. Happy to be home, are you?'

Hal nodded with vigor. 'Did Dido decorate the tree?'

'I told you I did. Here's Daisy's trick bridle.' She had fetched it from a peg in the passage.

'At least she didn't ride the pony in that skimpy thing right up to the brickpits,' Coral said. 'It was against her mum's wishes to go there at all, I may add.'

'I described it all to him in a letter.' Dido spoke with hauteur, and fiddled with the bridle, holding it aloft. 'I wrote how I fell in and nearly lost my life.'

'Silly girl you were –when you don't know who's going to be wandering about that place.'

'I only *imagined* a murderer there.'

'Did you pray on your bended knees to be spared?' Hal was trying the bridle over his head. He threw it on the table and they both went away to examine the tinseled tree.

John called to Coral, 'Please tell Alf when he gets back there's a trunk in the outer hall I'd like him to take to Hal's room.' To the children he said, 'I'm going for a walk round the fields. Want to come with me?' adding in a lower tone, 'That girl's a hefty lass,' as they followed him outside.

Coral, overhearing, pulled a rude face. She was on the verge of dozing again, when the phone rang and a moment later Constance appeared. 'I'm just crossing the road to the Almshouses. I won't be long.'

Oliver Seaton had rung. He wanted her to advise him about his uncle's belongings. They amounted to very little, and she suggested that it could all go into the local sale-room.

Oliver glanced about him and nodded. 'Right. That sounds a good idea. But it's just struck me that Ned would have liked you to keep an object to remember him by – be it ever so trivial.' He gestured at the untidy interior. 'Will you have a look?' He thought how attractive she was in a close-fitting grey-blue dress beneath her coat. He liked the occasional pleats. An image of her husband jogged his mind; handsome, affectionate John Burnett, lunching with Constance at the George Hotel.

Constance moved slowly round Ned Fewing's sitting room, and then back into the room he never slept in, but which contained a wardrobe and a chest of drawers for his clothes. There were various ornamental trinkets, a vase, a pair of insipid water-colours and a reproduction of Constable's Hay Wain. Nailed above the table where Ned had his meals was a picture, painted on glass, of a seated youth in velvet jacket and trousers, fondling two deerhounds. The frame consisted of four crude pieces of varnished wood overlapping each other at the corners. It was rather pleasing, and Constance lingered beside it.

'Why don't you take that?' Oliver asked, moving to her side. 'I've no idea where it came from. But I know Ned liked it.'

'Then you must keep it.'

'I've enough pictures on my walls.'

'It's charming and unusual. Surely you, or someone else, would be happy to have it?'

'I'd be very happy to know you had it,' Oliver responded.

After another quick glance round, Constance thanked him and he lifted it from its nail and handed it to her. Then he took it back and went to the window to dust it with the curtain.

Constance laughed. 'Now I should offer to wash that curtain.'

'It'll all be seen to in the official quarters,' he said solemnly. 'I wonder who they'll find to replace Ned.'

'Plenty for the gossips to speculate about.'

He walked her to the road and pausing to say goodbye, Constance saw Hal hovering at their gate opposite. Before she could wave to him, Oliver laid his hand on her arm.

'You're a very kind and delightful lady,' he said.

'The kindness is yours – parting with this,' she replied. She gave Hal his wave and turned back. 'Thank you Oliver– and all the best,' she said.

He stood, watching her crossing the road and greeting her son. He watched them walk away up the drive together. When the boy glanced over his shoulder, Oliver returned to Ned's rooms.

'Who was that?' Hal asked.'

'Mr Fewings' nephew. The old man died just recently.'

'Why have you got that picture? Was it his?'

'Yes. Mr Seaton thought we might like it as he has enough pictures.'

Hal took it from her. 'It's been painted on the glass. That's quite rare. It may be valuable!'

'Possibly. But we'll keep it to remember him by.'

Dido joined them, and explanation of the picture was repeated, without mention of Ned.

'Has Mr Fewings got tired of it?'

'He's dead,' Hal said.

Dido gasped, and appealed for explanations. Her hands flew to her mouth. 'The hospital bed killed him! They shouldn't have taken him away.'

'He was very shaken, and he had to have his hip mended. He was in pain,' Constance said.

'Just as the gypsy foretold,' Dido lamented. 'No-one should make anyone defy the gypsies. I'm very shocked – and not at all happy.' She turned and walked away.

'Christmas in two days. You'll be hideously happy then,' Hal called after her.

Chapter 15

'Happy Christmas!' John greeted his wife as he took his place at the dining table.

Constance half rose to receive his kiss, and expressed the same wish. 'Are the children not down yet?'

'They're still busy with their stockings. They like to spend time with the contents.'

John passed his cup to be filled with tea. 'They're a bit old for stockings, aren't they?'

There came the sound of feet pounding the stairs. Hal and Dido appeared, flushed and cheerful.

'What are all those presents out there?' Hal nodded back into the hall where wrapped parcels lay under the tree.

'Oh – one or two things for everyone,' said Constance. 'You've had enough to be getting on with. Come and eat breakfast.'

'If only it was snowing today, wouldn't it be perfect,' said Dido, spreading butter with fastidious attention.

'Christmas is seldom perfect, whatever the weather,' John remarked, pushing marmalade over to her. Dido declined it, and ate the buttered toast pensively. 'But we'll make sure it's a happy one all round,' Constance said lightly.

John met her ironic expression with large innocent eyes. She rose to her feet, went to fetch a rack of toast from the hatch, retreated to her chair and consulted a list of those who had sent them cards.

'I take it we'll be going to church?' John glanced at his watch. 'In half an hour from now, we must be ready to walk down. Do you hear, you two?'

'What's church to do with Christmas?' Hal asked in jest.

'Everything,' Dido said with her mouth full of toast. 'We'll sing carols. It'll be all right.'

‘Make sure that the shoes you wear are suitable and are cleaned properly. I shall want to inspect them before we set off,’ their father said, managing both to respect and offend the spirit of Christmas.

The children fell into silence; but their optimism continued to bubble not far beneath the surface. John, self-critically unhappy, and struggling to immerse himself in the role of parenthood, was rapidly irritated with their intermittent quips and gestures; and now that he’d imposed a traditional appearance at church on his family, he was beginning to dread even a trivial interest shown in him by members of the congregation.

‘Have you eaten enough?’

They nodded merrily.

‘Then you are welcome to leave the table.’

Constance heard them leaping up the stairs with a humbling sense of regret. Their presence had been comforting even in that atmosphere of mild disgrace. They loosened her tongue and strengthened her identity as happy mother, if not happy wife. Seizing a subject of concern that had been lurking in her mind, she launched into it with a sense of fatal mistiming.

‘John, it’s hardly a matter to discuss on Christmas morning, but I’m uneasy about money.’

He glanced at her, one eyebrow raised, his expression blank. ‘What about money? Why should you be worried?’

‘Not worried exactly. But the last things we need are financial problems. You must be sure to tell me if you feel this house is an unreasonable expense.’

‘As you say – hardly a concern for today,’ he responded. ‘Don’t stress yourself. We’re very lucky people who can afford a good lifestyle.’

She sat with his rebuke and her good fortune; then dismissing both, she said, ‘I’m glad we’re going to the morning service. Whatever else happens at Christmas, it’s never quite the same without a religious aspect.’

‘The same as what?’ he asked.

‘Well – the same as what one was brought up to value . . . and believe in.’

‘Like being brought up not to spend what one doesn’t have? Not to borrow?’ He mumbled the words, looking down, self-conscious or mocking – she wasn't sure.

She allowed herself to laugh. 'I suppose that's a fair parallel. Not wanting to risk one's money – or one's soul. Treating each with respect.'

'I know you attach great importance to respect.' He still avoided her eye.

'Yes.'

The silence lingered. He glanced at the clock and then at his watch. 'We'd better get ourselves ready, and chase up the tiddlies.'

They stood together for inspection.

'Does she wear a hat?' John asked his wife, contemplating Dido.

Dido shot a look of wild surmise at her mother.

'Oh – not necessary . . . and her hair's tidy.' Constance smiled.

John scrutinized his childrens' feet. There was a general fidgeting.

'Come on then.' He led them out of the hall through the porch and down the drive. They all wore overcoats. Constance had a neat wool hat with a rosette over one eye, and John a dashing Trilby with a narrow brim. They exchanged greetings as they passed into the church, and settled along a right-hand pew to themselves.

Constance lingered after the service. There were families she was ready to approach and to wish a happy Christmas. But John was adamant. He wouldn't offer himself to the town gossips for Constance's sake, the vicar's sake or even for the infant Jesus. Without a hint of rush or rudeness, he conveyed his family trio through the lych gate and across the square and up their road for home.

'When are we supposed to have the main meal?' John asked as they entered the house, unbuttoning coats. 'Can I help at all?' His manner was now of a figurehead displaced. Authority had become humility. He was Constance's subservient husband. Indicate what's expected of me, his tone said, and I'll fall in with orders; but allow me some privacy.

They had a light lunch, Constance remarking on people seen at church, and fielding the children's jokey comments. John ate and spoke little. Hal and Dido's cheerful spirits still prevailed.

'We can open our presents now lunch is over, can't we?' Hal insisted.

'That's what we agreed. Let Daddy light up the tree first . . .'

'Before you open presents, what about clearing this table and helping Coral with washing up?' John regarded them with what seemed to his children as benign malice. 'It's Christmas Day for Coral and Alfred too, you realise.'

Hal and Dido exchanged glances. Hal shrugged. 'Yes – we know.'

'Off you go then. Help clear and wash and put away. Then we'll see.'

The children disappeared into the living-room and beyond, to talk with and oblige the Sherwoods.

Constance went into the drawing-room, her forced conviviality ebbing. Even while she was hoping John would follow, she became aware that he was going up the stairs.

The house became very quiet. Then came a resounding crash.

Constance hurried to investigate. She found Dido in a state of remorse, the long apron Alf had tied round her having tripped her on the scullery step and caused a tray of crockery to hit the ground.

Constance said, 'Never mind – these things happen. Help Coral clear it up quickly.'

'Before he sees it,' Hal said, cryptically. He knelt with Alfred to hasten the task. Coral removed the apron from Dido and continued to put clean items away. Still cheerful, Dido followed her mother through the hall and met her father at the bottom of the stairs. As she tried to slip into the drawing-room, John caught her arm.

'Whatever was that noise?'

'It was an accident,' Constance was quick to say. 'No great damage done.'

John stared at his daughter, waiting for her to speak.

She twisted a little and said, 'I tripped.'

'The apron she was wearing came undone. It wasn't her fault,' Constance explained.

'Well? What happened?'

'I broke some china,' Dido told him.

'So you're a very careless child. I hope you told your mother you were sorry, and helped clear up the mess?'

'Yes,' said Dido, eyeing Constance.

'You should be more careful on Christmas Day.'

Dido looked down at her church shoes and made the toes knock together. She was tempted to lay the blame on them.

'Go away now, and do something outside. You can't hang about indoors. Come back together in about an hour.'

Constance smiled at Dido's disappointed face, closed the door and went to sit down. 'That was a rather sudden change of plan.'

He muttered something she couldn't catch. After a moment's uncomfortable silence, she added, 'I don't think you've put your cards up? I've an idea some arrived for you?'

John responded by walking to the fireplace with the cards in his hand. He placed one between two others in the central row on the mantle-piece. Then he found room for cards from Army colleagues. Constance could see that the first card displayed was of a coy puppy gazing upwards at the beholder. Her heart began to thud.

'May I know who sent that one?'

He declined to answer, so she rose and went to read the inscription. It was signed Vera – after a declaration of affection.

Determined to show the same absence of emotion as her husband, Constance replaced the card and went to sit again. John also sat, and began filling and then lighting his pipe. The silence lasted until John informed her that he too needed some fresh air. He wouldn't be long. Another mumble . . .

She had no idea whether he was intending to drive off, take a walk, or just find fault with the children's activities. She had seldom felt her self-confidence so sapped and her hopes so lowered. She rose and reached for Vera's card again. His adoring little puppy Vera. Whatever could she be like, to make that her choice ? What a hateful intrusion into her first Christmas with John for years. They'd spent only one Christmas together, and that was before the war. Oh . . . the sentimentality of Vera's offering!

Today was to have been a special experience, binding them together. It might have worked. John's sense of fun might have sprung into life. Hal and Dido's excitement might have lit a paternal touch-paper somewhere.

Constance decided to phone Hove; wish her parents a happy Christmas again . . . learn more about their day. She'd rung them earlier. She needn't let them know how wretched things were here.

She thought she could trust herself not to sound upset. When there was no answer, she remembered that her parents were going for a drink with neighbours.

Deeply depressed, she picked up the book she was reading and tried to remember what was happening in those fictional lives.

The children reappeared. They were bright-eyed and disheveled. 'Where is he?' Hal asked.

'I think he went for a walk. He'll be here any minute.'

'We've been ages. We biked over to Lound and back.'

'Well, go and tidy yourselves. Save a bit of time.'

'There doesn't seem to be much hurry,' Hal grumbled. 'Though he's so fussy about punctuality.'

Ten minutes later, they heard John come in. He also went to tidy himself before reappearing in the drawing-room. He was wearing a casual sweater.

'Can we light the tree now?' Hal suggested for his father's benefit.

John, standing by the window, re-lit his pipe and puffed complacently for a space while the children watched, interest in the process banking the fires of their impatience. Finally, he left the room and pressed the switch. The swags of small clear bulbs sprang into light from top to bottom of the tree. Red and silver baubles glowed among a miscellany of lesser nick-nacks cluttering the stems. The large square hall was otherwise in darkness. The grandfather clock ticked mordantly.

Constance called, 'Bring your presents in here.'

The children lost no time in obeying, stooping and hobbling to and fro with packages. The sound of wrapping-paper being ripped and crushed filled the room, followed by exclamations.

Constance addressed John, having failed to catch his eye. 'Perhaps we could have a glass of wine to celebrate?' she said. 'I could do with something to warm me up.'

Making no reply, John left the room, and returned with a bottle of red wine and two glasses on a silver tray which had been a wedding present from Ivo Collard. He handed her a glass and she said, 'Here's health and happiness!'

'Cheers!' shouted Hal. 'Can we have some wine?'

'Not until you're eighteen,' his father replied with a friendly glance. 'You wouldn't like it anyway.'

'Just a sip,' begged Dido.

'Did you find a couple of parcels under the tree?' Constance asked, still unable to meet John's eye.

He indicated the floor on the other side of his chair. He lifted and began to unwrap the handsome car rug she'd given him, nodded, smiled, and said primly, 'Thank you.'

She in turn opened a scent he knew she was fond of, and a sum of money to spend at Oats and Mussens, the large store in Stamford. 'I wish you'd let me replace that old watch of your father's, John,' she said when she had thanked him. 'You tell me it isn't reliable. You have to keep checking it.'

He dismissed the notion with a wave of his hand.

Constance swallowed a long draught of wine.

A little later, she saw that he had a present on his lap of which she knew nothing. She watched him take out a tie: in her opinion, a hateful tie. Cheap colours. She half expected him to put it on, but he merely laid it aside. She had no need to ask the name of his benefactor; she'd seen the complex expression on his face: smug, ashamed, defiant. Why shouldn't she demand the name and aggravate his discomfort? Anger overtook sadness; it was more bearable to be angry.

'Have you had Dad's present?' Hal asked his mother suddenly from out of his own preoccupation.

Constance pointed to the perfume and the envelope, and said she certainly had.

'But what about . . .?' He glanced at his father and back to her again with a cheeky perplexity. 'You know . . .' and he mouthed at John. Constance's expression was alert and John's embarrassed. No explanation was given.

Hal encircled his neck with his hands, still addressing his father. 'You know . . .' There was silence. Then he spoke with reckless abandon: 'For your wife!'

Further silence.

'You're talking in riddles Hal,' John said abruptly. 'My unreliable watch tells me it's time for dinner.'

Still perplexed Hal departed, ignoring Dido's signals for enlightenment. They took their places at table. Alfred brought the turkey in and John began to carve. Coral appeared with vegetables and accessories, and filled their plates. The need to comment and to inform dwindled away, and a dour formality settled over the scene. Constance made several attempts to encourage conversation; but John chose not to respond or look at her. They were all shut out. The children became increasingly nervous, and ate in silence. Constance wondered how the Sherwoods were interpreting the atmosphere.

They struggled through Christmas pudding, delivered with cheerful bravado by Coral and set alive with a purple flame. 'Careful how you eat it,' Constance warned the children.

'Are there coins?' Hal asked, with a surreptitious glance aside. His mother nodded. It had cost her dearly to eat a small portion herself. Before she had time to ask if John wanted tea or coffee, he left the dining-room. They heard him going upstairs. This is intolerable, Constance thought, his moodiness is blighting everything and everyone. But he's been through so much in the Far East – and of course he's unhappy too . . .

Hal and Dido stayed in the drawing-room with her for a while. She attempted to make excuses; but they remained baffled and disillusioned.

John didn't come downstairs that night. After Constance had seen the children to bed, she sat alone with Vera's card for company.

The tie had disappeared.

Chapter 16

They had just come back from a walk down to Will Hillis's piggery, John preserving a moody silence, on the twenty-seventh of December. He had spoken only to order some hay from Hillis, and then had started for home in the same baleful manner. Approaching the house they saw a car parked by the front door. A figure was stepping from the back and pulling a small suitcase after her. The woman handed money to the driver and the car slid away towards the west gate.

'Vera!'

John, ahead of Constance, stood stock-still.

'Hello John!' Vera stretched out a cool hand. 'And Constance.'

John spoke casually. 'Constance – this is Vera. I have to say, I'm taken aback.' He bit his lip as the two women shook hands. 'As I recall it, I explained why this was out of the question.'

Vera stooped to pick up her case, and he immediately took it from her. There was a tense moment.

Constance said, 'Well Vera – at least we've had Christmas.' She resolved to remove Vera's card on the instant. 'This is Hal. This is Dido.'

Vera smiled graciously at the children, who said nothing.

John led Vera through the porch and into the hall. 'A splendid tree!' she exclaimed. 'I can guess who decorated it.'

'Who?' Dido demanded.

Vera didn't hesitate. 'You and your brother.'

'Wrong,' Dido replied. 'My brother had nothing to do with it.'

John said, 'Come on Vera – what's the meaning of this unannounced visit? And what's the suitcase all about?'

'Presents!' guessed Dido, eyes shining.

'Wrong!' Vera retorted, echoing Dido. 'My over-night things. Would it be shocking bad manners to ask stay? It sounds feeble, but London's a lousy place to be friendless in at this time of year. I've never felt so blue.'

Constance's expression was inscrutable. She was thinking, those feelings are relative. She told herself, this woman ought to leave immediately. But what is more humiliating than a resentful confrontation in front of the children?

'Well . . .' John hesitated, clearly annoyed. Then he lifted the case and started up the stairs, retreating from the atmosphere. Vera smilingly followed.

Constance said, 'Would you children warn Coral that we have a guest for lunch.' Then she went into the drawing-room and removed Vera's card from its place.

Five minutes later John joined her, still looking agitated. Constance said, 'How dare Vera invite herself here? Or is it by invitation?' And she slowly tore the card into pieces.

Using a conciliatory tone, John refuted the idea. He added, 'She needn't stay long. I'll make sure she keeps out of your way.'

'And have her to yourself?' Constance grimaced. 'In any case, Vera seems to call the shots. And how long is not long? Until the New Year?'

'Of course not.' He sat down, crossed his legs and met her eyes. 'Look Connie – I'm mortified she's sprung this on us. I'd no idea she might come. I feel furious with her.'

Constance slipped the quartered card into her pocket. 'To quote Dido, my kind heart runs away with me. I'm a fool not to have ordered her straight back to London before the taxi got away.' She faced him again, colour rising. 'Imagine how I feel, hearing you say you'll keep her out of my way. That's so insulting!'

'I just meant that she won't expect to be entertained.'

'And what does *that* mean?' Pent-up feelings of resentment were escaping. 'Vera will be no trouble! She'll be treated like a member of the family!'

She broke into unsteady laughter. John smiled nervously. 'She's got a bee in her bonnet about being on her own this Christmas. It's when you live abroad and lose touch with friends. You know how it is.'

'I've no idea how it is! Where is her family?'

'She doesn't have any. Well – a sister she doesn't get on with. I admit her behaviour is outrageous to you and to me; but she's had to be an independent girl . . . and I admire her spirit. It's just a rather selfish personality. She lacks your breeding and integrity, Stupe.'

Intensely angry, Constance said, 'Since when did manners influence men more powerfully than sex?'

'Well, you have both in abundance; and you know I love you Constance.' He sat on the arm of her chair with his hand behind her neck. 'Forget sex. She's simply a nurse I've reason to be fond of.'

'I've been an independent war wife for five years, supporting you in every way. Have you no reason to be loyal to me?'

'Every reason. But she's only coming for twenty-four hours. That won't affect us much.'

'Believe me, I shall be aware of everything. Though my good breeding might fool Vera.'

They fell silent. It occurred to Constance that at least Vera's appearance had loosened John's tongue. Silences had been more painful than rows. She said irrelevantly, 'I can manage this house perfectly well with daily help. I think the Sherwoods should go.'

'Our income's plenty for my needs in London, and for the upkeep of Westbourne. Of course you must have living-in help; and we keep Hillis on for the garden.'

'I could engage a cleaning woman to come in daily. Or twice a week. That's the sort of help people are looking for nowadays.'

'My training costs me nothing. I have my army pay, and there'll be something substantial coming to me from Mother. You should have a housekeeper who can help with the children and can cook – and a woman coming in to clean. I want you to have a good life here, without worries of that kind.'

'What about other kinds? I'm not likely to enjoy peace of mind on my own while Vera has you in London.' She touched his arm, close to tears. 'You can hardly wonder if I'm putting pressure on you. Tomorrow, Vera goes.'

He was touching the top of her head when the children and Prince came into the room.

'Is she really here for the night?' Hal asked.

'She is.'

'But we don't know her!' Dido cried, tribal instincts roused.

'How long's she staying?' Hal pursued.

'Just a day I expect.'

They pondered. Then Hal wanted to know whose friend Vera was .

'She's our friend; only your mother hadn't met her before.'

'And we haven't met her. So she's just your friend.'

Dido put on a tragic voice. 'My one friend was Mr Fewings – and he's dead! I really liked him – and he called me Jezebel.'

'That's a Biblical name, and spells doom,' said Hal.

'Doctors don't always know best. But he didn't even listen to *my* advice!'

'We've heard this lament so often,' Hal said, kneeling down to interact with Prince. 'It gets less sad every time.'

Footsteps were descending the stairs. Vera smilingly entered the room. 'Why is it called the Milky Way room?' she asked, seating herself with a swish of her full skirt.

'The stain on the ceiling,' Hal replied. 'It looks like a smudge of stars.'

'Haven't you a family?' Dido enquired, sternly stroking Prince lying sphinx-like on the carpet.

'I'm afraid they've passed away.'

'Oh, don't start her off again!' said Hal. 'Dido's in mourning for an elderly gent who wouldn't sleep in a bed.'

'And when he did he died,' Dido muttered. Then as a thought struck her, 'You're too late to open presents with us, Miss Vera.'

'Not Miss Vera!' said John. 'Call her Miss Savage, or Vera – if she doesn't mind.'

'Savage!' Dido was entranced. 'I'd love to be called Savage. It's much more exciting than Burnett.'

'Do you like it?' Hal glanced at Vera and back at the Labrador, rolling him on to his side. 'Because you'll have to give it up if you get married.'

'Not every woman will give up her name,' said Constance. 'Occasionally she keeps her own, or uses both names.'

'I must confess at once,' said Vera, 'that I've no plans to get married – and no presents to put under your tree.'

After an antagonistic silence, she added, 'It was on the spur of the moment that I came . . . and all the big shops were shut.'

Coral announced that lunch was ready. Constance introduced her to Vera, and they trooped through.

‘Hasn’t Coral any family?’ Hal thought to ask. ‘Or are you going to tell us they’re all dead too?’

‘Don’t be facetious,’ said his father. ‘Coral has Alfred, and they both have families. But this year our house is their home. They’ll have the afternoon to themselves, and prepare the meal this evening. I suggest we walk up to the woods after lunch. It’s such a sunny day, more like spring. Have you suitable shoes for walking, Vera?’

‘Oh – these won’t suffer,’ Vera replied lightly. ‘I’ve others to change into.’ She turned away from the table and stretched out an ankle on what Constance judged a shapely but solid leg. ‘What will the young people do?’

‘We’ve walked to the piggeries and back,’ said Hal. ‘We need a rest.’

‘We could rest at the brickpits,’ said Dido. ‘Riding Daisy there and back.’

‘No,’ said her parents in unison.

Constance went on, ‘You could call at the Almshouses and give them all a small package.’

So Hal and Dido crossed the road to the Almshouse precincts with festive packages. Passing the door that was Mr Fewings’ house Dido, showing signs of sorrow, was frog-marched quickly on to Mr Hare who was beyond compare, and after him the mean Miss Elliot, and then to gossip-prone Mrs Baxter, where Snap met them with uncharitable yaps . . .

The adults set off up the road, where houses yielded to chestnut trees standing in fields, and a track turned right into the woods.

‘Where did you grow up Vera?’ Constance asked.

Vera began to describe her upbringing in the West Country, and they climbed the gentle rise between areas of mixed deciduous trees and conifers.

‘You have a sister, then?’ Constance addressed her across John as they walked three abreast.

Vera chuckled. ‘Alive and kicking. Though there were periods during our childhood when I could cheerfully have killed her.’

‘Sentiments that inspired your nursing vocation?’ John quipped.

Vera threw him an ironic smile. ‘My sister lives in Surrey with her conventional husband and their tiresome offspring. But I don't visit much because I'm bad with children.'

'John didn't warn you we have a couple?' Constance said.

'Theirs are the wrong kind of children,' Vera amended. 'Yours seem very tolerable!' And now she threw John an amused glance. 'My family loved sandy soil and ferns and old-world roadside pubs and commuting to the City. I prefer East Anglia and dear flat Lincolnshire, with those huge skies and rolling farmland.'

'Constance's family are Sussex people. Not so very different from Surrey.'

'Tell me about your family, Constance.'

Constance said phlegmatically, 'My father and his brother owned Plumpton Racecourse.'

'Much more my scene!' said Vera. 'I'd love to have cash to fling about at the races.'

'Actually, you're rather careful with money,' said John.

'How can a poor nurse be anything else? But I quite admire those who are lavish.'

They made their way by a circular route back to the main road. Constance felt she'd learnt little about Vera; nothing to explain her appeal to John. Was it her sheer cheek? Or those wide cheekbones . . . and the slight tilt up at the corners of her compelling blue eyes?

Chapter 17

Vera sat in one of the easy chairs, smoking and watching the children's movements, privately amused.

'Were you teasing when you said you had no presents for us?' Hal asked.

'I was not teasing,' she told him. 'But I have something for your parents.'

'We don't mind,' Dido assured her. 'You don't really know us.'

'Dinner is at seven,' Constance said. 'We've half an hour to have a drink.'

John brought them glasses of wine. Vera reached down a hand and picked up a square object bound with an ostentatious ribbon. She rose and crossed the room, avoiding the children with their drawing books and pencils, to offer it to Constance. 'Happy Christmas!' she said, and went back to her chair with an air of satisfaction.

Constance unwrapped and held up a box of chocolates weighing two pounds. 'Audrey's chocolates! Very special,' she said. She laid them aside. John, raising his glass, proposed an uncomfortable toast to them all. The three adults drank.

Vera smiled indulgently at Hal and Dido. 'Can you draw portraits?' she asked.

'No. We don't do them.'

'Try sketching your parents.'

Hal cast his eyes rapidly at each. 'I could have a bash at doing you,' he volunteered.

Vera lifted her head and leaned back. 'Very well. I'll keep still as a rock.'

'Oh, don't worry. It won't be a bit like you anyway.' Hal turned on the carpet and set to work, the pad propped on his knees.

Dido leaned close and watched him. 'I'd rather sketch Prince.'

She began to put her words into action, using the pencil with reckless energy.

'You were very good at drawing ships and aeroplanes in Mooi River,' John commented.

Constance said, 'Dido drew children.'

'And I called them dog-faces,' murmured Hal, concentrating on his model.

The minutes ticked by.

'I must break the spell to have a drink.' Vera emptied half her glass then resumed her pose. More minutes ticked along on the grandfather clock.

Dido leaned over again and hooted with laughter. 'Hal's made you look like a cartoon woman!'

'How clever,' said Vera. 'There's big money in cartoons.'

'The only films we've ever seen were 'Snow White' in Durban, and 'The Mummy's Hand' at the cinema here,' said Hal. 'Neither very suitable for young children.'

Vera extended a hand for her likeness. 'Aha! I am like a figurehead for one of your ships. A little practice is needed on the human form.'

'I think we should have dinner,' said John.

Coral, under Constance's supervision, had produced a casserole of left-over turkey. After a while Vera said, 'That girl's a good cook! I've never made chicken taste so good – let alone turkey. Perhaps the Aga makes a difference. But my favourite food of all time is Malayan. Every sort of Asian cooking – unlike the nursing staff out there, and a few other Brits, with their squeamish insularity. I expect you've tasted the peanut sauce they do in Malaya, Constance?'

'Will you pass me the salt please Miss Savage,' said Dido, show-casing her lisp.

Hal leaned over and muttered, 'Call her Vera. It sounds better.'

'Don't whisper at table Henry. It's rude, as you should know,' John rapped out. Hal fiddled with his knife and fork. He regarded his father from under his lids. What was that secrecy with the necklace all about? Why wasn't his mother allowed to wear it? He glanced furtively at Constance on his other side, and was discouraged to see her tight expression. Christmas in Mooi River had been nothing like this.

John refilled their wine glasses.

Vera said, 'I have a Malayan friend in the Earl's Court Road and I chat to him now and then, and he tells me how broken-hearted he is to see all the bomb damage in London. He adores London as his own city. And I adore Singapore!'

'And we adore Mooi River,' said Dido, carefully scraping her plate.

'We wish we were there now,' said Hal.

'Never mind. Think how lucky we were not to be drowned at sea coming home,' Constance reminded him. 'Perhaps you don't remember those colossal waves attacking us from all directions in the Bay of Biscay – and the helmsman losing his head – and in the lull after the storm, the mine that floated past so close to the ship . . . and no-one turning a hair!'

Both children claimed to remember vividly. 'Broken arms and legs and crockery everywhere.'

'Then be thankful we're able to begin our lives again in our own country, near to our families. We've much to be grateful for.'

'I'll drink to that!' declared Vera, raising her glass. 'Make the most of your childhood, you two. It never comes back.'

'We never supposed it did,' said Hal. 'Thank goodness.'

'I never want to be grown up,' said Dido. 'Though I'm not as happy as I used to be.'

'What makes you say that?' Constance asked.

'She has nightmares about the Tiplers. And her so-called friend has died,' Hal recited.

When dinner was over, and they had retired to the drawing-room, Hal took his sister aside. 'Let's call on Ernestine.'

Dido fetched her knitted collar for Willoughby and leaving the adults drinking coffee, they slipped into the darkness and rang Mrs Dunbar's front door-bell.

Mrs Ablewhite opened it. 'What a surprise!' she exclaimed. 'Come on in. Mrs D is just having a dram of something seasonal.'

As they entered the drawing-room, Willoughby rushed at them with shrill barks. It was a few moments before they could pay attention to Ernestine. She was in her usual chair, in a black evening dress to her feet, and wrapped with a woollen stole. She waved a gracious hand at them and they instantly felt they were on friendly ground.

'Willoughby and I were very dull together. Now we can both brighten up,' she said. 'Mrs Ablewhite's staying the night; but she's listening to something on the wireless.'

Dangling their hands at Willoughby, the children moved to two chairs close by their hostess. 'Look,' Dido told the pug. 'This collar is for you – and I made it.' She fixed it round the folds of his neck, and regarded him critically.

'A very dainty ornament,' Ernestine observed. 'You are fortunate indeed, Willoughby. Now – what am I going to offer you people to drink?' She pointed to a glass-fronted corner-cupboard. 'Fetch two sherry tumblers from over there, and you can join me with this,' and she lifted the bottle of port at her elbow. Sipping measures of port, both children expressed themselves with wry mouths and licking lips. 'It will warm the cockles of your hearts.'

Ernestine's colour was high this evening, and her voice at a lower pitch. 'A kind angel has sent you to visit me,' she said, 'when I was feeling in need of comfort. Christmas time is full of memories. Going back to when I was your age. A totally different world . . . and not a soul left from it!' Her eyes were moist as she smiled at them. 'I am the only person in the whole world now who knows about any of those dear friends and relations; no-one else has a scrap of knowledge about any of them. That is a very sad fact, which you have yet to experience. It's the essence of loneliness.'

'We can imagine,' said Dido.

'No-one can imagine,' Ernestine contradicted. 'It's all in here.' And she tapped her forehead below the grand pile of her hair. She fixed her gaze on Dido. 'You remind me very much of my daughter,' she said.

Seeing the children glance at each other, she added, 'My adopted but very dear daughter. Your Aunt Unity.'

'Really?' said Hal. 'Did you really adopt her from Granny Burnett?'

'She became like my daughter. She used to come round to me every day she could. I was more able-bodied in those days. She was a lonely child, and we got on very well. Her father was a man I loved and respected – and he encouraged Unity to come.'

'Was that why Granny Burnett went off?' Hal asked. 'You can't blame her, if no-one liked her the best.'

'We loved her terribly!' Dido said. 'Every day I miss her more.'

'She wasn't a natural mother,' Ernestine replied, as though that was fact enough.

'But when our father was a boy she was good with him – in some ways?' Hal suggested.

'Natural mothers shouldn't favouritise. That's what I mean.' Ernestine broke off to re-fill the glasses. 'Florence was fond of your father. But even he had a rough time of it.'

'What a muddle,' said Dido, blinking her eyes to see clearer. 'You're a lucky dog Willoughby – everyone loves you.'

'You've such a look of Unity,' Ernestine repeated. 'I wonder if you'll have her instability! To think that lovely person came to such a sad end!'

Unnerved and enraptured, the children stared round the room, seeking a distraction from Unity. 'You don't bother with a Christmas tree?' Hal was inspired to ask.

'Oh dear no! Not for Mrs Ablewhite and me.'

'And Willoughby.'

'Well . . .' Ernestine took a moment to drink more port. 'He might have been tempted to disgrace himself against a tree.'

They sat with this idea. Then displaying her left hand, Ernestine said, 'You may look at this ring. The one with the emerald.'

They peered at it with imperfect sight. 'What a lovely ring!' Dido obligingly said. It was rather large and heavy.

'Can you guess who gave that to me?'

'Mr Dunbar!' said Hal at once. 'I mean, Reverent Dunbar.'

'No.' Ernestine touched the ring with a gentle finger. 'Henry Burnett. Your grandfather. The man airbrushed out of history.'

'Except by you,' said Dido.

'If only you'd known him. We could have reminisced about him. Your mother never met him. Think of that!'

'We were born too late,' sighed Hal.

'Mrs Baxter talked a lot about you and Henry,' Dido said.

'Mrs Baxter? Now who is she?'

'Over the road from us – with a snappy dog.'

Ernestine's brow cleared. She raised her eyes to the ceiling. 'Oh yes – Mrs Baxter . . .'

'Who will you leave your ring to?' wondered Dido.

'It's still too much part of me to know,' Ernestine said. 'You can't try it on I'm afraid. It won't come off my finger.'

Hal said, rousing himself, 'We have a guest staying with us. A lady from London. She's a friend of our father's – but none of us likes her much.'

'Good gracious.' Ernestine sat in silence. Then she asked, 'Why?'

'She didn't give us a present,' Dido said.

'That's not a real reason,' her brother hastened to say.

'I'm sure the lady likes your mother?'

'Anyone would like our mother,' said Hal.

'Dear boy,' said Ernestine. 'Let me fill your glass.'

'I think we should get back.' Hal laughed. 'Your wine's very strong.'

The children stood, and set down their glasses. Willoughby jumped up and followed them to the door.

'He'll see you out,' Ernestine said, and waved again as they left the room. 'Be sure to go home slowly . . .'

Mrs Ablewhite's wireless was still on, turned up loud. She didn't hear them as they parted from Willoughby, closed the door, and went along the path in the dark with a strange uncertainty.

'I'm glad I look like Unity,' said Dido. 'But I hope I don't go mad.'

'Why worry, when you are anyway?'

'Because,' said Dido, bumping into him at the gate, 'she did really kill herself. I'll show you at home.'

Their parents and Vera were in the drawing-room, but no-one seemed to be talking. The children hovered in the hall, sensing hostility. The Christmas tree lights were on, but complete silence struck an unnatural note. Through the doorway they could see the adults reading. It was like peace after a quarrel.

Constance heard them coming in. She put down her book and went to greet them. 'Coral's tired and has gone to bed, so keep your voices down, won't you?'

They nodded and went softly up stairs and into Dido's room where Unity's letter to her father was produced and analysed.

'Catatonic. That's how I feel sometimes,' Dido confided to her brother.

'Catatonic only means unhappy.'

'But people can be so unhappy they get ill. The husband may

have taunted her to kill herself.'

'Uncle Max? No. He's got a temper, but he hasn't harmed Aunt Bunty.'

'He may have killed Unity with his own hands.'

'Of course he didn't. Our father doesn't like him because he can be bloody rude. He's not a killer. I wish Unity wasn't dead. It would've helped to know more about our father.'

'I don't want to know if I'm going to go mad,' Dido said.

Vera had gone to the room that had been prepared for her. Constance returned to the drawing-room where John was standing at the window with the curtain pulled aside, staring into the dark.

Constance shut the door behind her and moved nearer to him. He said, 'It's all going reasonably well, isn't it?'

'Not reasonably, nor well. Hal's explained his pantomime over the necklace. He found the receipt in your pocket – presumably after your gallivanting with Vera in London.'

'In terms of money, it wasn't a valuable necklace, Stupe. Just something to indicate appreciation to her.'

'For services rendered.'

'Oh, come on Connie. You know the situation.'

'A hundred and seventy pounds you spent on her! I hate to sound grudging, but it does reveal your priorities.'

'And they are you and the children.' He kissed her cheek. 'I'm so lucky to have you.' In this happier mood, he was able to use his sheepish tone.

'She saved your life. She gave you the will to live. I do know! As Hal would say, it gets less touching every time. But does Vera know that in my heart I fought the war with you day by day and inch by inch. I shan't remind you again. Bear in mind too, that I came to this house for your sake. Nowhere near my family . . . or friends. And what happens?'

'What?'

'Vera takes you over! You'll be in London together. I can't fight *that* war day after day.'

John pulled her against him. 'I'll be coming home as often as possible – and you'll get up to London. Another reason for keeping the Sherwoods. Come on your own – and we'll do some shows together.'

'You're putting her on a train first thing tomorrow,' Constance said.

She left him, and he went back to the window.

He imagined Vera upstairs, getting undressed. He tried to remember that room in the days of his boyhood. His parents sleeping apart. That patch on the ceiling. How did it get there?

Damnation to Vera. If he could only make love to Constance again. Her physical attractions were still palpable; it was her psychology somehow that let him down . . . her lack of involvement . . . and passion. Perhaps he should have died. In the worst times on the front in Burma, he had fancied he'd be happy dying at thirty-three. He was past that age now by four years.

Chapter 18

Vera woke at a little after six o'clock next morning. She left the bed and pulled her dressing gown round her to walk down the passage to the bathroom. As she neared the far end, she heard sounds of distress coming from the Sherwood's room. She halted, listened closely, and made out agitated little screams from Coral and urgent interventions from Alfred.

Never one to hesitate long, Vera knocked on the door while opening it.

Coral lay disheveled on the bedclothes, her knees drawn up and her face distraught. Alf stood over her, lanky and helpless.

It was plain what was amiss: Coral was in the throes of giving birth. Vera hastened to the bedside, grasped the girl's hand, and instructed her calmly to breathe fast and shallow. 'Don't panic Coral, you're doing fine . . . and I've delivered quite a few of these.'

Alf retreated in relief, and having been told to fetch a sterilsed knife, watched for the next fifteen minutes as Vera saw his baby into the world. It was a tiny but seemingly healthy boy.

Vera cut the cord and the house was filled with lusty yells. Alf hurried in and out for towels and flannels, while Coral lay on her pillows in a state of sweat and tears and relief.

'I'd better call Colonel Burnett to come and see you, Coral,' Vera said, exuding gratification. 'That was a good job well done! I take it you weren't completely innocent of his existence?'

The Sherwoods exchanged glances. 'We did know of course,' Alf admitted. 'But not that it would be so soon. We were going to tell Mrs Burnett.'

'Don't bring the Colonel,' pleaded Coral. 'I'd be ever so embarrassed.' Holding out her arms for Vera to place the wrapped baby in, she said, 'I can't thank you enough. What luck it was you who heard me.'

'I'll have to let them know now,' said Vera. 'What about baby clothes? And have you a crib?'

'A sleeping suit and two little vests – and toweling nappies. If Alf can get down to my parents, Mum will give him the crib and other stuff we've got. I was waiting on more clothes till I knew if it was boy or girl. Oh dear, isn't he terribly small?'

'Now relax,' Vera told her. 'Find a nappy Alf, and I'll fix it for you. Someone can take you down and bring the things back. I must announce the happy news; then I'll bring a pot of tea and some breakfast.'

'This is ridiculous,' was Constance's exclamation. 'We take Coral into the house. Then it's Coral and her man. Then it's the pair of them with dog. Now it's a family!' These words masked her personal foolishness, and resentment of Vera's dramatic role.

'We can't give them notice – but they'll have to leave of course,' said John. 'I'll call Gallatly to look in. Plenty of time to decide their future.'

Vera had gone humming to the kitchen. Constance confronted him with implacable purpose. 'Promise me you'll put her on the Peterborough train this morning. Chance is a fine thing, and she'll use this baby to prolong her stay. But it's out of the question. I don't want to see her here when I come home.'

'Of course. I accept that. So you'll take Alfred down to collect what's needed? I'd better have a word with Gallatly . . . and Vera might as well make herself useful to Coral before she goes. You realise there's no train until two-something.'

He and Constance looked in at the door to offer their congratulations to Coral; then Constance drove away with a still awestruck Alf and at the last minute, the children who begged to go too.

John had decided to put himself out for his children. As soon as the old car growled away, he climbed up into the loft which lay the length of the bedrooms, and located a large box full of his old electric train-set. Three large boxes. He wished he'd asked Alfred to liberate himself from his new responsibilities for a further ten minutes, to help him down with them.

Laying out a magnificent complex of track on the bare boards of what had been the spacious front morning room did much to lift his spirits. Empty of furniture other than a corner cupboard, the lines spread right across the bare floor, and before long there was a station and level-crossing and foot-bridge and a couple of tunnels in strategic places. As his enthusiasm grew, he began to wonder if the children should be allowed anywhere near this newly created world. He had unpacked two full sets of engines with coaches, each to run under power from two transistors; also a goods train of open trucks. Handling the engines and their dependent sets brought memories back to him which put his childhood on a higher level. For it was these trains which had inspired him in his youthful interaction with staff up at the local station.

Dr Gallatly arrived at a little before midday. He didn't stay long. John saw him to the bedroom, and gave him a sherry before he left, recalling local events before the war.

On her return, Constance hurried to confront John and saw him disappearing into the garden.

'I trust you've checked on the time of that train?'

Before he could answer, they heard the sound of another car on the gravel. Together they rounded the front of the house to investigate, and a moment later, Vera joined them, her full skirt swinging and her face bright with interest.

It was Roddy who stepped from the Land Rover. Katie remained inside.

'Just the man we wanted to see!' he called. 'John old chap, it's good to have you back.'

The two men shook hands, and Katie climbed down. She put an arm round Constance and was introduced to Vera. Roddy lost no time in seizing Vera's hand. 'A pleasure to meet you Miss Savage!'

John thought, I was never a friend of yours, Roddy Crawley.

Katie and I have been two old fogies this Christmas,' confided Roddy smugly. 'Our young have had plans of their own. Come and cheer us this evening. I've a new delivery of claret.'

John's eyes met Constance's. 'Well – Vera needs to catch an afternoon train.'

Vera's glance intercepted theirs. With a defiant tilt of her head at Roddy, she replied, 'I have to confess, I shall be in disgrace if I stay.'

'Nonsense! Don't you be swept away Vera. Let John and

Connie bring you down this evening. Then you'll know a few folk when you visit again.'

'Out of the question,' Constance cut in. 'Vera can't stay, and we've made other arrangements already. I'll give you a ring, Katie . . .'

Roddie lifted despairing hands, shook a wry head at the two women, and clambered behind the wheel. 'Another time then. Adios!'

They drove through the further gate.

'You have your marching orders Vera,' John said. 'Two-twenty on the platform up the road. Roddy will get over it.'

Constance regarded him impassively. Then reluctant to prolong the moment she retreated into the house. Vera sauntered into the garden. John followed Constance indoors as Hal came running through the hall.

John called 'Hal!'

His son stopped and was caught by the shoulder. John said, 'Listen – you had absolutely no right to get into my jacket pocket in the train. Or nose into its contents. Do they teach you no ethics at school?'

Bewildered, Hal said, 'It was only to get another Polo. I wasn't snooping.'

'But you were! You behaved in a very silly and misleading way the other evening – and upset your mother. You're a little nuisance.'

'She should've been glad to be given a necklace costing a hundred and seventy pounds. Was she shocked at how much you'd spent?'

'That's none of your business. Don't interfere again; and please respect other people's property in future.'

'Sorry,' said Hal, feeling sorry only that his father could make such a fuss about nothing. His mother too. Couldn't she be pleased, instead of getting people into trouble?

John frowned at him, acutely aware of using the boy as a scapegoat. Against his better nature again, he escaped to the garden to find Vera.

Hal went in search of Dido. She was pleading with Constance. 'Now can we see the baby?'

'We don't believe there is one,' Hal said, bringing psychology to bear.

'Just go quietly up then – and don't stay long. If Coral's asleep, creep away. You could try again after lunch.'

They tiptoed along the passage and put their heads round the Sherwood's door.

'Come in,' Coral murmured, her face pink and damp. Her red hair clashes with her cheeks, Dido thought. They had to peer over the side of the bed to make out the baby's head.

'Has he got red hair?' Dido wondered. There was so little, it was hard to tell.

Coral's finger lightly stroked the pale hairs. 'He's very fair,' she said. 'But who knows? He may go dark like his dad.'

The baby winced, twisting his features and screwing up his eyes.

'Is he in pain?' Dido gave a dramatic jerk.

'No, it's wind. He's still asleep. I'll try to feed him when he wakes.'

'Didn't you know you were going to have a baby?' Hal asked. 'I thought people always knew.'

'Well, I did know. But he decided to come much earlier than planned.'

'Our mother seemed surprised. You won't have to go now, will you?'

'Not straight away,' said Coral. 'We can always find a few little jobs for baby to do around the place.'

They laughed, and Hal wanted to know what he would be called.

'We were thinking of Michael. Or maybe Ben . . . after our two dads.'

'Would you call him Rory?' Hal looked wistful. 'I wanted to call our dog Rory – not Prince.'

'Perhaps we'll call him Prince Rory,' joked Coral. 'There's your mum calling. You'd better go and have lunch.'

'They won't call him Rory, I know they won't,' said Hal as they ran downstairs.

'I've warned Alf that if there's any trouble over feeding, or with Coral's health, they go straight to the Cottage Hospital,' John said as they were sitting for lunch. 'Gallatly was typically relaxed about the whole business.'

After an uneasy meal put together by Constance, John invited the children into the new playroom, his main purpose being to avoid Vera. Early darkness was gathering outside, and he'd closed the heavy shutters to create a gothic emptiness. On top of the corner-cupboard sat a squat figure, from which fluttered a soft light. Dido stared up in alarm.

When John switched on the main light, she and Hal were overcome. 'How fantastic!' Hal cried. 'What wonderful trains!' and he immediately knelt beside a transistor and sent the brown coaches into action.

Dido lost no time in monopolizing the green set. Her eyes followed the coaches on their journey, taking in the decorative details of their bodywork.

'Were all these yours when you were a boy?' asked Hal.

'They were. Unity and I used to do just what you're doing.'

'You kept them very well,' said Hal, reaching over the track to move a goods-truck aside.

'See that you do the same,' said John.

When he'd left them on their own, Dido stood up and took a closer look at the candle-lit figure. It was a large brown earthenware Buddha, with a night candle on his hollow lap. She switched off the light. The candle flickering through his eyes and grinning mouth produced a ghastly image, and sent shadows shuddering up the walls.

Hal uttered a shout of protest at being thrown into darkness; but glancing back at the Buddha, he went to stand by Dido. The light shed from it was golden, and they gazed round the moving room in awe.

'I'll start the train and let it run in the dark,' Hal said, settling back on his knees. Dido joined him, and the two trains rushed and slowed and reversed, and in due course met their inevitable fate.

'I wish the Tiplers were still here,' Dido said, staring about her. 'Think how scared Mister would have been.'

'I thought you were so sorry for him,' said Hal absently.

Dido sat on the bare floor in silent homage to Mr Tipler, resenting his wife's fall from grace. 'Come on,' Hal called, 'I've master-minded an extra long train of mixed coaches and trucks with an engine both ends. Come and watch.'

Up at the station, John said to Vera, 'You've invaded my house, sabotaged the spirit of Christmas, delivered a baby and captivated Roddy Crawley. Pleased with yourself?'

'Content enough,' Vera murmured. 'For the short term. Then I may be taking a new direction. Men come along, you realise?'

'Of course,' said John with mock solemnity, 'and you'll fall for every one of them.'

'I'm discriminating to a fault.'

'To a fault,' he repeated.

The train was approaching. John bent to kiss her and moved to open a door. She stepped up, he handed her case over, and slammed the door. I might be his wife, Vera thought with irony. She was wearing a dashing red outfit and had put on her Christmas necklace for the journey that was to separate them.

'Can we say goodnight to Rory?' Dido asked later that evening.

'Rory?'

'She means the baby,' Hal explained, a touch embarrassed. 'It hasn't really got a name yet.'

'You may,' said their father. 'But don't overstay your welcome.'

They scrambled from the table, were called back, left again with ironic grace and headed for the stairs.

They found Coral feeding the baby, and were duly fascinated. Alfred was sitting by the window, reading the local paper. Coral's high colour had faded but excitement showed in the smile on her face. 'He's a quick learner,' she said.

'Do they fill up again?' Dido asked, directing a finger towards Coral's breast.

'Oh yes,' she laughed. 'They both fill up.'

'Has he a name yet?'

'We think we'll call him Michael Ben. And use Ben,' Coral replied.

Hal's interest waned.

'How about this,' Alf said, holding wide the paper. 'The Tiplers of Fanfare Lane . . . Vincent Tipler died last Tuesday – assumed accidental. Possibility of manslaughter . . . Well!'

Coral's quick frown indicated the children, who were processing these facts.

Dido demanded, 'Not our Mr Tipler? He's not dead?'

'Seems he is. He had an accident.'

'Is manslaughter the same as murder?' Hal wanted to know.

'Not as bad,' said Coral, reversing Ben to the other side.

'Did she hit him?' asked Dido.

'Nobody knows,' said Alf, guardedly.

There was silence. Then Hal said, 'We never knew he was called Vincent. We just called him Mister.'

Dido mouth went down. 'I won't want to hear the musical-box again.' She pushed her face into Coral's eiderdown.

Hal said, 'You will – in about a day.' He felt a drab sensation grip him and he added, 'When I'll be back at school.'

Dido flung her arms round him. 'I don't want you to go away.'

Alf stood up, dropping the paper, and put a hand on each of them. 'Now then – you'll be upsetting Ben. Say goodnight – and don't worry about what you don't know.'

Sniffing, Dido followed Hal to get ready for bed. Constance came to say goodnight. 'Where's my father?' Dido asked.

'I'm coming up the stairs,' John called.

Seeing her daughter's woebegone face, Constance asked what had happened and was given a stark reply. 'I can't believe our Mr Tipler has died,' she said.

'Nor can I,' said Dido resolutely. 'Will you read Doctor Dolittle?'

'Yes,' said John. 'I want to know what happens next to the good Doctor – and to wise old Polynesia and to Jip the dog and to Dab-Dab the duck . . .'

'And to Gub-Gub the pig!' said Dido, giving a hoot of laughter with her hands over her mouth.

'Get into bed, and I'll read,' said John.

Constance left the room. Dido stuffed a half-sucked sweet under her pillow, then sat up while he read, staring at a picture on the facing page.

'Good night,' he said when the chapter ended. 'Tell yourself you're on a train, going for a long journey.'

'Mister's on a long journey,' she mumbled. 'I was nice to him, anyway.'

'Good,' said John. 'Well done.'

A wakeful hour later, Dido slipped out of bed because her fingers were sticky. Turning into the dark passage to the bathroom, she saw a white figure at the far end. It was Coral, who had herself been to the bathroom and was gazing happily through the window at the stars.

Dido, imagining the ghost of Vincent Tipler, uttered a scream; and history repeated itself.

Chapter 19

'Max and Unity are arriving!' called Hal in a warning tone.

Dido's head shot up. 'Unity?'

'Uncle Max and Aunt Bunty, you mean,' said John mechanically. 'Oh damn – what on earth has brought them here!'

The children exchanged glances. Cursing relations was surely too far.

Constance opened the front door. 'Hello, and welcome,' she said. 'What a surprise!'

'A happy new year to you all,' Max declared as though with peace-making intentions. It was the first day of January.

The adults embraced, and the four children hung about. 'Take them in there and show them the trains,' John said. Hal and Dido led Serena and James into the darkened room, and set about demonstrating the power that lay at their hands.

'I'm going to open the shutters,' Dido said. 'We'll shut them again later when we play our trick.'

Serena's eyes met her brother's. They knelt on the bare floorboards and watched their cousins activate the railway scene.

Max expressed interest in going outside. John took him into the garden and beyond, up to the furthest boundary. Max asked sensible questions and made positive comments; John responded in his most diffident and conciliatory manner.

'Bunty hasn't been at all good lately,' Max confided. 'We imagined it was just winter . . . and the cold. But she's been having tests and Xrays, and they say it's breast cancer.'

'I'm terribly sorry,' John said.

'It seems she can have radio treatment. The success rate isn't bad.'

John confirmed this. 'The thing is to catch it early. Any idea how long it's been going on?'

'The doctor said it's at an early stage.'

John thought, You're not lucky with your wives. Or your wives aren't lucky with you. 'Keep her feeling hopeful,' he said. 'If you believe in the power of positive attitudes – as Constance does. Mind over matter. There may be something in it.'

'Oh, it takes more than a tumour to get Bunty down,' Max asserted. 'She has bags of British grit. I just felt you and Connie ought to know. No need to mention it around.'

Constance had introduced Bunty to the Sherwoods; Alfred was at home until his evening shift. 'Little Michael Ben came as quite a surprise to us – including Coral,' joked Constance.

'Imagine how I felt!' Coral said. 'Proper foolish. I'd no idea I was so far on.'

'I must call Serena to see him,' said Bunty, and ventured in her nervy manner into the noisy train room. Serena appeared, duly paid her respects to the pram, and swiftly returned to her trains.

'I'll put the kettle on, Bunty, and rustle up some tea,' said Constance. 'Or perhaps we should fill glasses, and drink to the New Year?'

Bunty prefered tea. When the men joined them, John offered Max a glass of red wine. Despite the early hour, it was accepted. 'Only just gone five o'clock – but dark already. That makes it more respectable.'

'I'll join you,' said John, though he drank very little on any occasion. He wanted to be as hospitable as possible.

They sat in comfortable chairs in the drawing room, and the children were called through. They all shared their Christmas experiences and exchanged ideas for the coming months. John watched Bunty with guilt, reinforced by his behavior to Constance. He'd always approved of Bunty, if only to balance his dislike of Max.

He got up to offer the bottle of wine again. Constance and Bunty joined the men with small glasses. They were on the point of raising them to each other and to all that life would bring, when another car drew up on the gravel and stopped behind the Measures'.

Hal jumped up and announced, 'It's someone in a baby Austen. A big man in a little car.'

The large man walked to the front door. John left the room

and went to investigate. 'Ivo!' he called loudly for Constance to hear. 'What a shocking thing!'

'I've come to wish you joy and happiness. Constance!' He enveloped her in his heavy coat-clad arms. 'High time we met again in the old country.'

She was delighted. 'Ivo, this is a wonderful start to the year! Come and meet some more members of the family.'

'Aha! I remember that old belching clock! Does the clock-man still cycle up the road to mollycoddle it?'

'Rather.' Constance moved him out of the hall. She introduced him round, and John put a glass of wine into his hand. He was easily persuaded into an armchair. They all toasted the year, each other and themselves.

'It's not all that much a good new year,' said Dido. 'Our old house-keeper has murdered her husband.'

'Good heavens.' Ivo regarded her sternly. 'You were safer in Durban . . . in those golden days! Tell me – have you still got the dog I gave you – Sibbie, wasn't it?'

'I assure you – no blood has been shed, and no sentence passed,' John said. 'A plague of rumour-mongering seems to have infected our house.'

'My dear fellow, I will over-look the housekeeper,' conceded Ivo. 'But one person I must remember. Your redoubtable mother. I was her devoted acolyte, you know. We shared a sense of humour – we were seldom serious together. Such fun we all had in Durban. She and I were living in the same hotel in those days,' he told the Measures. 'Shouldn't admit to having fun, with the war going on. But Florence and I kept our spirits up together.'

Same old story, John thought. A couple of spinsterish years abroad with Mother . . . and this endless nostalgia. Is he losing his marbles? 'I heard what jolly times you and she had, when we met at the RAC,' he said; instantly regretting his mistake.

'Oh yes – I expect you did,' said Ivo, smiling imperturbably. 'The happy days of yester-year. The dear old Cumberland. You're perfectly right: we reminisced at the Club – and you were with a lady friend . . . what was her name now? Rotten at remembering names. You'd been shopping in the West End.'

John stood up with the wine bottle, avoiding Constance's eye. She cleared her throat with mute exasperation.

Max, for whom Florence Burnett was anything but lamented, asked if Ivo had driven down from London.

'You're perfectly right,' said Ivo. 'I have. And the last time I made this trip I was in an earlier model of that little jallopy outside. A darling car. Never wanted anything else. Florence used to tell me to get myself something suitable to my size and station. When I drove down here, she'd stand at the window and shake her head. And laugh. I'm an inveterate bachelor, you understand,' he explained to Bunty. 'No wife. No family. The last time I came here, and Florence welcomed me, we were both unhappy people. Her husband didn't love her. He'd lost his heart to one Ernestine Dunbar . . . she who succeeded in driving poor Florence away.' He glanced bullishly about him. 'No wonder Florence cleared out! Lost her daughter to that woman, too. Ever meet Unity?' he asked Bunty.

'No, I never did. But Max was married to her. I'm his second wife.'

History does indeed repeat itself, John thought. I cannot bear this ghastly tittle-tattle. Repeaters of other people's business. Like Mother, I shall have to leave. After suffering the nonsense Crawley talked – Ivo has to arrive, and begin it all again . . . Ivo added, 'Unity was a charming girl. Clever too. But she was awful to her mother. Awful. And the Dunbar woman encouraged it!'

'Ivo, this is all in the past,' said Constance. 'None of us wants to recall it today. These are painful memories, best forgotten. We're drinking to the future.'

'Forget Florence? Never! Not many women I'd raise my glass to - but here's to our happy times in Durban . . . my dear old girl! Nothing romantic between us: just true friends.'

'Here's to only five more days of happiness for me,' said Hal, quietly.

'How's that?' Max asked leaning forward, glad to turn the subject. 'Sounds a bit bleak for someone your age.'

'School,' said Hal, pulling a face. 'Can you remember school?' He refused to notice his father's glare.

'I enjoyed school days,' said Max, glibly.

'I don't think he should go,' Dido said loyally. 'He won't learn anything if he's miserable.'

Hal shrugged. 'I'm planning to run away.'

'Aha,' countered Max. 'I've heard youngsters say that before. But will you do it?'

'Please don't incite him to be stupid,' John interrupted, more annoyed than amused.

'Hal, I'll rephrase that: only run away if in dire straits – not to prove a point.'

'It's not going to happen.' John still looked piqued.

'It was only meant as a joke,' said Constance. She glanced at Bunty and smiled.

'Rather a reckless joke, Max,' said Bunty, leaning over to lay a timid hand on the arm of his chair.

'I'm sorry,' John said, speaking to Bunty. 'I over-reacted.'

'You're convinced I'm a mischief-maker!' Max gave a short laugh.

'My apologies for stirring this up. Seem to have stumbled on a hornet's nest,' Ivo said. He motioned to Dido. 'Fetch my old friend Sibbie, will you?'

Dido slipped out of the room. When she returned, she held the well-worn stuffed animal and placed him in Ivo's hands. Then she passed John a piece of paper.

He bent his head over it, and began reading what his sister had written to their father in the depth of her depression.

Reaching the bottom, John stared out of the window. Then he flicked the paper with his finger and addressed Max. 'This is Unity, written to our father . . . 'trying to explain to Max when I become catatonic . . . a bad mother and a bad wife . . . It was the farm that made him happy . . . I make him violent. My head is full of dark noise . . .' John raised an eyebrow.

Ivo jogged the toy dog up and down on his knee. 'Woof woof! That's how he used to greet me when you scamps arrived for lunch at the Cumberland! You remember old Joseph the Head Waiter? He certainly never forgot us till the day he died. Connie dear, they were golden days.'

'Ivo, they were. For all the horrors of the war, we had happy times. I feel we were so lucky with your friendship – and to have Florence there.'

Hal turned to Serena. 'Was Aunt Unity a bad mother?'

Serena shrugged in the way he had done. 'No! She was a nice mother. A bit on and off . . .'

'Ernestine called Granny Burnett an unnatural mother,' Dido ventured. 'That's why she adopted Unity.'

John laughed. 'Wherever do you hear all this rot? Mrs Dunbar wouldn't tell you what wasn't true. Ernestine Dunbar was simply a friend of our family.'

'But what about the ring?' asked Hal looking down, and recalling how irksome jewelry could be in conversations of this kind.

'What ring?'

'She wears it on her wedding finger,' said Dido. 'Diamond with emerald.'

'I think Mrs Dunbar's been having a joke with you two,' Constance said, joining the laughter. 'It's her poor husband's ring she wears, surely.'

Max, still preoccupied with the letter, said quietly, 'Unity was ill when she wrote that to Henry.'

'Catatonic,' prompted Dido. 'I get like that.'

'Wait till boarding school,' said Hal. 'These are 'golden days', compared.'

'Well, I refute your innuendos John,' Max declared. He winked at Hal. 'And will say no more.' He tossed the letter next to his glass. 'Having drunk to past, present and future, I suppose it's time we moved on.'

I shall move on, thought John. I must escape from this house and neighbourhood. I'll leave tomorrow . . .

'We haven't shut the shutters and given them the Buddha trick,' said Hal. 'Can Serena and James stay another ten minutes?'

'Heaven forbid I deny my children a Buddha trick, but go we must,' Max insisted. Though four faces fell, none of the children sincerely wished to prolong the occasion. The visitors pulled on coats and stood ready to leave.

Constance saw them all to their car, thanking them for coming.

In the house, Ivo was assuring John that no, he wouldn't stop – rather not . . . he'd booked himself into The Angel Hotel, down on the Square. Very comfortable place, The Angel.

'Oh, stay for a meal first,' Constance urged as she came in. 'And don't go to The Angel. Why not stay here? We can make up a bed in the spare-room.'

'Bachelors like their space,' Ivo responded. 'I know The Angel. But I'll accept a spot of dinner, thank you kindly. Then I'll take myself off and get an early night.'

Back in his chair, he was still holding Sibbie, making him sit up and look him in the eye. 'Will you come to The Angel with me?' he asked the dog.

John spoke to Dido. 'What has Mrs Dunbar been saying to you about your aunt's childhood? That she used to come over here and interfere? I don't believe she would have told you any such thing.'

Hal approached. He said, 'She seemed to love Unity more than Granny Burnett did. She loved Mr Burnett too, and when Granny left, Ernestine took care of them. Nothing wrong in that. The ring was probably in gratitude.'

'I'm tired of you children airing your views to our friends and causing misunderstanding. It's a form of showing off, I realize – but it can do a lot of harm. You're a couple of mischief-makers.'

'There's no more to say,' Dido told him. 'We've told you everything.'

'And a good few other people into the bargain. Now – not one more word on the fate of the Tiplers, either. D'you understand?'

'Not really,' Hal admitted. Then in the manner of his Uncle Max, 'But we'll say no more.'

When Ivo had enjoyed his dinner and was sitting over coffee, Constance found a moment on her own with John. Before she could speak, he broke the news of Bunty's cancer. Her own troubles at once receded.

'Poor Bunty – and poor Max . . . and the children! I do hope it can be treated.'

'I feel very ashamed of going for Max the way I did – after hearing this news. I behaved like a boor. But I'll always regard him as a scoundrel. I let you down Connie. I'm no good to you.'

'Is that regret? Or is it expedience?' She stared at him with hard eyes.

He said, 'I never expected to hear cynicism from you.'

'War ruins more than buildings and monuments. It ruins human decency.'

John didn't answer. She went on, 'Do you want to return to normal life . . . to the children and to me? You wrote in one of your letters you felt so ill you couldn't face any life – with or without us.'

He hesitated. 'I did say that. I was ill.'

'Not a vote of confidence. We weren't worth recovering for?'

'I got over that feeling.'

'You must decide.' Her heart hardened, and anger mounted. 'So Ivo met you Christmas shopping in the West End with your lady friend. Did you show him her necklace, by any chance?'

He gave a resentful laugh. 'Of course not!'

Her eyes were still on his face. 'Vera managed to ruin Christmas for us . . . landing on us when we so needed privacy . . . that precious time with the children . . . and now she's tapping her foot impatiently for you to return to London, I presume.'

'I've told you. There's no other woman for me. Not in the way you imagine.'

They were both silent. Then Constance thought again of Bunty. She struggled against tears.

'Look,' he said. 'I do need to buckle down to some work in London the day after tomorrow. And I've got to get away from gossip-mongers – ancient and infantile. You can always come up as I suggested.' His eyes were avoiding hers. He sounded sulky.

'You bet I'll come up. I feel very much at home in London. I'll meet friends, and see a show or two.'

He said, 'In my view, we'd be doing better by Dido's education if she boarded. Both children seem tiresomely hypersensitive. There are at least two girls' schools near Hal's. It would toughen her up, and give you a life.'

Constance made no immediate reply. Then she turned on her heel. 'We've left Ivo long enough. I hope he's decided what he wants to do.'

They went downstairs together.

Offered the spare-room again, Ivo was adamant. 'My dear girl, I insist on getting out of your way. My room at The Angel is already booked – and I'm off now. Do you remember those splendid rickshaw men in Durban, with their black skins and huge coloured ostrich feathers on their heads? No better way to travel in this world . . .'

Ten minutes later, the Austen made its exit through the gates.

John and Constance sighed with relief.

Hal expressed disappointment. 'We were going to drag a stick up the bannisters so he'd think it was the ghost.'

Chapter 20

Mrs Ablewhite opened the front door to him. She was wearing a faded overall, and for a moment seemed perplexed.

'I'm John Burnett – from next door. I've come to see Mrs Dunbar – if I may?'

'She's upstairs just now. I'll go and tell her you're here . . .'

'How are you keeping, Mrs Ablewhite?'

'Oh – so-so, thank you. Mrs D's the one to worry about. Been poorly all over the holiday. Some bug got her I suppose.'

'I'm sorry to hear it. Has Dr Gallatly been to see her?'

'Oh no. She hates to make a fuss.'

Before he could speak again, she was halfway up to the landing. He could hear the two women talking.

Mrs Ablewhite came down. 'Mrs D's indisposed; but she'd like to see you, Colonel Burnett.'

He began to remonstrate but she hurried off to the kitchen. John mounted the stairs and walked through her open door, tapping lightly as he went. The room was large and struck him as a very satiny and flouncy place. A capacious wardrobe was the only piece of furniture without embellishments. The walls were blue with a floral pattern, and the carpet was blue. Mrs Dunbar was ensconced in an armchair under the window, writing a letter in green ink. The pug was asleep on her lap, snoring rhythmically.

John skirted the big billowy bed and said, 'Good morning Mrs Dunbar. I hope this isn't an intrusion.'

Willoughby woke as with a seizure, eyes rolling, and leapt to the floor with a volley of yaps. 'Hush Willoughby dear,' his doting owner said; and then, 'Please call me Ernestine. Your small children do. This is Colonel Burnett, Willoughby.'

The pug pranced up and down, barking. Ernestine lowered a languid hand to him. Her appearance was somewhat slatternly, her hair disheveled and hanging down her back. Her large face was creased and lack-lustre, without a smudge of makeup. She was dressed in an elaborately fussy robe de chambre, her bare feet in feathered mules. She showed no trace of discomfort at being in that state.

He said, 'I came round to see how you were. It's a long time since we met.'

'I hear you had what you term a good war.'

'It was an interesting one. I was very lucky.'

'And is your gallantry crowned by domestic happiness . . . as it should be?'

Was she being ironic? What had his small spies been feeding her? 'How are you?' he asked again.

'The festive season never agrees with me. I'm too old and unwell to eat and drink much– and I've been foolish and done both. Please sit down somewhere, and tell me why you're here.'

'I simply wanted to make sure you were happy about the wall, now Hal and I have finished it. Thank you for agreeing I could raise it. It's actually an improvement – don't you agree?'

'Colonel Burnett – tell me your real reason for coming to see me.'

He pulled up a delicate chair and sat with caution. 'Ernestine, I'm very sorry to find you in poor state of health, and hope by spring you'll be feeling better. I'm planning to stay in London as from tomorrow. I've decided to make eye surgery my specialty. I'm hoping Constance will make regular visits to see me, and I'll be coming back here when I can.' He cleared his throat. 'But it's been galling to have our children trotting out garbled history – supplied by you, it seems.'

'I wonder what period of history that would be?' Ernestine carefully fitted the cap over her pen nib, and laid the pen down.

'On two occasions, when we were entertaining friends, Henry and Dido talked about your importance to my father – your affection for him, and for my sister Unity – but giving very false impressions.'

'Nothing false there,' she said briskly.

'The way they were talking, it was obvious you gave them the idea that my father encouraged you into Westbourne at any time of the day or night; that you virtually took over from my mother almost before she left home.'

'I was most particular to respect your mother – critical though I felt of her on your father and Unity's behalf. You can't accuse me of behaving out of order towards anyone.'

John wished he'd been quick enough to notice the fingers of her left hand. She had them both folded in her lap now. 'The children informed us that my sister wasn't a good mother, and that Florence turned Henry into a sad and lonely man. That you replaced her. I begin to wonder how many people were aware of it.'

'I have never, ever, been a vulgar person,' said Ernestine. 'All my life I've detested vulgarity. I always acted from goodness of heart and primarily unselfish motives. I never created the scandal you accuse me of.' She drew a deep breath, and sat tall in her chair. Willoughby was back on her lap, regarding John with eyes bulging with fun.

'Well.' John glanced down at his own hands. He wondered what more he could say. He spoke directly again. 'Dido mentioned a ring my father apparently gave you, which you wore on your fourth left finger, and regarded as a wedding ring. Is that true?'

She flourished her left hand at him. 'I have such a ring,' she declared. 'And I have nothing to say about it. I'm old, and a hermit, and all my associates – friendly and unfriendly – have passed away. You really shouldn't trouble yourself with my past, John. You have two lively children with a quick interest in life. I hope they keep coming to see me. We do each other good.'

'Very well. But please don't put inappropriate notions in their heads. Dido is highly strung and has a tendency to nightmares – and my son is building up a crisis for himself about boarding school. Let them keep their innocence.'

'You're calling me a corrupt influence?'

'Inadvertently – yes.'

'May I ask how successful you're proving as a husband and father, home from the war?' Ernestine asked quietly.

John stood up and offered Ernestine his hand. She took it and seemed to sag into the chair as he went to the door.

'My apologies if I've distressed you,' he said. 'Of course it was all a long time ago. But certain memories rankle, and stir one up. I'm trying to go forward.'

'Do so,' she said, 'and take your family with you. See how

much better you can manage than your parents did.'

She made a gesture so melodramatic that it had to be natural; and John quietly let himself out.

Constance was looking for him.

'Wherever have you been?' There was still a coldness between them, hers from hurt, his from mortification. 'Ivo's been on the phone. I gather he's cutting short his visit and you've arranged to drive up to London together in that silly little car?'

'Correct.'

'Couldn't you and I have gone up together, and fitted it in with seeing Hal off? Did that even occur to you?'

'I prefer to be back in London two days earlier.'

'I won't ask why.'

'Why should you, when you know I've a lot to see to.'

'I won't ask what.'

'Ivo's coming around midday.' John checked his watch.

'Then I take it he won't want lunch. That simplifies things.' Constance walked into the house with her heart knocking. It was hateful, reaching this level of recrimination. But now her pride was touched. She went to talk to Coral about meals for the day, and found her wheeling Ben indoors. 'Just a bit nippy out there. He's due another feed anyway.'

Constance bent over the pram and was transported into the small space of a baby's happiness. She smiled at him and he smiled back, full of fresh air. Coral remarked that Alfred was mending fences at the far boundary, both dogs keeping him company.

'We'll finish the lentil soup for lunch,' Constance said. 'There'll only be the children and me. And just three for supper.'

'Oh – is Colonel Burnett back to London again?' Coral asked in a bright tone.

'I'm afraid so.'

Constance hovered, unwilling to settle to anything before Ivo arrived, and uncertain where John had gone. No symbolic mending fences for the two of them! How different things were at this new point of separation from how she might have hoped . . .

The Austen crunched to a halt with disproportionate brio. Ivo hooted three times to alert the household. Constance, hearing the hoots, grimaced. What a cheek of Ivo – to sit there in his ridiculous car making an imperious din. She heard John moving upstairs, and the sound of him coming down with his case.

Nothing personal left behind, she supposed.

The children were quickly on the scene. 'Come and visit me one day,' Ivo invited them. 'Lots to do in London. Madam Tussaud's . . . and the Tower.'

'I'll be in a worse place than the Tower,' said Hal. 'School – remember?'

'So you will, so you will. We all go through it. But whatever else befalls you – prison, pestilence, earthquake – it'll never be as bad again.'

'Thanks,' said Hal, moving away.

John appeared. He greeted Ivo through the open car door. 'How was your night at the Angel? Did they give you a good breakfast?'

'Both excellent,' said Ivo. A man of goodwill, easily pleased. 'We'll break the journey along the route, and find some lunch.'

'Why not take it with us?'

Ivo shook his head. 'No need to bother your dear wife. I daresay we'll be able to stop at a nice English pub for a sandwich and a pint.'

'What happens in Madam Tussaud's?' Dido asked.

'You see a lot of famous people as wax effigies,' Ivo told her. 'People who have died. The good eggs are flattered no end, and the bad eggs are made to look twice as ugly as in real life.'

'Are the bodies preserved in wax?' Dido wrinkled her nose.

'Not the actual bodies. What a gruesome child!' Ivo chuckled. 'You come up on a visit and I'll take you. Not keen on zoos myself. Too fond of seeing animals in the wild.'

Constance joined them. 'How did you sleep, Ivo?'

'Oh, very well, very well. We're pretty much ready for off now.'

'I'm sorry you're away so soon.' She watched John preparing to enter the car on the other side. She hesitated, then went round the bonnet. 'Well – goodbye John!'

He recollected himself, took hold of her shoulders and aimed a rapid kiss at her face. 'Take care, Constance.'

'Goodbye Father,' called Dido with purposeful reproach. Hal bent over to squint under the Austen, studiously unconcerned at being ignored. The men drove noisily away.

'We're not good at having a father,' Dido said.

'It's a pity he ever had to meet us,' her brother agreed. 'Just the idea of us would have been best. We haven't come up to scratch.'

'What nonsense,' said Constance. 'Your father has a lot on his mind, so he didn't think to say a proper goodbye.'

'It would be nice if he approved of us,' Dido went on. 'But it's worse, us not approving of him.'

'Of course he likes you a lot,' Hal told his mother. 'But we tend to annoy him.'

'He did buy us a dog,' Dido pointed out.

'That's easy credit. Though I expect it's hard to be fun when you've got post-war stress. And it's so easy to be nasty with people below you.'

Dido remembered her father reading Doctor Dolittle. She had a sudden twinge of emotion. 'He'll be nicer when he's forgotten he was a soldier.'

'You say that because you're a girl. Anyone would think I was some base creature, the way he treated me. About school specially. But mainly not bothering to talk to me.'

'Not talking is safer. There was nothing to say.'

Hal scowled. 'I've said it all to him in my heart. I've told him he bullies our mother. But in my heart he's still got a chance. If my mother wants him with us, I could try to like him.'

Constance had been listening without appearing to, walking here and there on the lawn, head bent. This shouldn't have been a crucial parting from John, a summing up. But hearing the children's remarks, it seemed they had delivered verdicts. 'We're all the better for having your father with us,' she said. 'I've missed him, and I love him. If he could only stay here and settle down, we'd feel we were a real family. He can't help having to live in London for a year.'

'He seems to think well of Vera,' said Hal, morosely. He looked at his mother. 'Might you divorce each other?'

Constance was startled. 'Gracious no,' she heard herself reply. 'Divorce is the last thing any of us wants. Put that out of your minds. I love your father dearly, and I'm determined we keep him and make him happy.'

They entered the house, and Coral produced the soup.

Chapter 21

Mrs Ablewhite urged Willoughby through the gate of Trullers, delicately employing the toe of her shoe. He always liked to hang about, sniffing gate-posts. They set off down the road, and saw ahead of them Mr Belcher leaving the Almshouses, pushing his ubiquitous handcart. Miss Elliot was standing outside her door, haranguing poor white-clad Miss Poole. No sign of Mrs Baxter. She was the real trouble-maker, with her horrid little dog, and her nasty remarks about Willoughby . . . and her digs about the Burnetts . . .

These impressions glided in and out of Mrs Ablewhite's mind almost without her being aware of them. She turned in at the first gate for Westbourne House, using her foot to cajole Willoughby again. Surprised at the new direction, he swaggered on ahead of her, exuding good cheer.

Mrs Ablewhite crossed the lawn, rounded the great yew tree and headed up the side drive to the back of the house. No-one in the yard. Willoughby scanned this interesting area with all his senses, and had to be dragged after her to the door. Away in the garden, Mrs Ablewhite could see a pram under one of the pear trees. The Sherwood baby, she thought. What a carry on . . .

Coral opened the door. 'Hello!' she said. 'Can I help?'

'Is Mrs Burnett in?'

'Well, she was . . . Let me give her a call.'

Mrs Ablewhite stood very still, staring at the flagstones, not wishing to notice anything else. Her thoughts were broken by Coral's voice again, asking her please to come in. She was led through the kitchen and sitting-room into the hall, where Constance had come to meet her.

'Hello Mrs Ablewhite,' she said. 'How can I help?'

Her visitor regarded her without word or expression for

several moments. Then, still holding the pug's lead, she grasped Constance's hands. 'Mrs Dunbar has died,' she whispered. 'My dear Mrs D is dead.'

'Oh!' Constance exclaimed. 'I'm so very sorry, Mrs Ablewhite. When did this happen?'

Hearing it was yesterday, Constance drew her visitor into the drawing-room. She put her on the settee, and sat close beside her.

'She was very poorly over Christmas and since,' Mrs Ablewhite explained tearfully. 'I suspected she'd had a mini-stroke. But she wouldn't hear of it. Then yesterday it was the real thing. Carried her right off, before I could get the doctor.'

Constance was silent, thinking of her old neighbour and remembering their last talk. Lifting her head, she said, 'I wish I'd looked in on her again – last week. Or yesterday. I seem to have been busy . . . but I should have found time.'

'Colonel Burnett called in, of course. He popped round two days ago; the day before it happened.' Mrs Ablewhite blew her nose.

'Did he?' Constance fell silent again. The hall clock gave its cough and began to strike. Before it stopped, the grandfather across the room began its chimes. 'Was my husband's call just to see how she was?' Constance asked. 'A friendly call?' Her mind raced.

'That's what it seemed. Not a long call – just to see how she was. I said she'd not been well.'

'I'm so sorry,' Constance repeated calmly, staring at the pug. 'You'll miss her terribly, I know.'

'I don't know what I'll find to do,' Mrs Ablewhite said. 'I can't even think how my life will change . . . But maybe you can help me in one matter, Mrs Burnett.'

'Please ask me.'

Mrs Ablewhite joggled the lead. 'I'm nearly as upset about this little chap, to be honest. Mrs D thought the world of him, and he of her. Two spoilt souls, they were! He doesn't understand yet . . . but he'll be heart-broken without her.'

Constance could detect no sign of distress, actual or imminent, in the bright-eyed pug at their feet. But she said, 'I don't know how I can help . . . ?'

'He fell for your children and they were all over him. I was thinking – could you consider taking him in – like a sort of orphan?' A pale apologetic smile lit Mrs Ablewhite's face.

Constance said, 'We have two dogs already – but I know what Hal and Dido would say.'

'Think it over, perhaps?'

'Once it's done, it's done, that's the problem. Well, let him come on trial, and we'll see how he settles.'

Mrs Ablewhite stood up. 'You're very kind. I'd better be going back. The phone keeps ringing, and people coming round. I'd take Willoughby myself if I was in a position to care for him.'

The children entered the room. Not noticing Mrs Ablewhite's melancholic air, they rushed to greet Willoughby. The women watched their joyful reunion. Then Constance gave the news.

Dido stared at her mother with a fierce intensity. 'That's not true.'

'Dead?' repeated Hal, quelling Willoughby with both hands. 'Why?'

'Ernestine isn't dead,' Dido repeated. 'It's not true.'

'She wasn't very well, you see,' explained Mrs Ablewhite, apologetically. 'She lost the wish to go on, feeling that poorly. It's a mercy really, for the dear lady.'

'I don't believe it.' Dido directed her stare at Mrs Ablewhite.

'She seemed in good shape when we last saw her,' Hal stated. 'We chatted and drank port – and she was full of beans.'

Constance and Mrs Ablewhite exchanged glances.

'She wasn't all that old anyway,' Hal added. 'It seems a bit odd, I must say. I wanted to visit her again before I'm deported.'

Dido glared at them all, her mouth clenched, then ran upstairs and disappeared into her bedroom with a bang.

'I feel like that too,' said Hal. 'What a ghastly shock. What will Willoughby do?'

'Live with us?' Constance suggested. 'But you children must take your share of responsibility. Walks and meals, as well as Prince.'

'I'll tell Dido,' he replied, taking the orphan's lead.

Constance contacted John that evening. 'I feel I should let you know that Ernestine Dunbar has died. Mrs Ablewhite came round to tell us this morning.'

'I'm very sorry,' John said.

'Mrs Ablewhite was certainly upset. She'd been with her a long time.'

'What happened?' He sounded guarded.

'Very likely a stroke. I'll hear in due course.' She paused. 'I gather you called there the day before she died.'

Another pause. 'Yes, I did. I thought it was time I went to see her; hear how she was doing.'

'And how was she doing?'

'She was a bit decrepit. She said she wasn't feeling too well. So I didn't stay long.'

'Did you by any chance rake over old gossip?' Constance ruthlessly demanded. 'Did you indulge in taunting her?'

'How can you ask such things? Of course not!'

'You never accused her of damaging your father's life – and Unity's? Or of corrupting Hal and Dido with foolish talk?'

An extended pause. 'It was a perfectly civilized ten minutes,' John said coldly. 'It may please you to imagine I'm responsible for Mrs Dunbar's demise. But I'm not. So refrain from putting that around the neighbourhood.'

Disturbed and unhappy, Constance drew a deep breath. 'Max comes with good wishes and you're rude to him. Ivo appears and you rush off with him . . . and I'm left married to a man I no longer know.'

'Oh, come on Connie . . .'

Somewhere in the house, Ben was crying. The wails became more clamorous. Constance put the phone down. She hurried upstairs to her bedroom, and lay on her side under the eiderdown with a powerful desire to sleep.

When Coral called an hour later to announce supper, Constance was surprised to find it was evening – under the impression she'd been asleep all night. A bitter sense of failure returned to her.

The children were sitting at table when she entered the dining-room.

'Are you upset about Ernestine?' Hal asked.

Constance felt a pang of shame. Ernestine had slipped from her mind. 'I suppose I am. I hadn't known her well; but she was a splendid lady, and I felt sorry for her.'

'In a way I'm glad she's dead. She was lonely, and she couldn't do much. We couldn't keep going round there.'

Dido said, 'I think it's my fault she's died.'

Constance passed them plates of scrambled eggs. 'You can't say that, Dido. Start eating, both of you, while it's hot.'

'I do say it. Three people are dead because I liked them.'

'Who?' demanded Hal. 'Oh yes – your beloved Mr Fewings . . . and Mr Tipler.'

'And she's in gaol.'

'Not yet,' said Hal.

Dido said, 'When Mrs Baxter dies, we'll have to take her dog. Willoughby won't like that.'

Willoughby, perched on a chair between them, was ignoring the conversation with gastronomic focus.

'Mrs Baxter has years ahead of her,' Constance said. 'She'll outlive her dog easily. Try to cheer up Dido dear, and eat before it's cold.'

Upstairs, they could hear Ben resume his crying. Dido, overwrought, dropped her fork and left her chair. 'It's our fault our father's gone off, and poor Ernestine's gone, and poor Mister keeps appearing. I know I'll see him again tonight!'

'Of course you won't,' Constance said, pushing back her chair. 'You only imagine you see him. Or you dream it.'

'I've seen his ghost!' Dido shouted, her face pale. 'And I don't want Ernestine to start coming.'

'Don't invite trouble,' her brother said.

Ben's roars grew louder, and reached a frantic pitch.

Dido clenched her fists, staring with wide eyes. 'I hope I don't slaughter that baby,' she said.

Constance reached over and set the plate of egg on the floor. Willoughby jumped down to dispatch it, and Dido gave an involuntary laugh.

'Let's go and see what Doctor Dolittle's been up to,' Constance said.

The evil day had come.

Hal, dressed in grey shorts, blue shirt, grey jacket, long socks and black shoes, with his blue and purple tie roughly knotted, went down to breakfast. He walked as if his legs were made of lead.

'Hello Hal!' Coral greeted him cheerfully. 'You'll be back to see all your friends today.'

'Such as?' he asked dourly.

'Well – all your pals,' Coral said with a laugh. 'You'll have to tell me their names. Tuck into a good breakfast.'

Dido was at the table, poking pieces of toast out of the rack. She made no attempt to put one on her plate. She too was dressed for school, term having started the day before.

'Eat up Dido,' Coral urged. 'Set a good example.'

'She does,' said Hal, 'by not going to London and not going to St Satan's.'

'I would, if we went together,' Dido said, pushing her chair back. 'I hate him going by himself. It makes us both ill.'

'Most children enjoy school,' Coral persevered. 'You've been with grownups all the holiday. When you're home next, I bet little Ben will remember you!'

Hal said, 'Don't put money on it. I'll be sadly changed.'

'His hair might be grey,' Dido said. 'I hope you run away, Hal. If only I could help.'

'You could help by being more cheerful,' scolded Coral. 'You're both lucky, having breakfasts – and schools to go to.'

'Oh, we know all that about hungry children, and children who can't read. We'd swap with them if we could.'

Their mother appeared, looking flustered. She poured herself tea and reached for the toast. 'What a mess on the cloth,' she said, refilling the rack. 'We must hurry, time's going on, and you must start walking, Dido. Have you both finished?'

'They've not started,' said Coral, betraying them for the best reasons. 'Shall Ben and I come down with you, Dido?'

She nodded. 'And Prince – and poor little Willoughby.'

'Well, goodbye then,' said her brother as though for ever.

Dido gave him a hug. 'I'll write you one of my letters,' she promised. 'You may get it before you escape.'

Constance gave Dido a kiss. 'You silly child. Eat a proper lunch now, won't you – and I'll be home again for supper.'

With infinite longing, Hal heard his sister collecting the dogs into her charge, and Coral preparing the pram; Coral chatting and advising as they went out at the back.

'Hal, you must eat something,' said Constance, passing the toast. 'What about cornflakes?'

He accepted the toast, feeling it easier to relent now that Dido had gone.

They caught a train which brought them to London at half past one. Hal was silent all the journey, suffering that familiar nausea and enervation connected with returns to school. He couldn't stop yawning. He was a hollow, helpless, insensate stooge.

They had sandwiches and tea at the Victoria Station buffet. Hal remembered the other occasion, when he'd sat with his father in happier circumstances. He could have relaxed so much more that day, had he been with his mother. Life was never perfect.

'Aren't you seeing Dad this time?' he asked, with partial interest.

'I'm afraid not. He has too much to do, now he's begun his courses. I do admire him, beginning again in another area of medicine.'

'But he's still in the army? I thought he'd stopped being a soldier.'

'He's a peace-time soldier – and a doctor. When he's qualified, he'll be an eye surgeon.'

It struck Hal as going from one extreme to another: from blowing people up, to fiddling with eyes. After a moment, he had another question in his mind. 'You're not thinking of divorcing then?'

The cacophony of an announcement startled Constance. She gathered up her bag. 'Come on Hal,' she said. 'Perhaps I'll say goodbye to you before we're on the platform. And darling, your father and I are not divorcing. Don't mention it again.'

A tight ache gripped Hal by the throat. He straightened, and let his mother envelop him. He kissed her in passing, and moved to meet his fate. There they were, gaggles of daft boys messing about . . . and there was a dread master. And another. Hal began to swipe his night-case about in the accepted brainless manner, and sauntered along to say hello.

Chapter 22

Ernestine Dunbar's funeral was over.

Years later, before her death, Dido would say that 'Oh God our help in ages past' had been her favourite hymn since the age of five. She'd known the words in Mooi River, and loved the tune. Both had moved her profoundly. 'Time like an ever-rolling stream bears all our sons away, they fly forgotten as a dream dies at the opening day.' Metaphysical grief.

This hymn was chosen for Ernestine's service. The words and tune weighed Dido down.

A small group of mourners followed the vicar between ilex trees to where the coffin waited to be lowered. Before the melancholy ritual unfolded, Constance took Dido's hand and they wandered round a grassy area of grave-stones, noticing names and embellishments. Among the dark figures, she'd caught sight of Oliver Seaton.

'I think Floppyguts would have liked the service,' Dido told her mother.

'Sssh! Don't use that name now.'

'I said it because Hal's not here.'

'I'm sure Mrs Dunbar would have loved the flowers.'

'I wonder what will happen to her rings?'

Constance said, 'I've no idea.' She pictured John confronting Ernestine, bringing up grudges and losing his temper. How had Ernestine reacted? Was that the beginning of the end?

The committing of Ernestine into the earth now over, they went to greet Katie Crawley. 'Hello Katie,' Constance said. 'Are you going to The Angel for the tea? So few people have turned up.'

'I'm dying for tea,' said Katie. 'Hello Dido, fancy seeing you here!'

'I was her friend,' said Dido.

'She and Hal had paid Ernestine one or two visits, and Dido was determined to come.'

'I can't think she had many friends. Sad, really. Age and ill health can be so isolating.'

They walked in a light drizzle to The Angel Hotel. 'The end of another era,' Katie said. 'Not many left from her generation, and our younger ones will all be going further afield. Roddy and I are a good bit older than you and John of course . . . but we see a lot of changes. Not for the better in this town.'

'I read that the Tipler case has been decided; she's been given the benefit of the doubt,' said Constance. 'I'm very relieved.'

'Community service won't bring him back,' said Katie.

'But he does come back,' Dido said, under her breath. 'I see him sometimes.'

Katie smiled at her and went to wash her hands.

Constance led Dido into the hotel lounge where a crowd of strangers were gathering for another function.

Then she saw Oliver Seaton talking to a fair haired woman with dark eyes. Good clothes. On the heavy side – but rather stylish in that drab crowd.

She saw Oliver laugh with his head thrown back as his companion was speaking. A moment later he became aware of Constance. His face brightened again and he squared his shoulders.

'Hello Constance!'

He approached, and greeted Katie as an old friend. 'Let me bring you some tea. Then you must meet Georgia.' He threaded his way towards the rear of the room.

'Do you know Georgia?' Constance asked Katie.

'Yes, a little. I think you'd get on well. She's American.'

Oliver arrived with tea for two, and told Constance that his friend would join them in a moment. Her name was Georgia Chillcot. She had grown up in New Hampshire, had married an English businessman and lived in a house on the Dunsby road.

'Is her husband here?' Constance asked, glancing around.

'She was widowed in the war. He was in the wrong place. You've been luckier.'

Constance sipped her tea, meditating on the paradoxes of life as Georgia began walking over.

'Perhaps you have a lot of friends in London,' Georgia said, when Constance explained John's need to divide his time between London and Westbourne. 'You'll be dividing your time too?'

Oliver had noticed Dido. 'Hello there!' he exclaimed. 'I never saw you in the madding crowd. What would you like to drink? Orange juice?'

'Do they have Camp Coffee?' Dido asked primly.

'Why not orange,' Constance urged.

'Camp Coffee it shall be – if possible.' Oliver departed again.

'He's a dear,' said Georgia, watching him insinuate his way towards the refreshments. 'I shall miss him.'

'Is he going away?' Constance asked.

'I'm going away!' Georgia sipped tea while Constance considered this news. 'Back to the States. My family are there, and my parents are getting older. Maybe you'll come and visit me in in Vermont. I wish you would.'

Constance was processing this hospitality when Oliver returned, bearing a tall glass of coffee with ice-cream in. 'Not quite your order – but I hope it'll do.'

'It's my best drink,' said Dido.

'Are you seriously planning some time in London?' Georgia asked. 'Because my brother has part of a house in Canonbury. He's going to be on a course in Zurich in the first half of July, and I'm to mind his flat. See London in the summer. We could do a few things together.'

'Well.' Constance thought rapidly. Early July. There was Dido, of course . . .

'Yippee,' Dido said. 'It sounds lovely.'

'There'll be Dido to think about,' Constance spoke quickly. 'My idea was to stay at the Royal Overseas League, in Park Place – off St James's. I do know several people in London. But we could certainly meet. I'd like to.'

'I know the place – overlooking Green Park. Perfect! Anyway, here's my phone number.' Georgia jotted it down. 'And here's my brother's address. I think we'd have a whole lot of fun.'

'How are you Constance?' Oliver enquired.

She said she was well, and asked Georgia if she and Oliver would like to come for lunch. It transpired that Georgia was leaving for Paris.

Oliver tilted his head slightly. 'I'd like to accept – if I'm any use on my own? I'll need cheering up!'

'Of course you must come,' she replied, with a sense of being manoeuvered by events.

'I'll show you Mr Fewing's picture,' offered Dido. 'It's in my room.'

'I can't wait,' said Oliver. 'My word, that iced coffee's gone down fast.'

His wait lasted two days. He declined a sherry before lunch. 'I should have got in some beer!' exclaimed Constance.

'Have orange juice,' suggested Dido.

Constance shook her head. 'I'm sure you'd have liked a beer! How stupid of me.'

'A modest sherry would be more than welcome,' Oliver declared. 'A treat I rarely give myself.'

Constance handed him his small glass. 'Are you careful on health grounds?'

'From good example. My father owned a pub called The Castle in Bedford, and he seldom drank. He saw too many victims of the habit and became seriously health conscious. We lived in Foster Hill Road, which is close by a superb park. My dad used to run round it every morning, and we boys were encouraged to run with him.'

'Did you ever have to build a wall?' asked Dido.

Oliver pondered. Then he said, 'No. My Dad never thought of that.'

Constance raised her sherry. 'Here's to Georgia! I'm sorry she's going back to America.'

'I'm sorry John had to go,' Oliver reciprocated. 'Very tough on you both.'

'John at least has the challenge of new studies. Imagine operating on such a delicate scale! And he has such large hands. Eyes are very fascinating.'

'They are,' agreed Oliver, looking into hers. 'Of course, London's full of exciting opportunities.'

'He deserves to enjoy them. I hope he'll have time for friends – and some culture. We used to know a lot of people in London. We went to the Chelsea Arts Ball, and the May Ball, and they were enormous fun . . . and medical student rags. But after a war, one loses touch. All that gaiety's gone.'

'Do you really intend visiting? It's not the old London. Bomb damage everywhere. But you'll have seen it more recently than I have.'

'It's true. There's damage all around.'

It was as if they were both using coded speech.

They went in to lunch, and Oliver witnessed Willoughby on a chair of his own. The pug paid close attention as Dido poked at her food.

Coral cleared away the plates and brought a milk jelly to the table. 'I hope it's edible,' she said.

'You have a spoonful first,' Dido said.

Coral laughed. 'At least it's not poisoned.'

Oliver, watching a portion of jelly wobbling in his bowl, said, 'I wonder what will happen to Mrs Dunbar's house.'

'And the quantities of furniture and ornaments filling it.'

'Willoughby won't have to be sold, anyway,' said Dido.

After lunch, she took Oliver up to her bedroom and he was gratified to see his Uncle's glass painting on the wall over the fireplace. 'Hal has a thing called 'The If for Boys' on his wall,' she told him. 'I like Kipling. But my picture's nicer.'

'Really?' said Oliver. 'Well, you have good taste.'

They went downstairs. Constance said, 'Roddy Crawley's just rung to ask if they could borrow Daisy for a neighbour's child to hunt on.'

'Ragbag,' said Dido, with sardonic humour. 'Tell him I want her back, won't you?'

Coral brought coffee to the drawing room. Piteous cries reached them through the house. Oliver said, 'I heard what a stir your baby created.'

'It was a bit sudden,' said Coral, offhandedly.

'I must congratulate Alf next time I'm at the Nag's Head ,' Oliver said.

'If we kept a monkey it would throw Ben through a window,' Dido told him. 'It's the tradition.'

'I ought to get along.' Oliver put down his cup. 'It's been a most enjoyable meal.'

They went into the hall. 'Goodbye,' said Dido. She gave a quick light wave of her hand and darted up the stairs.

'Children are very enigmatic,' Oliver said. 'I do regret not having any.'

They stood in the hall, Constance deep in thought. 'I believe I might spend time in London ... take up Georgia's idea. But when one has children . . .' He waited. 'Hal's at boarding school, Dido goes locally. John's all for sending her away as well.'

'It's supposed to be the making of them,' said Oliver. 'Though I've always doubted it.'

They went out, and paused by his car. He reached forward to take her hands. 'Thank you for a splendid lunch.'

He was in no hurry to release her hands. Dido, upstairs in her mother's bedroom, watched intently with her nose to the glass. She saw him bend his head and kiss her mother; and in that second Constance became aware of Roddy, halter in hand, standing under the yew tree. He gave a salute. 'The trailer's in the road!' he shouted, and beaming from ear to ear, walked away to the paddocks.

Dido slipped off the ottoman and ran to her room to draw.

When Oliver Seaton had gone, Constance felt a baneful regret. Having him to lunch on his own had been foolish. Trust Roddy to appear.

Then a surge of defiance smote her. She and Oliver were both deprived of people they loved. John's paranoia about gossip, and Roddy's infernal innuendos, were enough to disturb anyone. She was behaving like Dido! To blazes with everything. Self-respect and a sense of proportion were called for.

She went to meet Roddy as he led Daisy down the drive. 'Her saddle and bridle are in the harness room. Has the boy hunted before?'

'A regular little terror on the hunting scene. No stopping him. Parents looking for a bigger mount.' Roddy brought out the harness. 'Katie tells me Oliver's losing his lady-friend.'

'Apparently. But she and I may spend time in London together in the summer.' She added, 'Between you and me, Roddy, Georgia found our community a bit stifling.' She ran her hand along the pony's back. 'Don't bolt with your young rider, Daisy.'

Roddy said, urging her forward, 'Once a bolter always a bolter.'

Dido had another nightmare that night: she dreamed she was

riding Mrs Tipler across a wide open space; Mrs Tipler bucked her off and she fell into a well and Mister was staring down at her as she sank . . .

Hearing calls, Constance hurried to her room. Dido begged to go to her mother's bed. For a while, they lay quietly together.

'I hope you never die,' Dido said.

'I'll try not to – at least until I'm eighty.'

'I was a happy child long ago,' Dido said, as Constance was nearly asleep.

'You're still happy. You've so much to be happy about . . .'

'I hate people dying. I hate bad feelings.'

'Write a letter to Hal tomorrow. That'll cheer you both up.'

'Yes I will.'

Constance remembered climbing the steep step into a train when they were leaving Durban, and slipping, and gouging her shin. She could remembered Dido's concern as she helped staunch the blood. Always been protective of me, Constance thought.

'I'll tell Hal how Ernestine's coffin sank into that hole, and I thought of her all wrapped up in shawls and wearing two wedding rings,' Dido was saying.

'Describe the beautiful flowers, and how we walked under the trees, and had tea at The Angel . . .' murmured Constance.

'Dropping down the well was like being buried alive. I'll tell Hal my dream.'

Chapter 23

Dido wrote, with her own spelling:

'Dear Hal,

I went to a dancing class at the Corn Exchange. He was called Professor Homer and he was fat and fussy with a red face. I was bored but at the end we learnt the Hokey Cokey which was very funny. I don't think I'll go again. Ernestine has been buried. We had the service and Mum and I walked about the graves while she was being sunk in her coffin. I hate her being underground. Roddy took Daisy for a boy to hunt. She hasn't come back yet. Our mother still pines for our father. Love Dido.'

Hal didn't write in return. He was as good as his word, and ran away from school.

The call came from the head master during Thursday afternoon. Constance could give Mr Hodgkins no help. She could only hope he was pretending to have run away, and would reappear. The head master's tone was defensive enough to dispel any such hopes. She rang her parents, supposing that Hal might have escaped to them in Hove; but they knew nothing of his disappearance.

When Dido heard the news, she was jubilant. 'Sucks to everybody!' she cried. 'I knew he'd do it.'

'I do hope he's all right.' said Constance. One heard of too many odd characters hanging about in towns since the war ended. What could have prompted Hal to do such a thing? What was John going to say? Certainly not 'Sucks to Max.' John would be quite likely to blame him, or herself, in some obscure way. The school could hardly come out of it with colours flying . . .

Two anxious hours later, her mother rang. Hal had caught a train from Eastbourne and made his way to Albany Villas.

Having exchanged cries of relief, and appreciation to heaven, and after Constance had rung Mr Hodgkins, facts emerged from Granny Parsons that Hal was unharmed physically and in a calm state of mind. He'd slipped on to and off the train to Brighton without a ticket, and had walked along the seafront, enjoying the fresh air and sense of freedom. He'd concealed his cap for fear of being asked awkward questions.

'I'm sure you'll want to speak to him,' said Granny Parsons. 'Here he is.'

'Hal.' Constance kept her voice level. 'What happened to justify giving us such a fright?'

'I hated football. And nobody believed anything I said.'

'Why ever not? Were you telling lies?'

'Of course I wasn't! I told them a bit about South Africa.'

'About life in Natal?'

'Yes. And they said I'd never been there, I was making it all up. I told them stories in the dorm at night about the River Mooi, and bands of African tribes and the Drakensburg Mountains, and they liked them. But they said everything was made up.'

'Did that matter? You knew what was true and what was story telling. There must have been more to upset you than some teasing.'

'There was Mr. Knott. He hates me because I'm useless at maths. I'm behind in lots of subjects, but he's the worst. The boys say I make Africa an excuse for being behind in class.'

'Perhaps they're envious of your experiences.'

'They call me cowardly for escaping the bombs in England.'

'In that case they accept that you were abroad!' Constance gave an impatient laugh. 'Let me speak to Granny, and arrange what we do with you now.'

'Anything – but not school,' Hal said darkly.

Constance and her mother decided that Hal should spend the night in Hove, helping Bampy paint tins in bright colours on spread newspaper for a charitable institution. Granny Parsons was willing to escort Hal by train to Victoria Station on Friday morning, where they would meet under the clock.

Dido was delighted to hear he was coming home for the weekend. Constance debated with herself the need to confess Hal's misdeed to John. She'd tell him once Hal was home. It was tempting to meet John in London, but instinct held her back.

When she and Hal had walked from the station down to Westbourne House early the following afternoon, Hal without a single item of luggage, Constance telephoned John.

'You mean you've taken him home!' John's voice was charged with disbelief. 'What a stupid thing to do! You should have put him straight on the first train to Eastbourne, and let him slog right up Carlisle Road on foot – the young idiot.'

'I thought it was time enough to send him back on Monday. He's showing a bit of bravado, but he's really rather wretched. I gather he was finding the work hard, and getting teased. One of us must have a talk with Mr Hodgkins, and sort out how real his worries are; and hear his side of the story. The school may not be right for Hal.'

'He can't change schools just because he's behind in class. He's a bright boy who certainly doesn't need to be behind in his work. St Andrew's must bring him up to scratch.'

'He won't do well if he's unhappy.'

'Heavens above – is our son turning into a sissy!' John expostulated. 'Every self-respecting boy gets teased and has weak subjects at school. I'll come down tomorrow and take him back to London on Sunday. It's a great pity you didn't ask your parents to return him promptly on Thursday. As for you traipsing to London and rewarding him with a weekend at home . . .'

Yes, words failed him. She'd spoiled the boy. He'd be sent back with troubles redoubled for the rest of the term.

'I wish we'd never left South Africa,' Hal told his sister as they walked up to the brickpits on Saturday morning. 'Now our father's coming here to criticise.'

'We could hide at the brickpits,' Dido said, weighing the phobias attached to both options.

They sailed a moderate sized boat on the pond and the usual routine unfolded: the boat became entangled in overhanging willow; Dido rescued it, with Hal directing operations, despite the extreme cold to her legs. 'Isn't it nice and warm?' she chanted, wading to a precipitous edge. 'My feet are quite hot . . . Oh lovely heat . . .' Practising the power of positive thinking, she endured the pain known locally as hot-ache.

Fortified against worse perils at home, they returned to the house and found their father had arrived. He was scathing when they appeared with wet legs after playing out of bounds, instead of awaiting him in repentance as befitted the situation.

'I want an account of your behavior,' he said, sitting Hal on the settee and facing him from a chair pulled close.

'I've explained to three people already,' said Hal. 'Four, if you count Dido.'

'I don't count Dido. I want to hear from you.'

'I just hate school.'

'Why? When two hundred and thirty other boys enjoy it?'

'You can't know they do.'

'Tell me why you ran away and worried your mother and grandparents.'

'I was as quick as I could be, arriving somewhere,' Hal objected.

'Did you feel badly treated at school?'

'I told you before about Mr Knott who does maths. And it's Mr Allsop too. None of the staff like me, because I'm behind in lessons.'

'Then you must have extra coaching. In the holidays, if needs be.'

Hal groaned.

'What about the boys? Is it true you get teased?'

'Only about telling fibs. And being backward.'

'Well,' said his father ironically. 'What's the bother then? Nothing serious there.' Hal remained silent. 'I suppose you saw yourself as a bit of a hero, running away?' Indignant tears came into Hal's eyes. 'It never pays to run away from troubles, or to use tears to avoid consequences. Brace up Hal, and look forward to seeing your friends tomorrow, and catching up in your work. Shall I arrange some extra lessons?'

'Please don't,' said Hal. 'I wish I could go to day school like Dido.'

Father and son regarded each other, one from a meditative distance, the other through a resentful blur.

'I'm in favour of Dido joining you in Eastbourne – not the other way about,' John said.

Hal rose to his feet and left the room as though his legs might collapse under him. He climbed the stairs and broke the news to Dido in her room. She stared at him for a full minute. Then she said, 'It's our fault. We've spoiled their marriage. We've put him off.' She sat on her bed. 'I'm not going to boarding school.'

'Thank God for Granny and Grandpa Parsons,' said Hal. 'We can always run away to them.'

Dido bit her lip. 'Ernestine would be sorry. If only she wasn't dead.'

'If only everything,' said Hal.

While they were eating supper, Max Measures rang to tell them that Bunty's condition had suddenly deteriorated. He sounded so distressed that Constance, who answered, offered to go to visit as soon as the weekend was over. He assured her that wasn't necessary, but that Bunty would indeed love to see her soon. A nurse had been calling, and it might mean Bunty being moved into hospital.

'Is it bad luck – or something more sinister?' John commented in a low voice. 'The Crippen syndrome.'

Constance flared up. 'John! How could you make such a tasteless joke?'

'Oh come on – nothing literal! But he drove one wife to death; and Bunty did seem nervy when we went there for tea.'

'No wonder – given your mood on that occasion.'

'The trouble is, you've lost your sense of humour, Connie; and the children are milk-sops.'

'I'm very fond of Bunty,' Constance asserted. 'This is awful news. Can cancer develop this quickly?'

'You've just been told it can.'

'Hal isn't a milk-sop,' said Dido.

'It's hard to believe.' Constance sat and imagined the worst outcome; it began to dawn on her that she could find herself without Bunty for company in an area where she still felt a comparative stranger. There were the Crawleys – but affable Roddy was a liability. Events were following one after another.

'Hal isn't a milk-sop,' repeated Dido.

'Oh, keep quiet will you!' exclaimed her father. Roused to anger by Bunty's plight and his own insensitive reaction, he brought his fist down on the table.

Dido jumped from her chair and burst into tears. She stood, stiff and shaking with distress, arms held aside. 'I've wet myself!' she sobbed.

Constance stood and putting an arm round her, led her from

the room. John and Hal heard voices next door and Coral came quickly in with a bucket and cloths. They heard Constance and Dido going up the stairs.

John made a pretense of finishing his food. Hal sat, his eyes cast down, wondering if he dared make a dash for the hall.

Constance helped Dido into clean clothes. She was quiet, sniffing now and then. She said bitterly, 'Your husband's sending me to boarding school.' She faced her mother. 'You won't let him, will you?'

Constance was in a quandary. It could be the ideal way to boost Dido's confidence and education, and to give herself freedom to win John back. Most children enjoyed boarding. Her two needed to mix more with their own ages; they were too reliant on each other. With Dido at school in Eastbourne, Hal might settle better.

'We'll think about it. Talk it over,' she said. 'Nothing's arranged. But I'm sure you'd find it fun, living with other girls.'

'I think I'd hate it.'

'You're usually so positive, Dido. So ready to like things!'

'Not any more.'

They could hear Ben crying along the passage. He cried constantly these days. 'I woke him up,' said Dido, listening with her eyes wide and her face pale.

'Come on. Let's go downstairs.'

'I'm bad for that baby. And for my father!'

'You're being melodramatic. Come along.'

Dido preferred to stay in her room. Constance descended slowly with her future shifting one way and then another. She met Hal escaping up, two steps at a time.

The telephone rang again, and she answered.

It was Oliver. 'Hello. How are you?' she said, her voice without expression.

His instincts warned him. 'I'm fine, thanks. I won't keep you. Just to say that Georgia left a book with me to give you. I'll drop it by sometime.'

He rang off. John called, 'Who was that?'

They went into the drawing-room together. 'It was Oliver Seaton, whose uncle lived in the Almshouses.'

'Oh yes – I remember him.' John succeeded in creating a nimbus of suspicion around his words. 'He tends to crop up.'

Constance began to laugh, and continued to laugh as if her cares had suddenly vanished. She sank into a chair and threw her head back. When she lowered it, she saw John watching her, with a half-smile dawning on his face.

'Bugger Oliver,' he said.

Chapter 24

John left with Hal after breakfast on Sunday morning.

'You'll find my letter waiting for you,' Dido shouted as they waved at the front door and began their solemn walk to the station.

Constance had offered to run them up in the car, before visiting Bunty at Haverfield. John refused the lift, and Hal assumed that trudging miles up a road was part of his humiliation; exercise he would gladly have taken any other day, with his sister. At least sharing a train compartment with his father was less intimate than being driven to London in the Bentley.

A little before twelve o'clock, Mrs Ablewhite came to the house. She knocked at the front door this time. Dido was drawing at the dining-room table and heard the knock, and Coral going to answer it.

Mrs Ablewhite came into the hall, and explained that she had something to give the children.

Dido hailed her through the open door. 'Hello Mrs Ablewhite! Come in. I'm doing a picture of Willoughby.'

'My – that's a living likeness,' Mrs Ablewhite generously said. 'Picture? It's a portrait!' She fondled the sitter's head, who was posing next to Dido on his own chair.

'Are you still very sad?' Dido asked. 'We are! I'm trying to keep Willoughby from thinking about her.'

'I'm very sad indeed. The house is that quiet. Mrs D wasn't really noisy – but she made herself felt.'

'Sit down, do,' said Dido, patting another chair.

'I won't stay, thank you kindly. I've just come across with these. Mrs D specially wanted you and your brother to have them.'

Mrs Ablewhite perched on the seat and brought two small bundles of tissue from her bag. Dido leaned over to peer at them as the contents were carefully unwrapped. One was a jeweller's box, and when it was opened, Dido recognised Mrs Dunbar's ring.

'Oh lovely – it's her secret wedding ring! If only Hal hadn't been dragged back to school.' She took the ring out and tried it on her thumb, where it fitted snugly. She flashed the emerald around.

'It seems right, you wearing that ring when you're grownup – since you look like Mr Burnett's daughter.'

Dido frowned. 'Please don't worry me.'

'That's a compliment. Unity Burnett was a nice looking lady. Keep it safe dear, it's precious in all ways. Now then – she thought this would be suitable for your brother.'

Dido peered over as the second bundle was unwound, revealing a man's gold watch and chain. 'It's what's called a half-hunter,' Mrs Ablewhite explained. 'I don't expect he'll want to wear it – when he's a man, I mean – but it's a nice keepsake from the old lady.'

'It's very important looking,' said Dido. 'Does it go?'

'Let's see.' Mrs Ablewhite wound the watch. 'No. It doesn't seem to.' She shook it. 'But I daresay it can be made to.'

'If it went, and Hal was here, he could take it to school and count the hours till next holidays.'

'No better way to make the time drag, I'd have thought.' Mrs Ablewhite stood up. 'Your mum's not around, then?'

'She's gone to see our aunt who's dying of cancer.'

'Oh dear. These are sad times! Give her my regards dear, and look after your momentos. They'll both have some value.'

Dido said, 'We won't ever sell them . . . unless we're utter beggars.'

'That's right,' said Mrs Ablewhite, pulling the door to behind her.

Dido finished her study of the pug, who was loath to pose again after his break. She kept Ernestine's ring on her thumb, and hung the watch chain from a candlestick on the table. Five minutes later, she wound the musical-box and began another letter to Hal, informing him of his legacy. Then she sketched it for him.

When Constance rang the bell at Haverfield, Max came to the door. The introspection on his face lifted, and he propelled her inside with an arm round her.

'Connie, I'm so grateful to you for coming. Bunty's a very sick woman I'm afraid. You won't believe how she's changed since Christmas. I know she wants to see you.'

'I've just brought these flowers. I wasn't sure what she can eat.'

'Very little. Leave your coat here, and come upstairs. She'll cheer up to see you.'

'I won't stay long.' Constance handed him her coat, which he slung over the bannisters. 'I expect she gets tired easily.'

'Wait a sec and I'll fetch a vase.'

Bunty was lying in their double bed in what was a large, light, attractively appointed bedroom. Her hair was caught back by a velvet band, and her face was narrower than Constance remembered it. She wore a plain, well-worn bed-jacket over her nightdress. From lifeless repose, she struggled at once into spontaneous greeting, pointing to a chair by the bed.

'You are a dear, Connie. I feel such a mutt, letting myself fall into this state. It's happened so fast, and I feel helpless to do anything useful.'

'It's only while you're ill. We're all expecting you to get better soon. Shall I put these chrysanthemums into water?'

Bunty watched the flowers being arranged and placed by the window. There was a view of green countryside stretching into the distance. 'The doctors have been perfectly open with me,' she said. 'I haven't got long.' She took Constance's hand. 'I've been thinking about you and John. Peculiar thoughts really. Max draws his own conclusions about things. He's got this idea that John isn't worthy of you. Isn't as caring as he should be.'

'Oh?'

'It's just how Max is. Overbearing. I knew both him and Unity years ago. He's a romantic, but we all knew there were rows between them. When I married Max I had to suffer his mood swings.'

'Bunty – I'm so sorry. I hate hearing this. He can appear very charming.'

'He can! He's good with the children, although they're frightened stiff when he loses control. But I've come to realize he's a dangerous man – and that he may have contributed to Unity's death.'

'Bunty! That's a very serious statement.'

'Unity was willful and highly-strung, but I'm certain she didn't kill herself. I think they had one of their quarrels out in the fields, and if he'd laid hands on her in anger, anything could have happened.'

'Has he hurt you physically?'

'Not really. He's threatened me once or twice.'

Constance closed Bunty's frail hand in hers. 'I don't know what to say. Shouldn't you have reported this to someone?'

'I daresay. But one expects the best of people; and of life . . .'

After a moment's silence, Constance said, 'You can't blame your illness on Max, at any rate.'

'Doctors do relate cancer to stress.' Bunty gave a wan smile. 'I'm not afraid of dying, Connie. I just hate leaving Serena and James.'

Before Constance could reply, she went on, 'I wanted to warn you; Max is sure your marriage won't last. Unity wasn't mad . . . but Max can appear to be! He has a great affection for you Connie – so be careful.'

The thought went through Constance's mind that perhaps cancer was destroying Bunty's reason. She said, 'Rest assured dear, I've no intention of losing my marriage, or of being wooed by Max. But I promise that if the time comes for any reason . . .'

The door opened. Max strolled to the bed. 'You've chatted long enough, dear. I'm sure Connie will come and see you again.'

Bunty lay back on the pillows. Constance leaned over and kissed her. 'Of course I'll come again.'

She and Max walked down the stairs together. Max helped her with her coat, his hands lingering on her shoulders. 'I'm sure you understand how wretched I am,' he said. 'Bunty's been told to expect two months at the most. She's remarkably calm about it, and brave.'

'Neither of you must give up hope. I'm a firm believer in miracles.'

'You're so sweet, Connie. No-one better for giving comfort.'

'You know very little about me, Max.'

'I know that John's a lucky man.'

'I've promised to visit again; but I'll ring first.'

'Please ring,' he said.

In her own bedroom, Constance looked across the drive and

lawn to the Almshouses over the road. She imagined herself in Bunty's room, with every comfort, and an attentive husband whom she feared. Horrible if Bunty was suffering cancer-induced hallucinations.

It was Wednesday morning. Dido was at school. Constance wondered how Hal was managing school life. John had reported taking him to Eastbourne and delivering him to Mr Hodgkins. He'd felt he owed it to himself to hear what the Head had to say about Hal's escapade. He claimed to have insisted that the bullying stopped; and that allowance was made for Hal's adjustment to the English system.

A Morris was nosing through the west gate, and scrunching to a halt. An ordinary kind of car. But it looked familiar.

She met Oliver in the outer hall. He proffered a paper bag. 'Georgia's book,' he said simply. 'It's a novel about Natal. She thought you might enjoy it.'

'Thank you for bringing it.'

'I'm afraid I rang the other evening when it wasn't very convenient.'

'It wasn't, as a matter of fact. But never mind. Can you come in now?'

'I was wondering if you could come out? Let me give you lunch?'

They drove to the Ram Jam. 'I've been wanting to do this,' Oliver said. 'You're thinking now of Georgia – I can see it in your face – and I'm thinking of John. The fact is, I am fond of you, Constance. I know it's unfair, and I know it's daft.'

They were sitting at a table with a garden view. Few others were in the room. Peace and quiet.

'I've never been in love with Georgia, nor she with me. I thought you could have had a false impression.'

'Well – I didn't dwell on it.'

'No, of course not. Why should you? Being a happily married woman.'

'Yes.' Constance regarded him steadily. 'Though not as happily as I could wish. Post-war blues.'

'I'm sorry. I'd gathered things weren't a hundred per cent.'

'I'm in love with my husband – and I believe he loves me.'

He nodded, his eyes on hers. 'I'm not expecting to be told

anything. I just thought it fair to express my feelings.'

After a moment she said, 'John used to be tremendous company, before the war. Now he finds it hard to relax. He's severe with the children. Then they blame themselves when things aren't right between us.'

'That's a shame. Tough on you. D'you suppose he'll warm to family life in due course?'

'He's at Millbank; and weekends at home don't help much. The children rather dread him coming.' Constance broke off for the arrival of their food. 'It's been quite a sad period so-far: the Tiplers' troubles, which upset Dido; then Mrs Dunbar's death, which has upset us all; now Max Measures' wife has cancer.'

'No love lost there,' he said. 'between John and Max.'

'Word certainly gets around,' she said. 'I wonder how you know that?'

'I know how worthless gossip is.' Oliver sought her hand across the table 'And I know what my heart is telling me.'

'Let's concentrate on this fish,' she urged him. 'I do enjoy your company Oliver. But losing John is causing me great unhappiness. I intend to fight for him. I'm ruthless enough to let Dido go to boarding school at seven, and I'll take up Georgia's idea of spending time with her in London.'

'So that leaves me – nowhere! Ah dear. Hope springs eternal, as they say. Keeping in touch is no sin . . . provided I don't add to your worries. I only need to be sure you're all right, and that I'm not in the doghouse.'

'You're a dear, Oliver. And I appreciate your friendship more than is good for either of us.'

'Amen to that,' said Oliver. 'Why don't we have a glass of wine after all?'

Chapter 25

Two months later, Dido was at boarding school for the summer term.

After an initial flush of enthusiasm for wearing a uniform, and levelling with Hal, came the panic. She woke from the dreams of possibility to the stark phantom of reality.

Sitting in the train to London, Hal had coached his sister in etiquette: 'Don't be too pushy, don't hang back, and above all, don't swear.' They were both due in school on the same day. Pale and shivering and yawning in turns, Hal clutched their shared Knockout comic and stared at the world flying by.

Dido's girls school stood on an eminence of front garden and drive, above the road: two elephantine brick buildings of asymmetrical shapes, with multi-styled windows, some generously proportioned. A paved covered yard linked the two houses.

There was no uniform. The pupils wore ubiquitous gym-slips with scarlet shirts in the week, but individual skirts, dresses and overcoats on Sundays. There were no prefects. A system of promotion had been devised that owed its inspiration to King Arthur; a head girl was a knight, followed by standard bearers, squires, service squires and pages. Their motto was 'Live pure, speak true, right wrong, follow the King.'

She was sleeping in a five-bed dormitory called Camelot, next to the Matron's room on the Astolat Landing. The first piece of information given her was that a pipe leading through the wall into Montsalvat next door was a private telephone, and to use it would cost three pence. Dido accepted this without question.

Then began a period of extreme home-sickness.

She'd previously spent only one night away from home, to have her tonsils out in Stamford. For that, she'd been put in a room with five other children who sang lustily, 'There's a party on the hill, will you come? Bring your own cup and saucer and a bun.' This merry-making was before the six operations were carried out. Afterwards, there were only sounds of moans and splutters from the beds. A doctor with attendant nurse came to Dido to remove a blood-clot from deep in her throat, with what she took to be a pair of huge sissors.

She hadn't cried then; but now the tears flowed. It was humiliating to cry. It was an impotent weapon for changing her circumstances; but the tears were beyond her control. At the end of every meal, exhausted by weeping, she asked the presiding mistress to be allowed to go home.

Matron, Miss Weldon, promised if she stopped crying she could phone her mother; but despite a supreme effort, the call was never made.

Gradually, progression into naughtiness brought an endurable status quo.

Miss Weldon was antagonistic to all the small girls. She had a fierce temper, and with her thin face and figure, she convinced them she was a witch. Going to the lavatory after lights out meant creeping along a narrow passage past her door, and at the least sound she would pounce out with suspicions and retributions. One Sunday morning Miss Weldon claimed to be woken by Sibbie falling from Dido's bed, and demanded to know who had been running about. After a silence, Dido confessed on Sibbie's behalf. Her face was slapped, and she was sent to sit in the Sickroom until the seven o'clock bell rang.

Before the children of Camelot fell asleep each night, Dido embarked on a story of a brother and sister who fell into serial adventures. This stream of imaginative suspense helped redeem Dido's image, and ward off homesickness; the same ruse that Hal had employed nightly in his dormitory to strengthen his morale.

There were wild games played in the large garden that sloped upwards to the Downs. Beyond the blue wooden door in high walls was a wood, and the children were taken on walks over the Downs: through gorse bushes known as Fairyland, or down Steep Hill, or into Paradise by the golf course. A longer walk was along the Downs towards Beachy Head, playing round the dewponds on the way.

Each afternoon, Dido and her class spread rugs on the Junior

Room floor and rested in silence for an hour, with four sweets each. On Sunday evening, they filed into the Blue Library, sat on the floor with handwork, and listened to elderly Miss Tizzard reading 'The Black Riders,' 'Light over Lundy,' or 'Raven among the Rooks;' and Dido, though barely aware of the fact, began to feel happy.

Constance, after nearly a week, was enjoying London, visiting friends and going out with them. She planned to stay one week more, then take the children home for the summer holidays.

John had been living in the Officers' Mess until now, but he'd been reluctant to let her have a contact address or phone numbers. She wondered if he had acquired a private flat for himself yet. When at last John rang on her fourth evening at the Overseas Club, she suggested he came round.

No . . . why not meet in the Tate Gallery? There was a café where they could talk; and a lot of pictures . . .

He didn't want privacy, or the personal touch. It was to be a refuge from all that, with plenty of human and creative distraction. Without enthusiasm, she agreed to meeting there next day.

It was sunny, with a blustery wind. She arrived first. It was too cold standing on the steps, so she went inside. Five minutes later, he hurried up looking immaculate and very handsome in uniform.

'Hello Constance!'

He gave her his perfunctory clasp and peck on the cheek. They went straight to the café where she removed her jacket and they faced each other over a small table. She'd been expecting to enjoy the Rex Whistler murals. She had assumed a level of civilized comfort far exceeding that of a mere café. The place they had come into was drab and functional indeed, and the murals around the walls, with their strange rustic scenes of rolling lawns, palatial houses, and mythical beasts, were in sad need of restoration.

'Tell me how you're getting on?' Constance put the onus firmly on him, and sat with an expectant expression, waiting to have his life of medical discovery revealed and illuminated for her.

'All right,' John replied, blandly.

'Tell me about it. Your routine . . . your fellow students. Anything!'

'The chaps are pretty decent. We get some time for lunch, and in the evenings. I like the work very much.'

Constance sat back, wearing an ironic look of curiosity satisfied.

'Nigel Walsh is an excellent man. Top of his sphere. Only smiles when he's dissecting an eye.' He set his cap on an adjacent chair. 'What news of the children?'

'Dido's been homesick. I think she's settling now. Hal writes saying he's so hungry, all he can think of is food. But the handsome watch and chain Ernestine Dunbar left him has won him a lot of credit. He must have smuggled it into his case after the holidays.'

'All schoolboys think they're hungry. Perfectly natural, they're growing fast. Fancy Floppyguts leaving him a watch.'

'That awful name! But more surprisingly, she gave a ring to Dido. An emerald with diamonds.'

'Well, well. Dear old Ernestine.'

'What makes me think that sounds mealy-mouthed? Tell me truly, did you upset her when you called on her that day?'

'I was very kind. I asked her about herself.' He mumbled the subterfuge with a childlike humour. Moments later, his large eyes discreetly sought the clock on a far wall. 'Is everything all right at the house?'

'Coral says there's nothing to report. Bunty's the real worry. Her condition is pretty grim. She was given two months to live, and she looks so frail. Now she's gone into remission, so we're all full of hope. I was driving over to see her twice a week, and she always managed to be cheerful.'

'How's Max taking her decline?'

'Not well. The idea of losing Bunty has hit him hard.' Into her mind came Max's repeated phone calls, and the occasions he had looked in at Westbourne on some pretext, and she'd felt uneasy.

'Don't indulge your good nature feeling sorry for Max,' John was saying. 'I'm aware of your generous attitude towards him.'

'I can't help feeling sorry for him. Bunty's improvement can't last. I feel rather mean being away now.'

'You're a martyr,' he said. 'You know my opinion of Max. Perhaps he's only getting what he deserves.'

With a quick change of subject, she said, 'I'm enjoying London, and seeing people; and meeting Georgia.'

'Georgia?'

'The American girl I mentioned to you.'

'Oh yes – of course. Of course I know. How long d'you think you'll want to be here?'

'John, it really depends on you! I've come to walk in the parks, go to exhibitions, see a show, see friends. But essentially, to spend time with you. For you to be honest with me. Share your feelings. Let me express mine. Each time you've come to Westbourne, there's been a virtual wall of silence between us.'

'It's difficult with the children. They're very intrusive.'

'Our marriage is important to them. They suffer from atmospheres. They need to know what's ahead for them.'

'At least they're both at boarding school. I thought them far too clingy.'

'You grumbled about them being too independent! Going to the brickpits, and cycling miles . . .'

'No – those are good things. I like that in a child.'

'John, I don't want to talk about the children. Have you been seeing Vera? She's the elephant in the room.'

He laughed. 'She can be a bull in a china shop, I grant you! Yes, I've seen her. Look – shall we have a cup of tea?'

He stood up, went to the counter and brought two teas.

'Vera is determined to marry you. Am I right?'

'There are several unattached nurses around. I'm not interested in any of them. Certainly none I want to marry.' He sipped his tea, while she ignored hers. 'I think Vera would be happy to marry me,' he conceded.

'And you really want to make her happy. Am I right?'

'Yes. But you put it too simply.'

'It's a straightforward choice, John!' She touched his hand. 'I love you. I haven't changed. But I'm paying dearly for it.'

'Finish your tea, and we'll go up and see the Turners. It's strange,' he said, 'how nice it is being with you, Connie, as if nothing had happened – the war, Vera – anything. I dreamt about your parents the other night. I was fond of them in those Croydon days.'

She drank her tea and watched him reach for his hat. She put on her jacket and followed him up the stairs and into a world evoking glorious storms, Italian vistas, English landscape.

Dido wrote to her mother:

'We like to climb along the walls of the loos. They are open at the top. Now they've put little nails so we can't do it. One loo is called Slapbang, the lid hits the seat when you get up, the next is Middle and it's big and sunny and the next is dark called Prison with a trick lock. We found a pistol buried in roots in the wood. One night a convict escaped. He was the Mad Parson and he climbed up on the flat roof by our bedrooms and stared in with a shiny painted face. He's been caught again now. We got in the Duke's summerhouse where the tennis is, and had our eiderdowns and some sweets. We had to write him a letter. Sometimes we hide in the art cupboard and smoke bits of cane it smells lovely. Love from Dido.'

She had a wart on two of her fingers, and was ordered to the Dispensary, where Dr Kent and Miss Weldon between them burned the warts away by the acutely painful process known as Snow. Dido gritted her teeth and the matron and doctor glanced at each other. 'We can't make her cry,' smiled Dr Kent.

Constance greeted Georgia and led her into one of the public rooms of her Club. As she threw off her jacket and sat down, Georgia asked, 'How did it go?'

Constance said, 'I begin to think all men are monsters. The game is always in their favour.'

'You met at the Tate. Reasonably conducive to airing emotions, I guess.'

'Entirely. The wretched tea-room wasn't crowded. We could have made love. Or had a row. As it was, we exchanged platitudes – and got nowhere.'

'You could certainly divorce him on grounds of cruelty.'

'I don't want a divorce! I don't specially want to make him suffer either; I just wish he'd explain himself. Next time it'll be in the National Gallery, or the Zoo . . . or Madam Tausaud's – as Ivo might recommend.'

'Who's Ivo? Another monster?'

'A harmless one – though I blame him for being in the RAC Club when John happened to breeze in with Vera.'

'These meetings smack of ritual humiliation.' Georgia stood

up. 'I've decided, I'm taking you out for dinner tonight at a fabulous little French place I've discovered in Conduit Street. We'll go there after the show, and you'll feel a million dollars again. Oh, and by the bye – Oliver rang. He sent his regards. He just wanted to check up on our health and safety.'

While Constance was in London, her parents offered to drive along the coast to Eastbourne; and one Saturday after half-term, they set off. They collected Hal first, then called for Dido. In great excitement, the children climbed into Bampy's car and they all headed for the sea front.

The sea was like sheet metal with the faintest hint of movement beneath its surface, and a light wind fluttered the flags adorning the pier. It promised to be a hot day, and throngs of holiday-makers were milling about. They walked the length of the pier, and agreed it wasn't as well-ordered as the West Pier in Hove, or as amusing as the Palace Pier in Brighton. The children kicked off shoes and paddled while their grandparents sat on pebbles beneath the wall, and the sun beat down, and cries of humans and gulls combined. At twelve-thirty they went into a fish-and-chip emporium with tiled floor and walls decorated with sea creatures and seaweed, and there was a tank with electrically agitated water and an orange plastic ball bouncing about on top. Bampy ordered four plates of fish-and-chips, and he and Granny Parsons heard a great deal about the heinous behaviour of Messrs Allsop and Knott, and Miss Weldon. After cups of tea, Granny Parsons felt she'd like to look out to sea from Beachy Head, so they drove up and parked the car and the children ran about, pretending to want to throw themselves over on account of school. Then they drove back into town and treated themselves to a grand tea, served in the comfortable lounge of the Cavendish Hotel, while a quartet of musicians played catchy music.

When the dreaded time came to be returned, Hal agreed to go in first as he had to tidy his lockers and desk before supper at half-past six.

Tearful at saying goodbye to Hal, Dido climbed out of the car and up the steps to a side door of her school, and wept in good earnest. Iron entered her grandparents' hearts as she fell on her knees in the covered yard and implored them, with bribes of money and Ernestine's ring, to take her away with them to sanctuary.

Three weeks later, and a few days before the end of term, Dido fell ill. She was put into the Sickroom, and on waking during the second night, suffered a crisis of hammering head pains. She called out, but no-one answered. Tipping herself off the bed she crawled across the Astolat Landing. Reaching stairs to the Dispensary, she lost consciousness and tumbled to the landing below.

Hal's school broke up. Constance met him in London and took him to Westbourne.

For a week after the school emptied for holidays, Dido was medically obliged to stay in a narrow bay called Slip off the Sickroom, with a brown linoleum floor. When the doctor called, Miss Weldon saw him in and out with unctuous respect. Then she dismissed herself from duty, and it was a jolly maid of sixteen who brought meals to Dido, and spent short periods of time with her until someone could take her away.

Chapter 26

When Constance was back in London, she heard that Dido was well enough to travel home. She took the train to Hove and stayed a night with her parents. Her original idea had been to stay in London until the children's term ended, and then go home with them. But Dido's illness, and a change of attitude in John, had made her alter her plans.

Granny and Bampy were instructed not to visit the patient meanwhile.

'It seems awfully heartless. But the school doctor advises complete quiet for the duration,' Constance explained to them. 'I've sent her a Knockout Annual to look at and to read. She has to sleep a lot.'

Which was perfectly true, and as fate decreed, John had made arrangements to meet Constance at Millbank Hospital and take her on a limited tour; he wanted them to see a West End matinee together during these extra days; and he suggested lunch at the RAC Club, which in the event she couldn't bring herself to refuse. They mostly talked over old times: their Chiswick flat before the war where Hal was born; her family and his mother staying at the same time at Oatlands Park Hotel. He recalled those 'comic' occasions when Connie broke her nose diving, and her collar-bone on the icy front steps; and she was reminded of his warped sense of humour.

'Perhaps we could slip over and just see poor Dido?' Granny Parsons had offered. After hesitation, Constance decided against making the child more aware of her isolation by an extra parting from family. Better to leave her another four days to get strong.

Staying in Hove, Constance tried to describe to her parents how disconcerting it had been having John courting her that week. He'd been his old self again, relaxed and fun, but never so as to encourage intimacy. Her own painful inhibitions had left her. She'd become so cheerful that decision-making issues hadn't arisen.

Constance's father reckoned that John's behavior was grossly unfair, better befitting a feckless girl than a doctor and an officer, and unworthy of his daughter. He wished he had the heart to convince Constance her marriage was over. Her mother spotted signs of contrition in John which in her view could and should lead to a complete reconciliation.

Dido was dressed when Constance drove up to the school in Bampy's car. Her trunk had been packed and sent on ahead. She carried a small over-night case and had Sibbie under her arm. She was pale and subdued, but cheered up when Constance appeared. 'Goodbye!' called the young maid, who had shouldered her responsibilities without ever realizing them.

They drove to Hove over the Downs and along the coast. Granny Parsons gave them lunch. They were told very little about Dido's incarceration with the maid; then Bampy took them to the station and they caught trains to London and home.

Hal had missed her, and expressed keen sympathy for her lost free days. 'At least you've had proof that school's bad for you,' he said.

Dido stared at him. 'It nearly killed me. I knew it would.'

'Did you have nightmares?'

'I didn't have any. Life was just a nightmare.'

Constance said, 'Do try, both of you, to think positive things. Think of all the fun you have most of the time – with your friends.'

'Friends!' scoffed Hal. 'Read enemies for friends. And most of the time was like a hundred years.'

'Dear little Willoughby. He's pleased to see me.' Dido stooped to fondle the pug, and stroked Prince in passing. 'When I've seen Daisy, I want to go to bed.'

Constance said lightly, 'That's a sensible idea. I'll bring your supper up – and read whatever you like.'

She was also surprised by the lack of resentment Dido had shown at being left alone at school; and the lack of interest in her mother's life in London. Constance had supposed she'd be returning for another autonomous week. But newly forged hopes were already foundering . . . and a wave of depression crept over her.

John had indeed found accommodation for himself outside the Hospital, and conveniently nearby, in Causton Street. The kitchen was well stocked. A large water-jug was filled with yellow roses. Their exuberance made him feel uneasy and disheartened. He was careful to repress these feelings. In his own company he brooded, longing to know his own mind. What he wanted, he didn't know. He wasn't even sure what he didn't want. With each passing day, his position became less desirable. Amusing himself with Constance had been like an escape into a time warp; a holiday from schizophrenia.

He imagined himself at Westbourne: the children furtive, unresponsive . . . or behaving like hooligans. Unstable Burnett streaks there, manic-depressive. Then all that baggage from the past resurfacing. He recalled the awful Christmas in his old home with wife and children, haunted by them, yet scarcely aware they existed.

Then Ivo came round with a box of little cakes and a tall young friend with floppy dark hair.

'This is Troy. He's been encouraging me to dawdle among the frivolities in Piccadilly's Burlington Arcade. All we succumbed to were these, from Fortnums– for you!'

He opened a box of teacakes, each a different pastel colour and surmounted with baroque ornamentation. Troy turned his back to look out of the window as Ivo arranged them on a plate. 'Can I interest you in a musical show one evening?' he asked. He began singing 'I'm a girl in a million, not a toy for a boy.'

'Possibly,' said John, perceiving problems.

'A musical would do you good,' Ivo insisted.

'Exactly. Ruthlessly uplifting.'

'What about that matinee you went to with Connie? 'Murder on the Moon?' That sounded fun. How about a murder, Troy? I love musicals – but Troy's not over-keen on them.'

'Being in full possession of my faculties,' Troy responded, as if that sealed the matter.

Ivo said, 'We were passing St James's, Piccadilly, and what did we behold but a wedding. The bride and groom were coming out and cameras were flashing and I had a sudden vision of Troy, smothered from head to foot in Brussel's lace. Curious how the mind works.'

'What poppycock, Ivo,' said Troy; and the pleased expression that crossed his sulky face exposed an inward revelation.

Ivo looked energetically about him. 'Constance likely to be with you again?'

'One of the children was unwell. I expect she'll come up.'

"Murder on the Moon.' Reminds me of New Year at your place.' Ivo chuckled. 'Got a bit close to the knuckle with that fellow – forget his name – married to your sister. A prototype for a murder story there!'

'Don't encourage me,' said John. 'Let's have those cakes. I've got the tea things ready.'

'And that chum of Connie's was staying. Can't remember her name. Who was it who said, one never loses one's memory – it just takes a few moments to claw the facts back?'

'Dickens, of Dickens and Jones,' Troy supplied wearily, tossing his forelock. 'Unless it was Swan of Swan and Edgar.'

'Troy's got a phenomenal brain. He can speak three languages. He's applied for a position with Hatchards bookshop. Meanwhile, he looks after my car.'

'What I'm doing,' said Troy with a repressive glance at Ivo, 'is translating. I'm translating into Spanish 'The Place of the Lion,' by Charles Williams. I've gone as far as chapter five: Servile Fear. I'm looking forward to The Triumph of the Angelicals – chapter twelve.'

'I've never heard of Charles Williams,' said John, pouring out tea. 'But it sounds addictive.'

'Trouble with entertainment nowadays,' Ivo said, stretching out for a yellow cake, 'is that it's all about family. Books are as bad. I've no primary family left alive, not counting my brother. I've no acquired family. Give me a thriller every time.'

'You're being a bit brutal,' John observed. 'Family entertainment is a reaction to the war. Give thanks for happy family memories.'

'What an extraordinary thing to say!' exclaimed Ivo. 'Your family, John, was no example: verbal sniping all over the place. Dear Florence excepted . . . and Connie too of course.'

I'll crack him over the head in a minute, John thought. He wished he could wipe out the present and exchange it for the cordon sanitaire of soldiers in Burma doing a bloody good job. Soaked with rain, lying in a trench with his precious plank, at peace with himself. Sitting here in Causton Street he despised himself for wanting to keep up appearances. 'What part of London are you from?' he asked Troy.

'Archway as it happens. But Ivo says I should get up into Hampstead. Better for my health. I tend to be bronchial.'

'I plan to take him on a tour of Scotland in the autumn. See the tints of Glen Lyon in the fall,' Ivo informed them. 'I tell Troy that parts of Lowland Scotland remind me of South Africa. Sounds potty I know – but the hills and the rivers . . . and stretches of mud cracked dry by the wind. That sort of thing. Very alike.'

'You surprise me. Will you share the driving?'

'We'll take turn and turn about,' said Ivo. 'And Troy will be in charge of the camera. And we'll both be in kilts!'

John said. 'Are you entitled to the tartan?'

'The question doesn't arise. Tourists won't be challenged. We'll show you Troy's photos when we're back.'

The cakes had disappeared and the teapot drained. Adroitly, John said, 'I've been rather stupid. I realize I've got a lecture at five o'clock. No need for you to hurry though. Stay as long as you like.'

Fifteen minutes later, Ivo and Troy were descending the stairs, and Ivo was calling over his shoulder to John, 'Tell Constance we promise to visit her on our way to the Highlands. No other family members to be there, though – Troy hates controversy!'

'I'll try to get hold of 'The Place of the Lion,'' John called after them.

He picked up a tea-towel and a wet cup and thought, Ivo has a three-track mind: my mother, my wife – and South Africa. Troy's an unexpected revelation . . . or am I being naive? John supposed he was. It had never occurred to him to speculate. Well, bless his heart, John thought, I hope Troy makes him happy and I need never see them again . . .

After tidying the kitchen he went into the bedroom, removed his shoes and lay on the bed. He recalled his parents in the heydays of their estrangement: his father deliberately hearing anything his wife said incorrectly, with the most wounding and humiliating effect. Any resentments his father might have stoked up during mealtimes he'd defuse in the drawing-room by folding his newspaper smaller and smaller with maximum force until it was a mere packet, then ramming it under his chair. 'A lung specialist for John?' he could hear his father demanding. 'I never know what you're talking about, Florence! Why must you put the boy out in all weathers? He's not a Highland beast!' And his mother, with sardonic civility, 'I often feel you are the one who needs a specialist, Henry.'

That lecture. He'd better get ready. But he actually had another hour.

He closed his eyes and drifted into a light doze, aware that when he came to his senses he would face the truth regarding the rest of his life.

Georgia said into the phone, 'We managed a few things, haven't we Connie? But I'd hoped to see a lot more of you. I thought we'd go down the Thames to Hampton Court.'

Georgia, in her brother's elegant flat, revolved a well-heeled foot in the air, which she knew was beneficial for circulation – ten times one way, ten times in reverse. Then she swapped legs, and swung the other foot.

Constance, staring out of the dining-room window at Westbourne, was saying how disappointed she was that they hadn't done more together.

'How is that young daughter of yours?' Georgia asked. 'Got over the mumps yet?'

'She's well again, but sticking to her vow: No more trauma. No more boarding school.'

'So –a bumpy ride lies ahead! Any follow-up from John? What a joyful week it was, when he was fixing up nice times for you together.'

'I know. You were so nice, sharing my pleasure and my misery. But as a matter of fact, he rang me this morning. Guess what he had to say.'

The tone of voice gave it away. Georgia groaned. 'Oh – what, Connie?' She jerked her foot and the shoe dropped with a thud.

'He's going to leave me. Or rather, he wants me to leave him.

He wants a divorce.'

Georgia kicked off the left shoe, and slumped from the chair arm onto the seat. 'That's sad, Connie. I just hate to hear it. I'm very sorry darling.'

'Something has made up his mind for him at last.'

'So he's decided you must stand in the witness-box?'

'Oh don't . . . It's an awful thought.'

'What a bastard.' Georgia straightened up in the chair. 'I apologise – I shouldn't call him that. But how unfair the law is to women. He's smashed your love-life, and you have to carry the can.'

'How long before you go back to the States?'

'Not long at all. Less than a week. I'll stay and see my brother arrive, and fill the freezer and take him out to a meal. Then I'm away.'

'Any word from Oliver?'

'Oh yes – he's been up in London for a day . . . And he's promised to fly over and check out Vermont! Says he's game to motor round a bit.'

'Really?' Constance was able to carry the phone while she sat herself down. She said quickly, 'Georgia, that sounds marvelous. You can show him all the sights.'

'Heaven knows what I've let myself in for.' Georgia began to laugh, but stopped abruptly. Another short silence. 'Constance – are you there? Look – I wish you'd come out and stay with me once things have been sorted. It would give me more pleasure than anything.'

'You know I'd love to, and I'm very grateful to be asked. If it's possible, I'll come.'

'Bring the kiddos. I'd be only too happy if they came as well.'

'I promise I'll think about it. I hear them shouting for me now. I'd better go. Thanks so much for everything.'

Constance rang off. The house was deadly still. The moments ticked by. She could hear both clocks distinctly. She could almost hear her heart. It had never felt so heavy and so sore.

Chapter 27

Coral and Constance were watching Ben crawling across the sitting-room floor. If the baby was aware of their admiration, he was too focused on his own prowess to acknowledge it.

'I ought to have told you right away when you got back,' Coral said, with a sudden flash of memory. 'Miss Poole, the old lady over the road – she died while you were in London. Ever so thin she was, and hadn't been eating properly. Like a living ghost, really.'

'I'm sorry to hear that. I don't suppose you've told Dido?'

'Only just thought of it now. I won't mention it to the children if you think better not.'

'Definitely not. There have been too many losses lately. Children can be quite sensitive in these matters.'

Constance could imagine Miss Poole's quiet death inspiring weeks of sensational nightmares and sightings. Miss Poole might even be co-opted into the No More Boarding School campaign. She said, 'I suppose I've missed the funeral?'

Coral couldn't say. She bent to abstract Ben from under the gate-legged table. 'Something I do know is what Mrs Ablewhite came to tell me while you were out this morning: she's inherited Mrs Dunbar's house, just like that! For loyal service. Don't you think that's marvelous?'

'I do. She deserves her good luck.'

Running a hand thoughtfully over Ben's reddish-fair head, Constance left the room. She, for her part, had news to break to the children.

They were up in Hal's room. He was constructing another model aeroplane with balsa wood and powerfully malodourous glue. Dido was drawing. Willoughby was snoring on the bed, his head against the pillow. Constance took a chair next to Dido. After a few moments spent watching them absorbed in their activities, she said, 'A letter came this morning from a solicitor, which affects you both.'

'Is it about a child's right not to be banished from the family home?' Hal asked, glancing up sharply.

'No, it isn't.'

Hal returned to his occupation with set expression.

'Have you crashed the SS?' Dido asked, crayoning busily. 'She's such a handful.'

'No. Perish the thought. It's something unexpected and nice – concerning you two.'

Both children's heads turned towards her, work suspended.

'Mrs Dunbar has left you £1,000 each in her Will. '

'Golly.' Hal sat back on his heels. 'I could buy a house with that.'

'As well as my ring?' Dido exclaimed. 'What a kind person.'

'And something else you'll be pleased to hear is that she's left Trullers to Mrs Ablewhite. I think that's wonderful news.'

'Oh good.' Hal resumed lining up his bits of wood prior to applying the adhesive. 'She did an awful lot of hanging around and cleaning for her.'

'What about Willoughby? She must have left something to him,' Dido said.

'Actually, she hasn't. She probably felt she's done enough for Willoughby.'

Hal said, 'I needn't go back to school now. I have means of my own.'

'Don't be absurd, Hal. That's not the conclusion Mrs Dunbar meant you to reach.'

'But I do reach it. Ernestine hated us to be miserable.'

'She would have hated you to grow up uneducated.'

'It's like slave money. I can afford to buy my freedom,' Hal insisted, fitting on the wings and applying great pressure.

'Well, it's our money. That's what matters,' stated Dido. 'We can always ask that solicitor, and he'll say we can do what we like with it.'

'He won't say you can buy your way out of school,' Constance said, smiling. 'I'll open savings accounts for each of you to put the money into. Perhaps one day it will help you buy homes of your own.'

‘We’re going to live together; so we’d be able to get a decent sized house,’ said Hal.

Constance stood up. Then she sat down again. After a few minutes she spoke. ‘There’s something else I must talk to you about. Not such a nice subject, I’m afraid.’

‘Dad is coming to stay.’

‘Well – it’s about him. He and I have been meeting in London and discussing our futures together. He must spend a year or more studying medicine there as you know, and we always supposed he’d visit us at weekends, and for holidays. That’s what I very much hoped would happen.’

‘But we’ve put him off,’ Hal said, to help her. ‘We always knew he thought we were mistakes. With just you, he’d have felt a lot keener.’

‘Hal’s right.’ Shaking her head, Dido continued to colour in. ‘If you’d only known not to have us. He should have thought of that before.’

‘Darling children – my life would be nothing without you. I can never regret it, whatever happens. You are my great comfort, and it was you two who held Daddy and me together. But he’s decided that if he’s honest, he knows he wouldn’t be happy coming back to this house and sharing our life.’

‘Vera Savage. It’s all to do with her.’

‘Not entirely, Hal. War changes people. As I’ve told you, your father’s been through terrible times. Those experiences were bound to alter him. A lot of men find it hard to return to their families. We can’t blame anyone.’

‘But of course, he’ll share himself with Vera!’ Hal got to his feet and going to his bed, sat roughly down, laying a hand on the reproachful pug.

‘There were no presents for us,’ echoed Dido, resentment still lingering for Christmas omissions.

‘As far as I’m concerned, these facts concern no-one but your father and me – and both of you.’

‘If she takes him over, will he bring her here?’ Hal asked in threatening tones.

‘That’s very much in the future. The question is, should I agree to give your father his freedom? He’s been honest enough to admit he’d like a divorce.’

'He wants to divorce you?'

'Yes. That's what he told me finally. But I need to know how you feel about it. You'll always have a father, you know. It's just a question of whether you'd be happier with one who lived here. Your happiness is all important.'

Dido nodded hard. 'Better without.'

'He can't divorce you, when you've done nothing wrong, and don't want to do it,' Hal said. 'I know the law's a donkey, but how does that work?'

'The law is tricky. But since I haven't done anything wrong, I have to be the plaintiff. Put the blame on him, so to speak. It's a horrid thought. I shall hate going to court, and answering questions. But it's the only way, if the fault is his.'

'Because of the necklace?' Dido suggested. 'We worked that mystery out.'

'And other things.'

'I'd like to go to court,' Hal said. 'Dido and I ought to be witnesses.'

'That's a kind offer,' said Constance. 'If only you could. But come on – let's get outside in this lovely warm weather. Harness Daisy for the trap, and we'll drive her through the woods.'

When Max rang Westbourne House, only Dido was available to answer.

Max spoke in a hushed voice. 'Hello – Constance?'

'Our mother's not here,' Dido said.

'Oh . . . That's a pity.' The sound of a nose being blown. In the same thick tones, and after an uneasy silence, Max continued, 'Please will you tell your mother that Bunty has died.'

Shock reduced Dido to silence. Then she said accusingly, 'Why couldn't the hospital save her?'

'The doctors tried. Will you ask your mother to . . .'

Dido abruptly put the phone down. She stood very still for a while, remembering Aunt Bunty's awkward figure hovering over tea at their house, and her kind face. Her thoughts passed to Serena and James, showing off their musical-box. She went to the dining-room and wound their own box. Tears began to drop on the slowly turning cylinder.

Some time later, when they were having lunch, she said to her mother, 'Uncle Max phoned when you weren't here. I think he was crying.'

'Oh! Did he say why?'

'He told me Aunt Bunty's died. So the hospital didn't save her. Like Mr Fewings.'

Hal watched Dido's eyes began to fill. 'Will Max marry again?' he asked.

'I haven't the faintest idea,' his mother said, in a different voice, 'Oh, what a blow. We so hoped she had a chance. Max will be devastated.'

'Another funeral,' said Dido, wiping her cheeks. 'I don't want to go.'

'There's no question of you going. But I will, and try to be some comfort to your poor cousins. They've lost their second mother now. '

She stood up, and went through to the drawing-room. She dialed Max's number.

'Dido has just broken the news to me, Max. I'm dreadfully sorry. When did it happen?'

'Last evening. Mercifully, she died here, at home. She'd gone early to bed, feeling very tired. I looked in on her before taking the dogs out, and when I came back, she'd slipped away.'

'Did she seem peaceful at the end?' Constance asked.

'Her face was full of peace. She looked beautiful,' Max spoke huskily. 'I'd been hoping against hope – and she was so plucky! No self-pity. Only anxious for me and the kids.' He blew his nose. 'This house is a miserable barracks now – not a home at all. The spirit's gone out of us all.'

'How can I help?' Constance asked, the situation she had foreseen coming upon her. 'What can I do for Serena and James?'

'We'd love it if you'd drive over. Could you possibly come?'

'Or should I collect the children and bring them here? Give them a change of scene?'

Max cleared his throat, took a deep breath. 'Would you come over, Connie? I'd be so grateful to see you.'

'Well yes – of course.'

'How soon can you come? This afternoon?'

Importunate Max. A flutter of distaste seized her. She wanted to say, 'What about tomorrow?' to give herself a little space. But she wasn't one to deny a cry for help.

'All right,' she said, 'I'll come now. But I can't stay long.'

He was there to greet her, and watched as she closed the car door and walked towards him in a neat skirt and jacket with a silk scarf. He wrapped his arms round her by the front steps.

'You can't know how glad I am to see you. We aren't close family – not blood related – but when you lose someone, you want people who know the background. Even good friends aren't the same.'

'I may be old-fashioned,' he went on, urging her up the steps with his arm snug at her waist, 'but a bit of history gives a sense of belonging. Kinsmanship.'

'Have you any other family who could come?' she asked. 'And what about Bunty's family?'

Max escorted her into the room where Unity's portrait was, and Constance was immediately conscious of being held by Unity directly, yet so enigmatically, in her over-the-shoulder stare.

Max said, 'I've contacted an unmarried sister of Bunty's, and she's in touch with a cousin. But I've no family worth mentioning. Just you – and John. How is he, by the way?'

The quizzical note needled her. 'He's very well, thank you. Enjoying his studies.'

Max's moist eyes gazed into hers. 'Good for him. Fresh challenges. Fresh faces . . . Now, what about some tea? My Mrs Avery is out buying provisions. '

'Yes, a cup would be nice. Let me get it with you . . .' She began rising from her chair, attempting informality. 'Where are Serena and James?'

'They're upstairs. It hasn't hit them yet that Bunty's irrevocably gone. She was such a sweet substitute mother to them – as you can imagine. I'll call them presently.'

'Why don't we go and talk to them now? Take tea up, and have it with them?'

'Very well.' Max set off down the passage to the kitchen, Constance following. She filled the kettle and he plonked four Wedgewood cups on a tray. 'We've got some biscuits somewhere.'

A worn tin of Palmers' biscuits was added to the tray. As the kettle reached the point of boiling, Max began to weep.

Constance hesitated, then moved nearer to him. With infinite caution, she placed a hand on his arm. 'Brace up, Max,' she said. 'Life has to go on, for you and the children.'

He was almost choking, and held his handkerchief against his face. She could see how wet his tears were making it. She was filled with contemptuous sympathy.

'Pathetic. Call me pathetic,' Max stated, stuffing the hanky into a pocket. 'The worst of bereavement is the regret, the bloody awful wishing undone things that shouldn't have been done – and things said that shouldn't have been said. I used to be so bloody rude to Bunty. But I did admire her, and I did love her.'

'We all talk nonsense if we're upset.'

'Do you sometimes shout at John? Do you ever get upset when he lets you down? I'm damn sure you don't!'

'What do you mean – lets me down?'

'Indestructibly loyal Constance!' He gave a spluttering laugh. 'For what it's worth, and for better understanding of yours truly, I always reckoned that John's spirited sister was unbalanced – and I always recognized that Bunty was weak. An endearing quality in her case. But you're strong and noble darling; and John is luckier than he deserves.'

He faced her as she withdrew her hand, and stared at her with his large dark eyes. He had a compelling intensity, with his olive skin and rough dark hair falling over one eyebrow.

Constance switched the kettle on again, catching it up as the water boiled. She filled the pot, and finding a spoon, stirred the tea with it. 'Come on – let's get up to Serena and James.'

Max drew close behind her. 'Hang on a second. I need time to pull myself together.' Tears were filling his eyes again, and he gripped her upper arms. Constance was obliged to replace the tray on the working surface.

'Forgive me please, Connie. Men don't blubber, of course they don't . . . least of all a churl like me . . . But honestly, I feel desperate. Remorseful, shattered, lonely, inadequate. How can I comfort my children when I'm in this state?'

'It will pass. You're suffering from shock. Concentrate on helping the children.'

'How like you to say that. You're so unselfish.' Max took his hands from her arms, and began to fiddle with the scarf at her neck.

Attempting to lift the tray once more, Constance inclined away from him and felt the scarf tightening.

'A moment, a moment,' he begged. She jerked aside, her heart thumping, and was immediately seized into a tight embrace. Struggling, her elbow knocked into the crockery, spilling hot tea into the tray. One cup exploded on the floor. Tea began dripping at their feet.

'Whatever are you doing?' Constance cried in exasperation, swiveling to confront him.

Max made no reply, but grasped her head with both hands and pressed his mouth against her cheek.

'What's been happening?' Serena asked, standing with her hand on the door-knob.

Max relaxed his arms and clearing his throat, bent to pick up the pieces of china. 'We were making tea,' he said. 'Not very efficiently.'

'I saw the Jaguar from the window,' James said.

Constance hastened to kiss the children. 'We are a clumsy pair,' she said. 'I wanted to see you, and tell you how very sorry we all are. Poor Bunty. But I think she's been spared a horrible part of her illness.'

'We're so unlucky, it happening twice,' said Serena in her well-modulated voice.

'Who wants tea?' Max asked. 'Here's a cup for you both – and this one for Constance. I'll pour myself another.'

The kettle boiled a third time, and they sat round the kitchen table. Max began mopping the floor with a tea-towel. Then he sat down beside Constance and laid his hand over her hand. 'It was a great act of kindness from Aunt Connie, coming to share our troubles.'

'I wanted to see you both,' she said, smiling at them. 'But I mustn't stay long. Hal and Dido are hoping you'll visit us, and take their old pony out in the trap with them.'

'Chocolate's mouth is too soft for harness,' said Serena. 'He's more suitable for showing.'

'I'd rather play with their trains,' said James.

'We'll see what the weather's like. I'll give you a ring, and arrange a day.'

Max shook the biscuit tin at Serena. She tossed her long fair hair. 'No thank you.'

'James?'

He put his hand in and stirred the biscuits. 'No thanks.'

Max blew his nose, then helped himself. 'I'll let you know when the funeral is. Will you come?'

Constance hesitated. 'Yes, please let me know. I hope I'll be able to come.'

'We've got to go now,' said Serena, slipping off her chair and over to the door. James instantly followed. 'Goodbye.'

Constance resisted an impulse to jump up and hug them. As the door closed, she said, 'Max, I think I'll go too. We'll keep in touch.'

'Please forgive my abominable lapse,' he said. 'I know you think I've insulted you. And Bunty.'

'Well, yes . . .' Her next thought was, this man should be on the stage.

He walked with her to the car, opened the door and made motions of helping her inside, without touching her. He looked very penitent.

'She had a merciful release,' Constance said, as the engine sprang into life.

Chapter 28

The postman had come. Constance picked up a letter addressed to her in unfamiliar writing.

'My dear Constance,

I seem to have been unlucky in my attempts to telephone you, both at the Overseas Club and at Westbourne. I'm very sorry indeed we haven't had another chance to talk. I've been thinking about you, and hoping sincerely that things are turning out as I know you wished them to. You were on my mind so much in fact, that I needed a complete change of scene. Georgia suggested I go over and see her part of the world, travel a bit, meet new people. Broaden my horizons, in other words. Your experiences made me realize how narrow mine are.

Wishing you every happiness, and with fond memories and great affection,

Oliver.'

It was the day of Bunty's funeral. Constance put the letter into her bag, and glancing at the clock, hurried to fetch her grey coat and small black hat. Yes, she looked all right. A touch of lipstick perhaps. She went through the house to tell Coral she was off, and heard the children calling to each other in the home paddock. 'I shouldn't be late back,' she added.

Her urgent wish was to avoid Max. She'd speak to him no more than was necessary – the feelings he induced in her being so mixed. She began to direct a prayer to any receptive power above that he would behave appropriately.

The service was held at the little church close by Haverfield. Constance parked with a number of other cars near the churchyard. Max was hovering inside the church as people were seen into seats. He caught sight of Constance, and taking her elbow, guided her into the front row, where several darkly clad strangers were sitting with his children. His appearance was in every way correct, and his manner quietly courteous. He looked the epitome of convention, and she took a deep breath of relief.

The service followed its usual course, and hymns were sung with their charismatic melancholy. It was a warm, late summer day, and the burial was accomplished with the sun shining and birds singing in a tangle of dark churchyard trees.

With the ritual over, Max moved to Constance's side. 'You'll come to the house, won't you?' he said, his eyes more eloquent than words.

She went up the front steps and introduced herself to Bunty's unmarried sister, and to her distant cousin. Max hung about, waiting for the last visitors and the vicar to arrive and be brought indoors.

A catering firm had delivered a choice of sandwiches and cakes, and two young women in black dresses and white aprons were there to serve them in the drawing-room from a sleek long walnut dresser. One waitress presided over the tea urn and coffee machine, the other encouraged people to help themselves from the spread of food.

After about twenty minutes, Max sidled up to Constance and nudged her into a window alcove. 'Forgive me for being such a creep the other day,' he muttered. 'I hate to remember how I behaved. It was most unfair to you. '

'It doesn't matter. I'm not dwelling on it.'

'Thank goodness. I was rather dreading this occasion – not least for having to face you.'

Constance shook her head. After a moment she said,' It was a good service. Your eulogy for Bunty did justice to her.'

'I'm glad you thought so. I'm no good at writing. Roger helped out here and there . . . the vicar, that is. He's such a nice chap, and knows the form. Let me introduce you to him.'

'Well – I'd rather not. I'm thinking I should leave.'

'Please just say hello to him. You've met Bunty's sister – and the cousin?'

'Yes. Both very friendly.'

Max drew her across the room to the vicar, which meant making herself known to the circle around him. Half an hour later, Max said goodbye to her at the front door.

'May I come with the children? It would help to have some time to talk.'

She was obliged to consent. Hurrying to the car she was aware of one threat withdrawing, and another taking shape.

Two days later, before any such visit could happen, Constance's mother rang. It was not happy news, and she sat for a while on the ottoman in her bedroom, thinking of her parents, and wishing she was with them. Hal and Dido were playing with their trains. She asked them to come and join her in the room next door.

'Darlings,' she said, tucking a lace-edged hankie up the sleeve of her dress. Her face was pale and her voice unsteady. 'I'm afraid Bampy isn't well. I want very much to go to Hove to see him. Coral will look after you, and I won't be away long.'

'We'll come too,' said Hal. 'Bampy will want to see us, surely?'

'We always make him laugh,' said Dido.

'It'll be easier for Granny if only I go. You can come later, when Bampy's better.'

It wasn't the time to dispute the matter. Looking into their mother's face, the children fell silent.

But wider forces brought a further change to their plans. Constance was not to see her father again.

Both the children became tearful when they were told of Bampy's death. Hal especially was upset, remembering their family stay with his grandparents on arrival from South Africa; and his grandfather's sensible attitude to bunking out of school.

'We must all go down and look after Granny,' he said.

'Well – we could all go. School doesn't start for another little while.'

'Forget school. For Grandpa's sake. He knew it was bad for us.'

Dido said, 'I just worry I never have school nightmares. I ought to have them.'

'I have them,' said Hal. 'Often.'

Constance wore a remote expression. They sat in silence. Then Dido said, 'Have you noticed how everybody's dying? I shall be next, if you send me back to school.'

Her brother gave a mirthless laugh. Constance made no reply. This circular debate had to end. But her thoughts were with her father.

Dido's eyes were on her mother's face, and her own expression became very strained. 'How old are you?' she asked fearfully.

Constance turned to reply. 'I'm thirty-seven.'

'That's dreadfully old,' cried Dido.

'No it isn't! Not really. Your great-grandmother lived to an astonishing age. I hope Granny will – and I will.'

'I want to die when you die,' Dido said.

'I'm sorry there's so much to be sad about,' Constance said. 'It isn't usual to lose people so close together.'

'It's this house,' said Hal.

Dido said, 'It's our father rejecting us.'

Constance said quickly, 'Now – I'll have to tell Uncle Max what has happened. He wanted to come here with Serena and James. But we'll all go to see Granny, and try to cheer her up.'

It occurred to Hal to say, 'I hope Granny doesn't die.' But seeing his mother's face, he merely thought it.

Constance again wore her grey coat and the little black hat that sat to one side of her head. Her mother's very elderly sister and husband weren't able to attend the funeral. A second cousin who lived in Sussex appeared for the service but disappeared after it was over. The crematorium was spectacularly sited, high above Brighton in beautifully manicured gardens. There were not many people in the pews: some casual friends from hot days on the beach; members of the historical society; Hove neighbours. A few arrangements of flowers.

Granny Parsons herself wasn't well. She walked with difficulty, and kept becoming confused with names and events. Constance realised that she was going to hate leaving her mother on her own in Albany Villas. She made a point of demonstrating her love for her, unaware that in later years she would regret not seeming closer to her emotionally.

Hal and Dido spent the afternoon with people next-door, and enjoyed going on the West Pier with them. They were allowed to run about on the stony beach, and paddle as the tide went out across the sand.

Albany Villas had it's own atmosphere. Comfortable worn furniture, large rooms with generous windows overlooking a fig tree in the garden and the road in front; and the long town garden at the back. The cornice in a small bedroom was decorated with plaster blobs that Hal and Dido called jam tarts when they had slept there together. They were happy to be in the jam tarts room again now. They re-discovered Bampy's large black elephants, and the picture he used to tease them with, saying a figure in it was waving from the ruined tower across the countryside – although when the children looked, that person had always gone; and Bampy's old desk, and the bone-handled cutlery.

'Will you come back to Westbourne?' Constance asked. 'Stay for as long as you like. It would be lovely for us.'

'I think I'll just stay here,' her mother answered. 'I want it all round me. I'll come and see you sometime, dear. But not yet.'

'You haven't met Daisy or Prince or Willoughby,' Dido pointed out to her grandmother. 'Or Coral or Alfred or baby Ben.'

'You tell them all I intend to come.'

'What about Christmas?' Constance suggested, thinking it wasn't the best time to travel, and that their house might seem cold.

'If they ask at school what's happened these holidays, I'll have to say, funerals,' Hal remarked.

'But you aren't going back,' said Dido.

Hal shrugged. 'Oh no.'

Two days after the funeral, the door-bell rang. Constance, going to see who was there, was greeted by a man's back; and when he turned, it was Max.

'Good heavens,' she exclaimed. 'Whatever are you doing here?'

'I wanted to see you.'

'How did you know the address?'

'I rang the house. Coral gave it to me.'

Constance stood as one trapped. She made no effort to conceal her shock.

'May I come in?' he asked with a quizzical smile.

Still she hesitated, untypically rude. 'I think I'd rather we had a walk. I explained to you my father had died. Mother won't be feeling like putting a stranger at ease.'

His wry smile became a grimace. 'Very well. Shall we go on the front?'

'Wait here while I get a cardigan.'

He turned his back again, and took in the neat front garden, the over-spreading fig with its grey bark and floppy leaves, the Regency villas opposite. He was wearing light trousers and a blue shirt, and had a bag slung from his shoulder.

'The children have promised to keep granny company. But I don't want to be long.'

'That's what you always say to me.'

She glanced at him, as he at her. Their eyes met. 'How are you feeling, actually?' she said. 'Any less wretched? It's early to be asking, I know.'

'Bloody awful – and for the same reasons. Remorse is agony.'

'Does it have to be so dramatic? Why so remorseful, Max?'

He shrugged. 'You knew Bunty. Not well, but enough. You know me . . . through other people, of course.'

They crossed the main road at the bottom of Albany, and headed for the sturdy iron railings that bordered the beaches. The front stretched ahead, sprinkled with people enjoying summer weather; senior citizens, families with young children.

'Dare I take your arm, Mrs Burnett?'

'I suppose so,' she said, with a certain ungracious charm.

'I'm booked into the Ship Hotel. In case you've wondered.'

'I hadn't given it a thought.'

'Quaintly historic, with it's nautical sign and creaky corridors – but a touch insanitary, I fear.'

'Oh well.' She spoke cheerfully, gazing out to sea. 'You'll survive one night.'

'What if smugglers invade?'

'I'd have thought a rough-house would be just up your street.'

'Now, why on earth should you say that?'

She filled her lungs with ozone, the benefits of which her sea-loving mother swore by, though science now held it to be detrimental.

'I take it you've deserted Serena and James at this crucial moment in their lives?'

He gave her another wry half-smile. 'It won't be for long. Anyway, they're very fond of Mrs Avery, who helps keep the house decent.'

They were approaching the Angel of Peace monument that defined the spot where Hove ended and Brighton began. Hal and Dido liked to stand with a foot each side of the line. When they reached it, Constance stopped in that position.

'A cup of tea – or an ice?' he suggested. There was a café behind them almost on the beach. She walked over to it. 'An ice-cream would be nice. Then we go back.'

He bought two cornets and they sat with them at a table. The sun was producing such a heat that she removed her cardigan and draped it over her chair. 'What has really brought you here?' she enquired, licking circumspectly at the melting ice.

'To escape from Haverfield. My memories. My self.'

'Which you can never do.'

'No. But I fancied you might help me.'

'How on earth can I help you?'

His shrug gave him a Gallic appearance. 'I'm simply a very stubborn and capricious man.' He licked carefully at his cornet, eyeing her. She sat in silence, seeing him as an irrelevance; the person she least wanted to spend sympathy on, and who was dominating her in an unreal situation. Behind the charmer was the man whom Bunty believed to be dangerous.

'Oh well.' Constance smiled briefly. 'Sun and sea air may do us both good at this sad time.'

'It gives me a silly sort of pleasure to think you're my sister-in-law.'

'Really?'

'Yes. It's an undemanding comfortable link. Don't you agree?'

'I'm actually your late wife's sister-in-law. Nothing special in that.'

'I felt you were special at Bunty's funeral. I was quite proud of being your brother-in-law. It's a kind of belonging.'

'I don't think a very healthy kind, to be honest.'

'You tend to be painfully honest about most things, Connie. Only you won't come clean over your marriage.'

'Please don't call me Connie.' She finished her ice-cream and tossed half the cornet to the gulls. 'And never ask me again about my marriage.'

'A cup of tea?'

'I must get back.'

'I'll be a good brother to you. Give me time.'

'I'm more interested in being a good aunt to Serena and James.'

He came round the table and took the sleeves of her cardigan. He loosely tied them together, and drew them close until his hands were under her chin. 'You have a very pretty neck,' he said. Then he kissed her forehead.

Constance retreated, pulling the sleeves apart, exclaiming, 'Why do you do these things?'

She sharply shook the garment, turning her back to him, and put it on with a show of dignity.

Then they began what was to all the seaside world their companionable stroll back along the front.

Chapter 29

When Max rang the front bell the following day, Mrs Parsons answered the door. He was wearing a linen jacket over a clean white shirt, and carried no bag. He passed a bunch of tulips into her hands.

'Forgive me for appearing unannounced,' he said with a well-crafted smile. I'm Constance's brother-in-law, Max Measures. I expect she told you we met yesterday and had a walk along the front.'

Mrs Parsons looked blank. 'No. Constance said nothing about it. Thank you for the beautiful flowers. Come in. She's taken the children to Hove Museum and Art Gallery, along New Church Road. She won't be long. What a nice surprise for her.'

'I'm very sorry you've lost your husband,' Max said, waiting as she seated herself. He laid a box beside her. They were Audrey's chocolates from their shop off Palmeira Square. He then took a chair for himself. 'My wife died recently – so this isn't a very happy time for either of us.'

'Oh dear, you have my sympathy.' She sat with the tulips across her knees.

Max sighed. 'I'm doing my best to back Constance up over her marriage. She says very little. But she must be terribly hurt.'

'You know John, then?'

'Oh yes. I was married to his sister Unity. I lost her in sad circumstances, and find myself widowed again. But Connie's a person who doesn't deserve to be on her own this way.'

'Has she talked to you about it?'

'Well – I'm only sorry things have gone as far as they have,' Max responded suavely.

'John seems to be adamant. He wants a divorce. Some nurse he met in the war. Poor Constance naturally feels the shame and stigma. It's a hard part for the woman to play.' The old lady brushed some water off her skirt. 'I liked John back then. Quite a shy man, with a good sense of humour . . . but difficult to know.'

'May I put those flowers in a vase for you?'

'No no. She'll be back any minute and knows where vases are. I think I hear the children.'

Hal and Dido burst into the room. They pulled up sharp on seeing Max.

To pre-empt deflating comment from them, he said 'Hello! Been improving the shining hour with culture?' He had a way of lifting his eyebrows rapidly up and down, just once, when he smiled, which Mrs Parsons found peculiarly conspsiritorial and attractive.

'We've seen some stuffed birds and old dolls,' Dido said to oblige him.

'And lots of portraits,' added Hal. 'Why are you here? You don't know Granny.'

Then Constance came in. She glanced in dismay from Max to her mother and back to Max.

'He tells me he's in mourning as well, poor fellow. We never met before; but John's our connection. You would have been at Constance's wedding?'

'I'm afraid not. John and I weren't ever on the best of terms. He thought his sister could have done better for herself.'

Constance took the tulips off her mother's lap, and hurried from the room. She had caught sight of the box of Audrey's chocolates in passing, and it galled her to be reminded of Vera at Christmas. Hearing Max gossiping about her wedding to John was more than she could bear. How dare he appear unbidden, and trade on a false friendship with her?

'Would you be a dear, and make us cups of coffee darling?' her mother said when she returned with the tulips arranged. 'Dido, you could find cups and saucers for five people, and plates; and Hal, will you put out that Fuller's walnut cake we bought yesterday. Do you take your coffee with hot milk, or black, Mr Measures?'

'With milk, Mrs Parsons. But please call me Max.'

Their stately good-neighbourliness made Constance want to grind her teeth. 'Wash your hands first, children,' she called coldly. 'You've been touching exhibits which everyone else touches

– legitimately or not.'

With showy bustle, Hal and Dido set out the plates and knives for everyone, and the white-iced Madeira cake studded with walnuts for sharing.

'The cake knife,' Granny Parsons cued them, and they sped away to locate a carving knife.

'Not what I meant,' their grandmother murmured. 'But never mind!'

'Uncle Max won't care,' Hal said. 'And he's the guest of honour. Where are Serena and James?'

'I left them at Haverfield.'

'Wouldn't they have liked a stay by the sea? I wish they were here.'

'They could've gone to the Aquarium with Granny and us tomorrow,' Dido added.

'Now, that is a swizz. However . . .' Max leaned over his knees, 'they'll be coming to play trains with you, don't forget - as soon as we all get home.'

'Where did these chocs come from?' Dido asked, as her eye fell on them. 'They're like the ones Vera gave when she gate-crashed. Yummy violet creams.'

'They belong to Granny. Nothing to do with you,' her mother said, returning with the coffee.

Conversation flowed, with minimum help from Constance. When an hour had passed, Max felt constrained to make a move. Constance gritted her teeth again in the face of his amiable courtesy. She could barely wait to close the door on him.

'That was quite a fun happening,' Hal said, going to inspect the carnage on the cake plate. He licked his fingers and poked the debris together. Dido was instantly at his side, licking and picking with him.

'Leave that cake at once, and rinse your hands again. Then you can wash up.'

Constance carried the stacked china into the kitchen. The subdued children appealed to their grandmother. 'Why's she so cross?'

Granny Parsons lifted her hands and shook her head. She indicated that silence was their best policy.

Before they set off in the car, Constance spoke to her mother.

'What a cheek he's got – landing on you out the blue!'

'He said he was family. I couldn't send him packing . . . and he mentioned he was widowed a short time ago. I felt very sorry for him.'

'He comes across as pleasant enough. But I seriously don't think he likes women much. He can be quite a bully.'

'Surely not! He was perfectly polite to me anyway, and a pleasure to chat to. It's a pity John didn't get on with him; but that was all a long time ago. Despite our sorrows, we had a few laughs before you came in.'

'Well, I hope he's going home today.'

'He didn't say, and I didn't ask. He looked rather Italian. Nice dark eyes.'

Tired of the subject, Constance called to the children to take jerseys and go to the car. The plan was to carry Bampy's ashes up to the windmills on the Downs.

'He'd have loved to be scattered at Chanctonbury Ring,' Mrs Parsons said wistfully, 'but he doubted a car would make it up there. Or else at The Devils' Dyke, he used to say. But without being superstitious, I'm not leaving him there.'

'Is it a pagan rite to scatter ashes?' Hal wanted to know. 'It seems a bit primitive.'

'Following a normal Christian service, it's perfectly acceptable,' Granny said. 'Most people choose cremation now, and some like to be scattered in a special place. It's a saving of precious ground.'

'I want to be scattered in my bedroom,' said Dido, improvising fast. 'Then my ghost can go back and I'll always be at home.'

'That's a daft idea.' Hal stood deep in thought. 'I'd like to be scattered from a helicopter flying low over the polo ground in Mooi River. Or,' he went on, also improvising, 'I want to be kept in an earthenware pot and left in our little museum at Westbourne.'

'What cheerful conversation!' said Mrs Parsons. 'Are we ready to go? Just as well it's not windy or raining for our ceremony . . .'

Max didn't come the following day.

The day after that was their last in Hove. They had been at Albany Villas for nearly a week. After hours of discussion with her mother, and research with agencies and maps, Constance warned the children that she had something to tell them. They sat kicking their legs in worn chintz armchairs.

'As you know, I went to London yesterday, and as I explained, I met your father; and we talked.'

'Was Vera there?' Hal asked.

'No. Just the two of us.'

'And you've won! He's agreed to come back?'

'Sucks to Vera,' said Dido softly. 'Though I did quite like her.'

'Vera's neither here nor there. It's a decision made by your father and me, no-one else. I thought you understood that. I'll have to apply for a divorce. And I've made up my mind not to stay at Westbourne.'

'How d'you mean?' asked Hal, aghast.

'I've decided to sell the house, and buy one in Sussex. Somewhere near Granny.'

'That makes me sound very guilty,' said Mrs Parsons. 'But this is none of my doing. I'd hate you all to leave your lovely home if you're happy there.'

'We are,' said Dido.

'It's not such a lovely house, as far as I'm concerned,' Constance explained. 'It's too big, the garden's too big, and it's too far from my family's county. Westbourne was Daddy's house, and now I'd rather be near where I spent my childhood.'

After a heavy silence, Hal said, 'I thought Westbourne was our ancestral home!'

'So it is – up to a point.'

'You'd be nearer your schools,' put in their grandmother with intended cunning. 'I'd be able to take you both out at least twice each term. And so would your mother, of course.'

'How can we want to be nearer our schools!' cried Hal, as if to a mad woman.

'And we won't be there anyway,' Dido reminded him.

'Oh no.'

Constance sat regarding them, looking weary. 'Let's leave school out of this for the moment. I think it could be really exciting to move to a different sort of house. You can have your say in choosing it. You'll probably make friends more easily; and anyone special from school could come and stay.'

'I thought we weren't talking about school. So that's very tactless,' growled Hal.

No-one spoke, until Dido remembered her responsibilities. 'What about Daisy? And Willoughby, and Prince? Can they all come with us?'

'If we agree to go,' Hal added. 'And anyway, what about the Sherwoods – and Race? So we can't go.' He swung his legs angrily.

'The Sherwoods will be wanting to find somewhere else. It's not easy for them, living with us. They'd be better on their own. Daisy's too old to travel – it might be kinder to leave her where she is . . . or perhaps she could go to the boy who took her hunting. The dogs could move with us.'

'We'll need to ask them. They may not be at all pleased,' Dido said. 'Willoughby's had traumas enough.'

'Pugs are very resilient,' her grandmother observed.

Another silence fell, broken by Hal heaving a sigh. 'The best time of my life was in Mooi River, and that includes school. Treverton was a lovely school. I liked all the teachers and the boys and the games, and football was taught by an old lady with irons on her legs. She was excellent.'

'Really?' Granny Parsons knew this for a fact, but pretended surprise.

'She sat on the side-lines and shouted what to do. Which shows that schools don't have to ruin your life – even weird ones.'

'I don't believe we have to leave Westbourne,' Dido said, tears responding to the pathos of her words. 'I just don't believe you mean it. You're upset because of the divorce. If only our father wouldn't blame us.'

'He doesn't. Of course he doesn't.' Her grandmother looked at Constance. Her daughter's mind was miles away in Croydon, in the garden at Castlemain Avenue, three years before that beautiful house was bombed to atoms. It was sunny, her parents were sitting in deck chairs, her mother holding baby Hal dressed in a white knitted outfit. John was there. They were in love. Then war ruined everything.

'Why don't you come and live with us at Westbourne, Granny?' Hal suggested.

'You can share my room,' Dido said.

'She'd sleep in the Milky Way room.'

'Or she could have Coral and Alf's room if they're going away.'

'Granny doesn't want to leave Hove. It's warmer here, she has friends, and she loves the sea,' Constance told them. 'I'm sorry it means you two uprooting again. I know you love the house. But it does make sense for us to settle in Sussex.'

'Always starting again.' Dido wiped her eyes. 'Hal's right. We should've stayed in Mooi River. You'd have loved it, Granny.'

'What? Granny share a corrugated iron bungalow with us, with a verandah and rough patch of garden? Just above the railway line?'

She had described perfection. They nodded eagerly.

'Wait till you've seen one or two brochures of houses in the Sussex countryside,' Constance said. 'We may indeed get a bungalow – and I don't want much garden. But you'll grow to like whatever we buy.'

'Mrs Ablewhite will miss us dreadfully,' Dido offered as a further obstacle to moving. 'Just as she's got so happy, too!'

Hal glared mutinously at his mother. 'We can't move house – and we refuse to go back to our schools.'

Max was on the phone to Constance the evening they returned to Westbourne.

'Connie. I hope you're not feeling too depressed. May I come round tomorrow? We both need cheering up.'

'Max, I'm perfectly all right because I'm busy. I've a lot to do tomorrow . . . the children's things to get ready – nametapes and so on. Clothes to shop for. Does your farm run itself?'

'Practically. I have a wonderful manager. I'll come over with my pair. They've been rather miserable and bored.'

'You left them in the lurch, larking about in Hove. I'm still annoyed with you for inviting yourself into Mother's house.'

'It bucked her up. Don't pretend you minded, Connie. I can't bear to let you live on your own, with a sense of being thrown over. Once you're through the divorce and a free spirit, you'll be up for anything; and I intend to make you happy.'

'You certainly astound me! As for gossiping with Mother about my private affairs – that rankles.'

'I know,' he said submissively. 'It was cheek. But forgive me if you can. I got back to my house and the emptiness was awful. I was a sobbing infant again. I miss Bunty more than you imagine.'

'Your behavior makes you rather difficult to read.'

'I realise. God forbid I'm having a breakdown! You know Connie, I end each day despising myself. However . . . it really was marvelous, seeing you by the sea.'

'Max, I prefer to manage my troubles on my own. I'm a very independent person. Dwell on Bunty's special qualities and the sadness will ease.'

'You're an angel. I must be allowed to say it.' Deferentially, Max cleared his throat. 'So – see you tomorrow at four'.

Chapter 30

Serena walked into the hall at Westbourne with her accustomed poise, and received her aunt's embrace. James returned an untidy half-hug.

'I expect you'll want to play with the trains,' Constance said. 'But why don't you have some games of croquet first – in this lovely weather?'

Hal shrugged. 'D'you want to play croquet?'

'We don't mind,' Serena replied with exquisite indifference.

'I want to,' said James.

They trooped back into the porch and wandered towards the harness room.

'We've been left a legacy,' Hal remarked. 'One thousand pounds – each.'

'Gosh,' James said politely.

Serena said, 'Our stepmother may have left us something. But we're not thinking about it.'

Hal felt abashed. He wanted to say, I'm sorry, I didn't mean it like that, I'd forgotten about your stepmother. We always feel we're in competition with you both which is very childish. But none of these words came.

'You don't have to wear black then,' said Dido, who also had knowledge of the world.

'Goodness no – not for *ever*,' said Serena. 'We're not Catholics, anyway.'

'Oh,' said Dido, further enlightened.

'Where's your old pony?' James asked. 'Can we see her?'

'She's going to be sold,' Dido said sourly. 'Our mother's selling the house and garden and getting rid of Daisy – all over our heads – though we've begged her not to.'

They reached the paddock and passed through the gate. 'She's quite small,' Serena observed. 'Only twelve hands, I guess.'

'But she can go like thunder,' boasted Hal. 'Once the bit's between her teeth, she can't be stopped.'

'Then you're using the wrong bit, and the wrong bridle I expect.' Serena shook back her hair. 'I could stop her with the correct aids.'

'Perhaps you'd like to buy her?' queried Hal.

'Why's your mother selling?' James wanted to know.

'Because our father's marrying someone else. This is his house, and she wants to get away from it.'

'D'you mind?' James looked distressed, the idea occurring that with Bunty gone, a similar shock might await him.

'We just say we won't leave. We like this house; and we've told our mother we aren't going back to our horrible schools either.'

'Gosh,' said James. 'Our father would kill us if we talked like that.'

Dido said, 'I had a nightmare about Miss Weldon last night. I knew I would, with all these plots hanging over us.'

'Who's Miss Weldon?'

'She's the hag who looks after us at school. I almost died last term – and she may have poisoned me.'

Hal said, 'I'm beginning to learn a lesson in life: things always get worse.'

'Bunty used to tell us that things can always be worse,' Serena answered. 'She meant, we should be grateful.'

'Yes, well – she died quite young didn't she, for a grown-up. Which shows she got the very worst.'

'Then I'll be saved some misery if I die at school,' said Dido glumly.

'Do you both go to boarding school?' Hal asked.

'I'm going to start at Cheltenham Young Ladies' College. James goes to a prep school.'

This reply was given with such complacency that there was nothing more to say.

They left the paddock, Daisy making no effort to approach. Hal banged the gate shut after them, saying, 'I'm banking on our mother seeing sense.'

'I don't want to play croquet,' Serena said, staring about her. 'I'd rather play with your trains.'

'Right.' Hal and Dido led into the house by the back door, pausing for Serena to fondle the dogs in the kitchen, and cast a polite smile at Ben who was being fed in his highchair. 'Come on,' she said to Willoughby,' you can play trains with us.'

'Much better not.' Hal scooped the pug back through the door. 'He's a terrible nuisance, trampling on the lines.'

'Indoors already?' queried Constance.

'We can do croquet later.' Hal hustled them into the large empty room, then immediately pushed his visitors out again. 'Wait there a minute!' He began closing the shutters, whispering to Dido, 'They haven't seen the Buddha. Find matches, so we can light the candle.'

Max was the soul of discretion today. He barely touched Constance's cheek when he kissed her, and he kept his conversation objective. She heard a great deal about his plans for the farm for the next five years. Like a Soviet commissar trotting out revolutionary ideas, she thought; and he gossiped a little about his neighbours.

'And how is your mother?' he asked, all sincerity.

'She's looking after herself, and coping well. I don't think she'll want to move house yet.'

'Very wise not to rush it. That's the advice we're always given.'

'I'm planning to move to Sussex, however,' Constance said.

'You're not!' Max stood stock still.

'Indeed I am. Much against the wishes of the children. I've an urge to go back to my roots. Spend time with Mother.'

'I do so understand.' Max resisted an impulse to put an arm round her as they walked about the garden. 'Funnily enough, it's occurred to me lately to wonder if one can produce a decent wine in Kent or Sussex. The chalky soil has all the elements for a good terroire.'

She faced him. 'You can't be thinking . . .'

He laughed. 'You're such fun to tease, Connie. It's a tempting proposition, but I'm not . . . because I think you're teasing me. You've no intention of leaving!'

'I fully intend to go.'

'In other words, John has wrecked the new life you were creating for him. The home you were making, after seeing him through the war. How does that rate in the selfishness scales?'

'They say that history repeats itself. I hear myself quoting it often enough. There was John, never very happy as a child, his parents separating. Now it's our turn to take a different direction.'

'Abide by that other bit of folklore I was spouting at you: don't rush into anything. After a couple of years here, you'll have made more friends, the children will be older and easier, and you'll almost certainly be happy.'

'You'd be happy – because you'll imagine you've manipulated me. It's an idiosyncrasy of yours, I believe.'

He shook his head. 'You're so naive.'

She replied, before she could have second thoughts, 'Bunty saw you as manipulative.'

They walked along the paved paths, under rose-covered arches, like two lovers, and then down the little bank by the ancient greengage tree. Constance glanced across at her husband's new section of wall, and Ernestine appeared in her mind. She waited for him to speak.

He looked stern. 'When did Bunty tell you that?'

'When she was ill.'

'And not herself; in fact, very confused.'

'By manipulative, I suppose she meant that you behave in an over-bearing manner. And have a hot temper.'

'Bunty wasn't the timid neurotic she was taken for. She had a will of raw iron and ruled me with it. And I respected her.'

'Max, it's rash to judge other peoples' marriages. That's why I feel indignant when you pass comments on mine.'

'Can't you try to like me?' he pleaded, anger leaving his face in a manner so specious it put the iron back into Constance's soul.

She said, 'Come and help me carry out the tea things. The children will like it in the garden.'

Tea on the lawn wasn't very entertaining. Serena daintily picked at her aunt's home-made cake, and James displayed an infantile fear of wasps; Max tended to be abrupt with them both. Constance exerted herself to keep the atmosphere pleasant.

'Shall we have a return tea next week?' Max suggested. 'How about it, cousins?'

Hal and Dido nodded. 'All right.'

Constance said, 'But you can't. Term begin in three days. You mustn't go on being in denial.'

'You gave me a real shock saying that!' Hal scowled at his mother.

They all embarked on goodbyes.

'One day I know you'll give me a champagne moment,' Max murmured in Constance's ear, as his children climbed into the car.

The Measures drove away before six o'clock; and the Burnett children fell into despair.

Hal stomped upstairs, denying his state of denial. Dido's weeping had reached a crescendo when loud knocks on the inner front door announced the arrival of Ivo and Troy. 'Hello hello hello! We appear to have descended into purgatory,' Ivo called in stentorian tones.

'What a surprise!' Constance greeted him warmly, with Dido's arm gripped in her hand. 'You couldn't have come at a better moment. A slight collapse of morale – and who better than you to lift it?'

'Have you lost something, or broken something? There's nothing that can't be mended or replaced,' Ivo declared.

'My heart can't be mended or replaced,' wept Dido, perceiving a ray of hope beaming between herself and her bombastic uncle. 'I'm being forced back to a place of great wickedness.'

'Well – you obviously don't mean school,' Ivo chuckled. 'Source of those happiest days.'

'I do, I do!' Dido's voice rose higher.

'Forgive me, my dear.' Ivo turned to Troy, and back to Constance. 'This is Troy, with whom I've set my heart on discovering Scotland.'

'I'll never see Scotland,' stuttered Dido.

Constance and Troy shook hands, the latter looking ill at ease. 'What are your immediate plans?' Constance asked, remembering Ivo's previous descent without warning. 'I hope you'll have dinner with me? And spend the night?'

Troy said, 'Excuse me, but I can't abide emotional excess. I go to pieces. I can't bear suffering.'

'Where's that stout fellow, Sibbie?' Ivo demanded. 'Can't he keep the peace?'

Hal, hearing voices, slowly descended the stairs. He said, 'She's still got a hang-up about the aunt who was catatonic.' He spoke with a painfully ironic smile.

'In that case,' Ivo said, 'school's the best possible place to be. A catatonic aunt wouldn't dare set foot amongst hoards of schoolgirls and their tormentors.'

Somewhere in the house, Ben began to scream. Troy winced. Constance touched him on the arm. 'I've a bottle of Burgundy which is said to be very good. This is just the excuse I've wanted. Come in here, sit yourselves down and I'll open it.'

She was moving into the drawing-room when Coral came into the hall. 'What a hullabaloo! she said, cheerily. 'Upstairs Dido, and help me quieten Ben. Then we'll read a chapter.'

Dido allowed herself to be helped up the stairs, walking as one acutely fatigued.

'What I really want,' Ivo said, following Constance, 'is to take you over the route Troy and I will be motoring. Up to Inverness and through Easter Ross and into Caithness to John o' Groats – and back whichever way our fancy leads us. I've got the maps – if I could spread them out over something . . .'

Chapter 31

'I've made a mess of my life,' Dido said. They were walking over the rough turf on Beachy Head, a robust wind blowing.

'You shouldn't have married Roland Recknall, my dear.'

'I was obsessed by him. I doted on him! It was a terrific experience – the best part of being at art college.'

'You spoiled marriage for me. I've never found anyone I liked as much.'

'I don't recommend it.' Dido shaded her eyes to scan the sea. 'We must go lower if we're going to see the lighthouse.' She linked arms with him. 'Must you go back to teaching at Treverton. I miss you when you're so far off.'

'I was only ever really happy in Mooi River. I'm moderately happy there now – so long as I keep the past separate. You can always come and visit me – as I keep reminding you.'

'I couldn't go back. Or to Westbourne.'

'Isn't it annoying to think of the Crawley son having Westbourne?'

'Andrew's probably nice enough, – despite his father's embarrassing behaviour.'

They approached nearer and nearer to the cliff edge. 'Do you remember how we ran wildly round threatening suicide when Granny and Bampy brought us here?' Hal yawned, and Dido yawned a moment later.

'That back-to-school feeling's hitting us again,' she said. 'Yawning on trains all the way from home to the dreaded doors.'

'Our mother shouldn't have married Max Measures.'

'He was obsessed by her. Like me with Roland. I think she gave in to him on the divorce rebound. Oh, to think our mother's gone – and Max is still alive. A widower three times. That makes him a terrific egotist, doesn't it?'

'Fancy Serena becoming Mrs Warwick-Percy. Sometimes people do what you imagine they should.'

'And little James with twins! Not so easily predicted.'

'I'd never have guessed you'd be a prep-school master, Hal. Of all things. You were a brilliant scholar, a great runner and you shot at Bisley. You could have done anything!'

'A morbid fascination with education, I suppose – compounded by nostalgia.'

'It's a respectable job. A vocation. My life has just been doing arty things. I envy you.'

'Come out and join me . You could teach art.'

'I dreamed through school . . . doodling and writing stories - while the clock hands crept round. I won prizes for English and art and Ancient Egypt and Ancient Greece. But never stuff that's needed.'

'D'you know, it's often struck me as strange that our mother never went to see you at school when you were so revengefully ill.'

'It didn't matter. Children don't expect things. That's one advantage of being a child.'

'I think we were odd children. Was it childhood neurosis – or a genetic dysfunction?'

'I haven't the faintest idea. Both probably. All I know is, I peaked at four. I understood adult things.'

'Oh yes – don't tell me: When you wanted something in Durban aged three, you said, Today is tomorrow because of yesterday. Brilliant.'

'And I remember our mother taking a dress out of the wardrobe at Ainsdale for me to wear downtown, and I lisped, 'I can't wear that – I must wear thomething dethent!' A definite drop in standards ever since.'

'Yes. Downhill all the way, Stupe,' Hal said in teasing tones. 'Our father used to call her that, didn't he? I don't remember him calling her Connie, as Ivo did.'

'Well, Vera and our father have lived happily ever after. Sometimes I get an urge to visit them again. With you of course . . . now he's in his sixties. Shall we go?'

Hal ruminated. 'I can hear our mother saying, Yes, do visit them. It would give your father great pleasure! She was remarkably lacking in all the vices.'

'Yet you were so critical of her for not fighting harder to keep our father – and then for giving in to Max. As for going to Cornwall, I went twice, and the first time I trod on a rusty nail and had a poisoned foot, and the second time I had a poisoned ear – and managed to lose Vera's mac in the sea.'

'And you smashed a folding table in their caravan.'

'But you were far worse the time you went alone. You brought up religion and politics, and were arguing even when I came to fetch you, hours later. Chasing after Dad across a field, in full cry . . . Look, there's the lighthouse. It's a pity this wire fence stops us getting nearer the edge. I want to see more of the beach below.'

'At least you aren't catatonic these days. That's one way you've improved since growing up. You don't fuss about being another Unity.'

'There's a lot of Unity in me,' Dido insisted. 'I'm glad I didn't have a child. It could never have lived up to little Willoughby.'

'Our life at Westbourne was all crying, dying and lying. Think about it.' Hal stood, reflecting. 'It was, wasn't it?'

Dido laughed. 'Put it all into a book.'

Hal gave a dismissive shrug.

They both stood looking out to sea, breathing the fresh air and feeling free of childhood, for better or for worse. The daunting drop of the cliffs was just out of sight.

'And history repeats itself,' Hal said unwarily, quoting what their mother used to say.

Lightning Source UK Ltd.
Milton Keynes UK
UKOW01f2102240117
292787UK00001B/111/P

9 780993 349331